The Heirs of
Southbridge

The Heirs of
Southbridge

a novel

JENNIE
HANSEN

Covenant Communications, Inc.

Cover images: *Summer Morning Landscape* © Michieldb; *Cowboy* © GaryAlvis; *Southern Belle* © Dszc; *Portrait of a Young Woman* © SigWest1. All images courtesy of iStockphoto.com.

Cover design copyright © 2012 by Covenant Communications, Inc.

Published by Covenant Communications, Inc.
American Fork, Utah

Printed in the United States of America
First Printing: March 2012

18 17 16 15 14 13 12   10 9 8 7 6 5 4 3 2 1

ISBN-13: 978-1-60861-892-7

With love and appreciation to my brother-in-law Chuck, who spent twenty months beside my sister's hospital bed, hoping and praying that one day they'd be able to go home together again.

CHAPTER ONE

1878

"Git! Leave! I want you off this place before morning!" From across the fresh grave of his daughter, Desmond Southbridge shook his fist at his Yankee son-in-law.

"There's never been any love lost between the two of us, but I didn't think even you would toss your grandsons out the day they buried their mama." Gavin glared at the older man, and Clayton could tell Papa was struggling to keep his voice even. He figured Papa meant to leave anyway, but not before he was ready. Clayton might be only twelve, but he knew Mama was the only reason Papa had stayed on the plantation since the war.

Then Grandpa growled, "Not them. Kathryn's boys are staying, and if you ever come near them again, I'll have you shot." Clayton's head jerked up. Not even Grandpa could expect Papa not to take Clayton and Travis with him when he went. There was no chance they would stay behind. Grandpa didn't treat Clayton too badly, but Clayton was well aware the ornery old man preferred him to his shy brother, Travis, who was three years younger. Poor Travis frequently got a generous share of the old man's bad temper and vile tongue. Clayton did his best to protect Travis, but without Mama or Papa . . .

"Where I go, my boys go." Clayton didn't have to hear Papa say the words to know he wouldn't leave them behind. Yet the declaration was reassuring. Even so, he wondered why Papa bothered to argue. Grandpa was stubborn and mean at the best of times, but when he was drunk he was beyond reason, and he'd been drinking steadily since Mama's crumpled body had been found in the woods two days ago.

Papa had gone looking for her shortly after her wild-eyed stallion had returned to the stable with trailing reins. He'd found Grandpa coming through the woods, stumbling and crying, with Mama in his arms. Blood dripped from an angry gash in her head where she'd been kicked or hit a rock when she fell. Grandpa claimed her stallion had thrown her and run off. Papa was convinced Grandpa knew more than he'd admit about the reason an exceptional rider like Mama lost her seat.

"I'm gonna shoot that horse too! Should have done it before now."

"You're not going to shoot Kathryn's horse. That horse belongs to me now!" Papa shouted. "If anything deserves shooting, it's you, old man." Though he vehemently denied it, Grandpa had gone hunting the morning of Kathryn's death, knowing full well the stallion was gun-shy and that Mama was riding in the woods that morning. Papa had accused Grandpa of deliberately frightening the horse, thinking that if the horse acted up, he could convince Mama to sell it.

"That horse is mine!" Grandpa screamed. "This is my land, and everythin' on it belongs to me. My sweat paid for every acre of this black dirt. Never shoulda let a Yankee set foot on it." Grandpa's speech was slurred, and he staggered as he turned toward the large house, just visible through the trees. He stumbled into the mound of dirt covering the fresh grave, causing him to swear even more as he struggled to steady himself.

"Quit your sniveling!" Grandpa's cane struck the ground beside Travis, causing him to duck. Clayton moved closer to his brother, steeling himself to ward off any blows intended for Travis. Mama had assigned Clayton to look after his brother when Travis was a red-faced infant. She said it was a big brother's responsibility to protect his little brother, and Clayton had always taken the charge seriously.

Papa started toward Grandpa with clenched fists, but as the old man staggered toward the house, Papa grimaced and turned his attention back to the fresh mound of dirt at his feet.

"Kathryn!" he said, his voice cracking as he sank to his knees and bowed his head.

A heavy knot settled in Clayton's thin chest. *Mama, dear Mama, is gone.*

* * *

Two days hadn't changed much for Clayton. He had gone to Mama's grave and couldn't seem to bring his eyes up from the flower-covered mound he knelt beside. His thin arm reached out to circle his younger brother's shoulders.

He knew Grandpa had been barely restrained from shooting Mama's stallion when he stumbled to the stable after coming from the woods with Mama's body. Grandpa had seen the horse impatiently waiting beside the barn door and went kind of crazy. Papa had stopped him then, but he and Grandpa had quarreled and fought for the two days since. They argued all of the time anyway, but without Mama to tell them to hush, their voices had gotten meaner, especially Grandpa's.

Sometimes Grandpa treated Clayton fine, letting him read the books in the library, teaching him numbers, and talking to him like he was already a grown man. Grandpa had told Clayton nearly every day that someday he would be master of the plantation and that he'd be a rich man. "Wealth is measured in land. All else fades away, but land remains." Clayton looked at the dark Alabama soil covering his mother's grave, and he wondered if Grandpa would trade all that dirt to have Mama back. Clayton knew he'd rather have Mama than any amount of land. Still there was a part of him that felt a kinship with the rich bottomland that was the only home he'd ever known. If only Grandpa and Papa didn't hate each other so much!

Being just a boy, Clayton wasn't sure how to go about comforting his younger brother. He patted Travis's shoulder and pulled his brother a little closer, as he'd seen his mother do when Travis had suffered some small hurt. He wished Grandpa wouldn't scare Travis with his cane or threaten to whip him. Travis was just nine and couldn't help crying. He couldn't help it either that he was the spittin' image of Pa, tall and lean, with an unruly shock of pale hair that gleamed with red highlights in the sun, while Clayton's resemblance to his mother was unmistakable, from his dark auburn hair to his compact build.

He was glad Papa was going to take him and Travis away. He'd miss the plantation—he'd always loved the broad fields, the big trees, and the river that rolled past the bottom of the hill beyond the east lawn like it was in no hurry to get to Mobile, and he had often dreamed about what he would do when the plantation was his. But if they stayed, he wasn't certain he and Pa could keep Travis safe. His little brother already bore several scars from Grandpa's blows. Clayton hoped he and Travis would get to take the horses Mama gave them. Clayton liked horses but not like Travis did. When it came to horses, Travis was more like Mama than he was.

"Come on, Travis," Clayton whispered to his brother. "Let's go check on our horses. Mama isn't really here, you know. She's up in heaven with Jesus." He helped his brother to his feet, and they made their way toward the barn.

"I keep thinking Mama will wake up. Then I see that box with all the flowers and dirt on it, and I know she won't ever come back, and I feel so lonesome and scared." Travis trudged beside Clayton, stirring little clouds of dust with his boots. Clayton tried to explain to Travis about being dead, but Travis just wanted his mama to be there riding horses or making cookies for him. He didn't care about Mama's stories about angels or Jesus, so Clayton stopped talking.

When they reached the stable, Clayton helped Travis push the heavy door open wide and welcomed the cool dimness that greeted him as he stepped inside. "Ew!" Clayton wrinkled his nose and Travis laughed.

Travis said he loved the smell of horses and straw, even when the stable needed to be mucked out. Clayton couldn't see how anyone could like the way the barn smelled. He reached for a pitchfork, and Travis picked up the shovel he usually used. Grandpa said they were big enough to keep the stable clean, so it was their job to muck out the stalls every day. Papa would be along in a little while to make certain they did a thorough job. He always came in time to help them fork the pile of droppings and dirty straw into a wagon to be hauled to one of the fields as fertilizer. Clayton looked around without enthusiasm and shrugged his shoulders. They might as well get started.

The restless stomping of hooves caught his attention, and he scrambled down the aisle to see why the stallion hadn't been released to graze in the pasture with the other horses. Standing on his toes, he peered over the top of the Dutch door at Mama's latest acquisition. Travis came to stand beside him. Zeus was the most beautiful horse Clayton had ever seen. The animal's hide was a rich roan red. Little tufts of white adorned each fetlock, and a small blaze of white highlighted the center of Zeus's long, narrow head. Now that Mama was gone, Clayton wondered who would exercise the horse. Clayton supposed Papa would have to do it. Papa was almost as good as Mama at training horses.

"Zeus doesn't have any water," Travis informed Clayton on seeing the empty tub in the stallion's stall. "I'll get it." He leaned his shovel against the wall and reached for a bucket that hung on a nearby peg.

"I'll help you." Clayton's pitchfork joined the shovel.

They were on their way back from the stream that ran a short distance from the stable when Clayton asked Travis if he needed to rest a minute. His arm ached from carrying the heavy bucket, but he figured his younger brother was probably hurting more, even though he would stubbornly refuse to admit as much or ask for a break. Taking care not to slosh the water over the sides of the heavy bucket, they lowered it to the ground, where it left a ring in the dirt.

Clayton straightened and looked to see how much farther they had to go. He was surprised to see Grandpa walking toward the stable. The old man didn't often enter the barn. When he took the buggy out, he sent Lucas to harness the tired, old mare he used to pull it.

An odd sensation crawled up Clayton's back. Something wasn't right. Grandpa was carrying his old squirrel gun, and Zeus was alone in the barn. He remembered the old man's threat. His feet began to fly; he had to reach Mama's stallion before Grandpa did. He heard Travis yell as he seemed to reach the same conclusion Clayton had, followed by his little brother's pounding footsteps racing after him.

* * *

Gavin knelt, heedless of the damage to his trousers, absently aware of the two small figures trudging with bowed heads toward the stable. It was inconceivable that anyone as vibrant and alive as Kathryn could be dead. They'd met toward the end of the war when he'd commandeered her father's house as headquarters for the battalion of Union soldiers sent to secure the outlying areas of Montgomery. Gavin Telford's first glimpse of Kathryn Southbridge, with her long auburn curls and flashing green eyes, had sealed their fate. There had never been any doubt from that moment on that he wanted the Southern beauty for his wife. In the ensuing weeks, he'd proven to be her protector and he'd done all in his power to engage the lively miss in conversation, while she did her best to ignore him. At length he'd gained her sympathy when he'd prevented the mansion from being burned when the army moved on.

At the conclusion of the war, chaos reigned and he'd seen many of the Southern mansions that hadn't been burned by the Yankee army fall into the hands of unscrupulous profiteers from the North. He hadn't been able to get the Southbridge plantation nor its beautiful mistress out of his thoughts. Instead of returning to his Yankee homeland, he'd returned to Montgomery to pay the taxes and claim the plantation before it could fall into the hands of carpetbaggers. Desmond Southbridge had never acknowledged Gavin's actions but had been livid when his only child married one of the conquerors and a hated Yankee officer became his son-in-law. Out of deference to his bride and new father-in-law, Gavin hadn't transferred the deed to his own name. Sometimes he regretted that unappreciated act of honor.

It was hard to feel sympathy for the man who had dedicated his life the last thirteen years to making his son-in-law's life miserable. Gavin respected the fact that the old man had spent his life building the plantation, but he resented that his father-in-law never acknowledged that without Gavin's intervention, the plantation would have been burned or confiscated because the taxes hadn't been paid. Desmond also failed to give Gavin credit for taking over the planting and harvesting of crops or for keeping the family and servants fed when Desmond's health deteriorated with age and too much liquor. It had been Gavin, too, who had recognized Kathryn's potential as a horse breeder and encouraged her to acquire the best animals their desperate neighbors were anxious to sell. When conflict between him and Kathryn's father worsened, he'd wanted to return north, but Kathryn hadn't wished to leave her papa alone. She hadn't wanted to part with her horses, either, and having no family of his own to return to anyway, Gavin yielded to her pleas.

Kathryn had invested an inheritance from her only aunt into the purchase of the stallion, Zeus, a few months ago. Her father had been livid when he learned what she'd done. He'd anticipated getting his hands on his sister's small fortune and blamed Gavin for thwarting his plans. Kathryn had been riding the stallion when a gunshot from nearby sent the horse into a frenzy. She lost her seat and fell, hitting her head on a rock. Desmond had been wild with grief since Kathryn's death. The local sheriff had listed her death as accidental, but Gavin wasn't as lenient; he assumed Desmond had been so sloppy drunk that he had fired his gun at the wrong time and had spooked the horse to spite Kathryn's purchase of the stallion. Desmond was indirectly responsible for Kathryn's death. His Kathryn.

Gavin no longer doubted his father-in-law meant every word of his threat to kill the horse. He suspected the old man was being eaten by remorse for his crucial part in the fatal accident. The old man had practically worshipped his daughter. She was the only thing he seemed to care about other than the plantation. No, that wasn't quite true; Desmond had some feelings for Clayton, misguided as those feelings might be. The boy had become another source of contention between the two men, as Desmond assumed it was his right to determine Clayton's education and discipline. Desmond was determined to tutor the boy himself, while Gavin wished to send him north to a respected academy for boys. At twelve, Clayton was old enough to be enrolled in a good boarding school.

Only Kathryn's intervention had kept Gavin and her father from coming to blows. Without her, Gavin had no reason to stay on the plantation. He was tired of fighting Desmond's thirst and his determination to countermand every instruction the younger man gave the field workers or his sons. Gavin didn't want his sons growing up under the tutelage of the old man's hatred and bigotry. Unlike Kathryn, he'd never believed the old man's versions of the injuries inflicted on Travis's face and back. Gavin would go, and he'd take Clayton and Travis with him.

He'd also take his gelding, the team he'd raised from colts, the mares Kathryn had given the boys, and the young stallion she'd prized so highly. He'd have to leave the other horses behind. No matter what had happened that day in the woods, Kathryn would want him to fulfill the dream they'd shared of using the stallion to sire a line of highly sought-after colts.

The sharp crack of the old squirrel gun brought his head up. Dark fury nearly blinded him. "The fool!" He began running toward the stable.

"Papa!" he heard Clayton shriek, and Gavin increased his speed. Flinging open the stable door, he saw Desmond struggling to reload his rifle and Travis lying motionless on the floor of the stallion's stall. The frenzied stallion reared and whinnied loudly, its front hooves pawing the air. Clayton was valiantly attempting to take the gun from his grandfather, but the boy was no match for Desmond.

A blow from the grief-crazed man sent Clayton sprawling onto the straw-strewn stall beside his brother. The old man raised the rifle in a determined gesture. Not knowing if Travis was dead or alive, but feeling certain the horse would crush his sons if he didn't act, Gavin lunged forward. A crashing fist to the older man's jaw left Desmond lying in the muck of the gutter that ran the length of the horse barn.

Dodging the stallion's hooves, Gavin reached for the maddened horse's halter, and he whispered calming words to the beast until the stallion stood with head down and damp hide trembling. Gavin tethered the animal to a post, then knelt beside Travis and Clayton, who were both struggling to sit up. "You all right, boys?" he asked while scanning the boys for any signs of injury.

"Yes, sir. But Papa, you've got to stop Grandpa. He's going to shoot Zeus for killing Mama. Zeus didn't mean to, I just know it." Travis held a hand to the lump forming on his temple. If the situation weren't so serious, he'd smile at his son's predictable concern for the animal ahead of his own injuries. He'd known since the boy's first stumbling steps that his younger son shared Kathryn's passion for horses.

Gavin pulled the boy close. "Grandpa isn't going to shoot Zeus. I promise," he whispered as he ran his hands over the spare frame of his second son to assure himself that the boy hadn't been injured. Clayton struggled to his feet to stand beside them. The red mark across his cheek would turn to a bruise in a few hours, and Gavin clenched his teeth as he struggled to comfort his sons.

"Sir?" Slowly Gavin turned to see Lucas, the large former slave who had belonged to Desmond for somewhere around fifty years. Lucas had proved his loyalty time and again as he carried his master home from his drunken forays, cleaning up after him when his indulgences made him ill, carrying out his master's inexplicable whims, and serving as a formidable bodyguard to the old man. Long ago he'd worked side by side with his master, chopping brush and clearing fields. The size and beauty of the Southbridge plantation were as much the result of the hard work and determination of Lucas as of the man who claimed every square inch of the plantation as his own. President Lincoln's Emancipation Proclamation had somehow failed to set the black man free—or he had nowhere else to go.

"Best you take Miz Kathryn's horse and go now," Lucas said in a soft, deep voice while his face remained impassive. "Dat boy be fine. Young Mastah Clayton spoil Mastah Desmond's shot, and he push his brother out o' de way so he not be hurt. Mastah Desmond's shot hit de barn wall. He ain't gwine hurt Miz Kathryn's boys." He seemed to be pleading with Gavin. Whether he was attempting to reassure Gavin that the old man wouldn't hurt his grandsons or urge Gavin to take them and run, Gavin didn't know.

"I'm fine, Papa, but we've got to hide Zeus before Grandpa wakes up." Travis pulled himself free from his father's embrace and stood steady on his feet.

"He's groaning. He's going to wake up pretty soon," Clayton warned.

"You go on. I be lookin' after Mastah Desmond. Take care of dat horse and dem boys. Dey be all de fambly you got, and fambly be what matter de most." Lucas bent and in one smooth motion swung the old man over his broad shoulder. With slow, easy steps Lucas carried Desmond toward the mansion.

Gavin looked at his sons and then at the roan stallion standing at the back of the stall, nervously pawing at the planks beneath the straw. Lucas was right; it was time to go. Grabbing a pile of feed sacks, he handed one to each of the boys.

"Take these to your rooms, and put your clothes in them and anything you can't bear to leave behind," he ordered. "And be quiet. Wait for me under that big oak beside the slave quarters. I'll join you as soon as I have the horses ready."

* * *

After they made it back to their rooms, Clayton stuffed some clothes in his bag, along with a couple of books, and then went to help Travis, who had so far put in his bag a few toy soldiers and a carved wooden horse. Clayton added an armful of clothing and then remembered the small framed daguerreotype of his mother that had sat beside his bed as long as he could remember. When Clayton and Travis could think of nothing more to add to their bags, they tiptoed to the back stairway, once used by the family slaves, and made their way to the back door. After a moment's hesitation, they dashed toward their rendezvous point. They waited for what seemed a long time, watching through the trees for Papa.

"Maybe we should help Papa get the horses ready," Travis suggested.

"He said to wait here," Clayton argued. He scratched his shoe back and forth through the dirt. He wished Papa would come. He looked back at the house and across a cotton field. He was glad they were taking the horses with them, but he wished they didn't have to leave. Grandpa said owning land was important. Clayton couldn't take the whole plantation with him, but he could take a little bit of the dirt that was supposed to be his someday. Taking a handkerchief from his bag, he scooped up a handful of dirt and put it in one corner of the piece of cloth. He tied it securely and dropped it into his bag.

"Why'd you do that?" Travis asked.

"So I never forget this place." In his thoughts he added, *One day I'll come back. If there's any way to return when I'm a man, I will.*

* * *

When Gavin finished saddling the gelding and the mares, he tied them, along with the stallion, to the back of the buckboard, where he'd already set his team in the traces. He paused at Kathryn's grave for one last farewell before making a quick trip to the room he and Kathryn had shared since their wedding day. He hastily gathered clothes and the cuff links she'd given him on that day long ago when she'd become his bride.

Thinking he should take along enough food to last them a few days, he turned toward the kitchen. Dulce, Lucas's wife, handed him a sack, already filled, without saying a word. When Gavin closed the kitchen door of the mansion a few minutes later, his steps lengthened, and without a backward glance he hurried to meet Clayton and Travis. They waited beside the buckboard.

With the boys settled in the back of the buckboard along with their makeshift luggage and with four horses trailing on lead ropes behind the wagon, Gavin drove down the lane and turned the buckboard south onto a worn road. Desmond would expect him to go north. They traveled on into the night, putting as much distance as possible between them and the search his father-in-law would begin as soon as he sobered up enough to discover they were gone.

CHAPTER TWO

Traveling mostly at night and hiding out during the day, they made their way toward Mobile, choosing the least-traveled roads. Occasionally Papa had to leave Travis and Clayton concealed in a thick stand of trees while he rode his gelding into a small town to purchase supplies. He'd explained, and Clayton understood, that it was best that the three of them not be seen together any more than they could help. Clayton felt the weight of responsibility as he attempted to keep Travis's fear mitigated and to keep a sharp watch for trouble. Travis had been skittish since Grandpa knocked him down in the stable, and he seemed to miss Mama even more than Clayton and Papa did. Clayton woke up more than once when he and his brother should have been sleeping to hear Travis attempting to muffle his sobs. Clayton was too big to cry for Mama the way Travis did, but there seemed to be an almost constant ache in Clayton's chest and a lump in his throat that wouldn't go away no matter how hard he tried not to think of her. Almost an hour had passed since Papa had ridden off, and the boys had been watching the trail for his return when they noticed an unfamiliar rider approaching their camp. Travis immediately grabbed the team's halters and disappeared into the brush with the pair of work horses and the stallion, and Clayton attempted to look unconcerned, even drawing his letters in the soft dirt with a stick, while he waited for the man to draw closer.

"What's your name, kid?" Clayton looked up at the sound of the stranger's voice. Something about the man made him uneasy. It wasn't just his bearded face and the hat pulled low to hide his eyes, but something in his arrogant bearing.

"Ain't none of your business," he attempted to sound tough, avoiding the man's question. He turned his attention back to the crooked alphabet taking shape before him.

"This paper says it's my business." The rider waved a paper before the boy. He nudged his horse closer, obliterating the letters drawn in the dirt, and Clayton feared he might be trampled next. Scrambling to his feet, he looked up with all the defiance he could muster.

Clayton read only one word. Big letters spelled out "WANTED." He began to sweat. He was just a boy, though tall for his age. Even though he was twelve, he wasn't sure he could hold his own against a grown man, but he'd try.

"I'm lookin' for a horse thief travelin' with two kids. Seein' a kid out here all alone looks mighty suspicious. Where's your pa?"

"He and Ma went with Uncle Dan to look at a piece of land they're thinkin' of buying," Clayton lied, using the story Papa had coached him to tell should anyone get curious about finding him and Travis alone. Papa figured that anyone looking for them would be thrown off by pretending they weren't traveling alone. Ma had taught him that he shouldn't ever lie, but he figured staying together with Travis and Pa was more important than a few small fibs.

"How come they left you behind?" There was suspicion in the man's voice.

"I ain't alone. My brother saw some birds he thought would be fine for supper. He took his rifle and went after them. He's almost as fine a shot as Uncle Dan. I wanted to go with him, but he said I had to stay here to look after his horse and collect firewood." Clayton nodded toward the horse that was still tethered near their makeshift camp. He watched the man's scowl deepen and watched anxiously as the stranger scrutinized the horse and the camp. The boy wasn't certain whether the man believed him or not, but he was glad Pa had made some changes to the markings on the horse's rump.

After a few minutes the rider grunted, pulled on his horse's reins in a manner that made the boy wince, and charged back down the dusty trail.

Clayton stared after the bounty hunter for a long time, until he was sure the man wasn't going to double back. Then he went in search of Travis.

Travis looked up with a question in his eyes as Clayton approached his hiding spot in the bushes. Clayton grinned, beckoning for Travis to follow, which he did. Clayton could see what seemed to be tears of relief on Travis's face.

* * *

Without taking time to cook supper, Gavin moved on that night as soon as he heard Clayton's story. He found himself watching their back trail and growing nervous each time he spotted a rider or a trail of dust as they drifted toward the Gulf and made their way from Mobile to New Orleans.

They arrived in New Orleans on a sweltering late-summer day. It would take most of Gavin's small reserve of cash to hire a ferry to transport them across the river. They were tired and needed baths and a decent night's sleep. Leaving his boys to watch the horses on a quiet side street, Gavin approached a storefront on a street a few blocks away. He'd heard rumors that the old man who ran the shop knew something about jewelry. It was said that he'd been a diamond cutter in Europe before villagers with torches and clubs had driven him from the town, forcing him to smuggle himself aboard a ship bound for America—determined to start a new life. The story, whether embellished or true, hinted that he'd arrived in New Orleans with a fortune in gems stitched into the lining of his coat and that he'd enhanced his financial standing by buying jewels from impoverished immigrants and selling them at vastly inflated prices to gentlemen currying favor with their Creole mistresses.

Knowing a great deal about horses but little of jewels, Gavin felt his shirt grow damp as he approached the man who was a blur behind a brilliant burst of light at the far end of the shop. For what seemed a long time, he waited for the jewel merchant to acknowledge him. Gavin cleared his throat several times. The wizened figure at last looked up.

"I've heard you buy jewelry. What are these worth?" He set a pair of diamond cuff links on the man's table. They caught the light, appearing almost like twin flames. Accustomed to dealing with horse traders, Gavin didn't miss the slight twitch of a muscle, the flicker of an eyelid, or the slight tilt of the old man's mouth that confirmed Kathryn's wedding gift to him was of considerable worth and the dealer wanted them. The cuff links were family heirlooms Kathryn's aunt had somehow hidden from Yankee raiders and had kept from her brother's grasp. They'd been a gift to Gavin from his bride on their wedding night.

When Gavin left the shop, his step was brisk. He'd never thought to part with Kathryn's gift, but he felt confident she would have chosen to keep the horses and sell the cuff links, which were the only things he owned of any value. He never doubted Desmond was still pursuing him to lay claim to the boys and the horses, which meant Gavin needed money to move fast.

Twice in the weeks he and the boys had been traveling, he'd heard the pounding hooves of horses passing by and feared posses were searching for them. He wouldn't feel safe until they put more miles between themselves and Alabama. Still, the distance they'd already traveled and the cash in his pocket lifted his gloomy thoughts.

The gelding was his, the offspring of the mare he'd ridden to war before he met Kathryn. He had papers to prove his ownership. The buckboard and matched team were the only wages he'd claimed for managing the plantation, and he'd received those only because Kathryn had demanded them from her father and had seen that he had papers for them. Desmond considered the stallion and the blooded mares his, just as he claimed ownership of everything and everyone on the plantation, though the stallion and the mares Kathryn had given her sons had belonged to her, purchased with her inheritance. As her husband, Gavin had legal claim to the horses, no matter what her papa claimed. Gavin's or Kathryn's name was on each of the papers, but Gavin knew his father-in-law well, and he'd witnessed Southern "justice" often enough to know that papers didn't matter as much as knowing the right people. Just as Desmond had ignored the law that freed the slaves who hadn't run away, if Gavin and his sons were dragged back to the plantation, the old man would ignore the papers Kathryn had signed to give Gavin and his sons the horses. He wasn't about to trust his life and his sons' future to Desmond or a Southern judge who made no secret of his contempt for any law that allowed a black or a woman to own property.

"Into the wagon," Gavin ordered the boys, who were playing with marbles in the shade of the wagon. When Travis didn't move quickly enough, Gavin picked the boy up by the seat of his britches and the braces that crossed his back and pushed him over the side of the wagon. In seconds the buckboard rattled out of town, with the string of horses tied behind, trotting to keep pace.

After crossing the mighty Mississippi, they became adept at dodging small-town constables and avoiding public scrutiny until they were well within Texas and another spring had come.

Reluctant to use all of the funds he'd acquired by selling the cuff links, Gavin found work on ranches as they made their way across Texas. They never stayed long on any ranch, and after two years of this nomadic lifestyle, he began to feel more secure. With what was left from the sale of the cuff links and what he'd managed to save from his wages, he considered settling in Texas, but something drove him on.

Their wandering led them farther south, and they crossed into Mexico. Both boys were large for their ages, and Clayton was increasingly mistaken for a man. Gavin found that not only were his sons growing taller and taking on more responsibility, but they were also becoming wilder, and he worried over their lack of schooling. Clayton seemed to eat up each small lesson Gavin gave the boy, but Travis was indifferent to learning his letters. It was also becoming harder to maintain their small but growing herd of horses. Their plight came to a head one night when a mare was stolen, and fourteen-year-old Clayton set out on his own with his rifle to recover it.

* * *

Clayton was furious when he found his mare missing that morning. The sun wasn't up yet, but close enough that he had no trouble seeing. He wasn't certain what had awakened him, but whatever it was, he figured it ought to be investigated. Pulling on his boots and britches, he grabbed his rifle and headed for the corral. He noticed the absence of his mare at once.

Staring at the ground, he could see where someone on foot had approached the hastily constructed corral he and Pa had built. The marks left by a cracked boot dragging an oversized Mexican rowel were unmistakable. Narrowing his eyes, Clayton followed the tracks to a thick cluster of brush. It was obvious that more than one horse had been hidden there. The boot marks disappeared, leading Clayton to assume the thief had mounted a horse.

He considered briefly returning to camp to inform his father of the theft and to seek assistance in tracking the thieves, but he'd lose a great deal of time doing so. Besides, he was as good as Pa at tracking, and he suspected he was faster and more accurate with a gun. He set off at a trot.

As Clayton followed the hoof marks, he noted there were four riders and one of them was trailing Clayton's mare behind him. He wasn't sure what he would do if he caught up to the robbers, but there was no way he would let them just waltz off with his horse. Not only was his mare a valuable animal, but it had been a gift from his mother.

A whiff of smoke floated in the air, and Clayton felt a tightening in his chest. He'd soon catch a glimpse of the thieves. Taking greater care, he approached the top of a hill covered with scrub brush, traveling the last few feet on his belly.

Slithering behind a clump of greasewood, he peered downward and was surprised to see a rough adobe structure. Tethered to a hitching rail in front of it were five horses. His mare was on one end. He lay still, considering the odds of freeing his mare without getting caught by the thieves. With any luck, they were either sleeping or eating their breakfast. If he was careful, he could get his horse and be gone before the outlaws even knew anyone had followed them.

Gripping his rifle in one hand, he crept toward the tethered horses while keeping watch on the door of the structure. With one hand he pulled at the knotted rope and was pleased when the knot loosened. He took a step away from the hitching post, leading his mare, when it occurred to him that the men might find the mare gone and follow him. He turned back to loosen the remaining horses' reins.

With two horses freed, he reached for the third. The animal's head jerked up, and it shied, bumping the horse next to him, and pandemonium broke out. Before he could mount his horse, the door of the house flew open, and all four horse thieves charged through the door. Clayton dropped his mare's reins and backed behind a tall, black horse while raising his rifle. "Drop your gun belts," he shouted.

Two of the robbers' hands moved toward the buckles holding their holsters in place.

"He's just a kid," one of the men shouted and reached toward his holstered six-shooter. The fourth man followed suit, and the first two began to reach to retrieve the guns they'd dropped. Clayton didn't hesitate; he squeezed off a shot, catching the man with a gun in his hand in the shoulder and then turning his rifle toward the next man. The man dropped to the dust, moaning.

"Don't touch those guns!" he warned the two who had begun to loosen their gun belts.

* * *

Gavin caught up to his son shortly after the sun turned its full glare on the high plateau. His heart nearly failed him when he crept around the side of the run-down hovel and heard Clayton order four armed men to drop their gun belts.

"Best do as he says," Gavin backed up the command just before Clayton fired again, sending a shot from his rifle that stirred up the dust at the men's feet while allowing him to stay out of sight. Gavin held his breath as the boy calmly collected the guns, tossed them into the brush, then mounted his mare. Before following Clayton, Gavin backed away and sent a reminder to the thieves not to move until his son was well out of sight.

After their run-in with the horse thieves, Gavin sold several colts to keep the number of horses in their herd down and to give him and his sons more flexibility of movement. The attempt to steal Clayton's mare wasn't the first problem their horses had caused. When they rode into established areas, the villagers eyed them with suspicion. When they approached the large landowners looking for work, they discovered that the wealthy ranchers made their own laws. Both their safety and that of their horses were constantly in question. Several times they managed narrow escapes as they fled dangerous situations. On more than one occasion they were forced to hole up in rugged terrain for lengthy periods of time. It broke Gavin's heart to part with any of the animals, and Travis cried himself to sleep every night for a week after the colts were gone.

One morning Gavin sat on a rocky knoll deep in Mexico, watching Clayton practice a quick draw. The boy had insisted on purchasing a six-shooter after the run-in with the horse thieves. Instead of being pleased with the boy's speed and accuracy, Gavin felt a surge of remorse. For five years he and his sons had wandered from place to place with no home to call their own. The boys' education had been neglected, and they'd forgotten the genteel manners their mother had taught them. The first couple of years they'd been constantly looking over their shoulders, but Gavin now felt certain the danger was past. It was time to settle down before Clayton's skill with a gun turned him into a gunfighter. That day they headed north.

CHAPTER THREE

1881

Lucy peered over the back of the buckboard, glaring at the man with a big star pinned to his shirt. He was a bad man, a Yankee. She'd heard Mama say it wasn't right for a Yankee banker to force them off the farm when they'd paid far more than they still owed. Papa had tried to comfort Mama, saying he had a plan. He showed her a paper, and she shook her head as though she didn't believe Papa's plan would work. Papa reminded her that with his legs no longer working right, he couldn't walk behind Duke and Dandy anymore to plow a field or properly care for the cow or pigs, so he really didn't have a choice when it came to leaving the farm behind.

"It's my fault." Mama buried her face in her apron, and Lucy knew she was crying. She didn't see how Mama could think Papa's sickness was her fault. Maybe she meant something else.

Lucy looked toward the pasture where Dolly the cow watched the departing wagon, her big head stretching over the top pole of the fence. Lucy wondered who would milk Dolly now. Lucy had been doing the milking and slopping the pigs for almost a year. The animals made Mama nervous, so Papa had let Lucy take over most of the chores, though Mama said she was too young and they weren't suitable chores for a young lady. Mama had been raised in a big house where black servants took care of most of the chores, and she made no secret of her desire for Lucy to grow up to be a lady. Lucy couldn't see why a lady couldn't milk a cow. Besides, she wasn't sure she wanted to be a lady—not if it meant wearing hoops and sitting still to have her hair curled.

Dust spun out from the wagon wheels as the buckboard moved slowly down the lane. Her stomach ached and her eyes burned as the farm—the only home she'd known in her short life—disappeared from sight. Bringing one of her long yellow braids to her mouth, she bit down hard to stop herself from crying.

It took a long time to reach the place Papa said would be their new home. They passed the village where they occasionally went to church and shopped at the store. No one waved or ran after them to say farewell. They passed several other similar villages. Sitting in the wagon became tiresome, and she wished Mama had let her keep one of Papa's books to read, but Mama said the books were packed and she didn't want any crates opened until they reached their destination. Eventually Lucy fell asleep, but she awoke when Papa pulled off the road and stopped in a grove of trees near a small river.

Lucy clambered out of the wagon to help Papa water the horses and loosen their harnesses so they could rest and graze on the tall grass at the water's edge. When she returned to the wagon, Mama gave her a slice of thick, brown bread and a warm peach for her supper. When she finished eating, she discovered Mama had spread quilts on the floor of the buckboard. She'd never slept outdoors before, and it seemed like a grand adventure with stars like tiny candles on dark velvet filling the sky. As she lay still, watching the spectacle above, she caught quiet whispers and then the sound of her mother trying to cover her sniffles, and she was afraid.

Mama prepared breakfast as soon as the first beams of light touched the wagon. It wasn't a good breakfast. The biscuits were burned and there was no milk, just the water they'd dipped from the river. She and Mama helped Papa climb down from the wagon, and Mama rubbed something that smelled awful on Papa's legs.

It was up to Lucy and Mama to bring up the horses that had been staked out near the river, and she showed Mama which buckles to tighten. Papa watched. His eyes were red, and he blew his nose several times. When all was ready, Papa climbed onto the wagon seat. Lucy and Mama steadied him until he was settled, then Mama sat beside him and Lucy scrambled into the back of the wagon.

The sun was blazing straight down when they stopped in front of a large gray building and Papa painfully made his way down from the wagon seat. He handed the reins to Mama and took several slow, deliberate steps up the stairs and through a large wooden door to enter the building. He was gone a long time, and Lucy grew almost as restless as the horses, but at last he returned. He was smiling and waving a piece of paper. Mama began to cry, but she was smiling too, and Papa climbed into the wagon without any help. He put an arm around Mama, then picked up the reins, and with a slap across Duke's and Dandy's backs, the horses trotted down the main street of the town and left it sleeping in the sun.

* * *

After crossing the border, Gavin inquired at several ranches until he found a rancher who was part of a group preparing to combine their herds for the drive north. Gavin persuaded the trail boss to hire him and his sons as wranglers to accompany the herd to a new rail line in Kansas.

"Your boy is kind of young." The trail boss, Luke Sorensen, looked askance at Travis when they were introduced. Clearly he didn't see Clayton as a problem since it wasn't unusual for boys his age to hire on for the trail drives.

"He's young, but you'll never find a man who knows horses better than my boy."

The tall foreman placed two fingers inside his hat and scratched his head a moment. "All right, I'll see what he can do. If he doesn't measure up, half wages."

Gavin wasn't sure whether it was the prospect of gaining two men and their choice string of horses that persuaded the man to agree to hiring Travis too or if the man actually saw something promising in the boy himself.

Clayton and Travis worked as hard as grown men, and though younger than the other drovers, they were soon placed in charge of the remuda that trailed the herd. It was their job to care for the horses and provide a change of mounts for the men as needed. Travis took some teasing for the coddling he gave the rough cow ponies, but the good-natured way he took it in stride soon made him a favorite among the men.

The boys took turns moving in unhurried steps around the rope corral they strung up at night to keep the horses from straying. While one boy slept, the other patrolled. Not far away, night riders circled the herd of cattle in the same way. Most nights were uneventful, but occasionally a coyote would stray too close, looking for an easy meal, and they would have to scare it away.

They'd been on the trail for a little more than three weeks, moving slowly through the deep prairie grass, when Travis woke Clayton from a sound sleep a few hours after he'd started his rounds.

"Something ain't right," the younger boy whispered. "Do you smell that?"

Clayton sat up, rubbing his eyes. He took a deep breath and nearly choked. "Fire!" he whispered. He jumped to his feet, balling up his blankets as he looked around. Several cows bawled, and a restless stomping betrayed the herd's nervousness. Far to the west, a pink haze spread across the horizon.

The horses' restless movements threatened to break down the slim barrier between them and freedom.

"We crossed a deep creek a ways back," Clayton said. "We need to get the horses there."

Moving in easy strides to keep from adding to the horses' natural fear of fire, they entered the remuda corral with ropes to begin tethering the animals to two lines. Cowboys slipped out of the darkness to claim mounts, and Clayton helped them throw saddles on any horse close at hand while Travis continued to link the remaining horses.

The fire was moving closer, and with a frightening roar, the bellowing cattle began to run. Dust and smoke nearly blinded Clayton as he groped his way toward the lead rope he'd tied to one side of the temporary corral. With the rope in hand, he looked around for Travis. A line of horses was disappearing through an opening in the corral, and Clayton could only hope Travis was leading them. Clayton began to run.

Once outside the corral, he gripped the lead horse's mane, thinking to swing himself aboard the animal, and noticed a saddle blanket tied around the horse's head. Travis! No wonder the frightened animal had followed him so readily. Without reins to guide the horse, he continued to run beside it and was grateful the string of horses behind continued to follow instead of stampeding as the cattle were doing.

He was gasping for breath, and his lungs ached by the time he reached the stream, but he felt like shouting in jubilation when he saw his brother leading a string of horses into the water. After coaxing the frightened animals into the water, they removed the blindfolds and used the wet cloths to drench their coats while speaking soothing words to them.

Keeping the tethered horses together, they stood in the water and watched the fire pass them by. It was close enough that they could see the flames leap high in the air and turn the distant chuck wagon into a silhouette against the crimson sky. Fearing the ground would be too hot for the horses' hooves for some time, they remained in the water until the sun sent its first rays across the blackened landscape.

Once Clayton felt certain the danger was past, he and Travis led their charges by a circuitous route back to where the camp lay unburned but in shambles. Silently they saddled fresh mounts for the men who were struggling to reassemble the herd and rubbed down, fed, and watered the exhausted mounts.

Clayton ordered Travis to curl up in his bedroll for a few hours, and it was getting on to late afternoon before some semblance of order prevailed in camp again. The two boys were headed toward the chuck wagon when Mr. Sorensen reined his horse in beside them.

"Good job, men!" He lifted two fingers to his hat brim before moving on.

"He called us men!" Travis puffed out his chest.

Gavin fell into step with his sons. "Your quick actions to save the horses won him over. I don't think you'll hear any more about half wages."

* * *

Water splashed against her bare feet as Lucy lugged the heavy bucket toward the old man's garden. He was gone today, but he'd be back. Lucas always came back, and it was a good thing he did, because Mama didn't know anything about growing a garden. Lucy was learning, but she didn't know enough yet. Sometimes she thought they might starve to death if Lucas didn't share his garden with them.

Papa was having another bad spell. Some days were better than others, but most had been bad days lately. When they first arrived

at the Southbridge farm, Papa had helped Lucas plant a field of
cotton, but the field was smaller this year because there had only
been her and the old black man to work the ground, and together
they weren't strong enough to guide Duke and Dandy down the rows
and keep them walking in a straight line. Lucas had been alone since
Papa's half brother had died a few months before her family arrived
at the plantation. Lucas had been happy to see Papa, and they'd
spoken in quiet tones of Papa's mama. As near as Lucy could figure
out, her papa and old Desmond Southbridge had been brothers,
though they'd had different mamas. She couldn't remember Papa ever
speaking of his family before. "Lucy!" she heard Mama call.

"In a minute," Lucy called back. If she went to the house now,
Mama would make her scrub herself and put on a clean dress. Mama
didn't seem to understand that there was no one to help Lucas but her
and keeping weeds out of the garden and their small patch of cotton
was dirty work. If Mama would just let her wear the britches she
found in one of the upstairs bedrooms . . . She thought a boy about
her size must have slept in that room not too many years ago.

It took several minutes to carefully tip the bucket so that the
water came out slowly and stretched to as many small plants as
possible without washing them out of the ground. Mama called
again, and Lucy righted her empty bucket with a sigh and trudged
toward the stable, where she was careful to hang the bucket on its
proper hook. Pausing for a moment to stroke the noses of the two big
draft horses, she promised to return to give them a good brushing.
She swept off the dirt that covered her dress then picked up her skirt
and ran to the house.

Mama stood on the verandah with her hands on her hips. Lucy
knew she was in trouble.

She attempted to defend herself. "The garden needed water."

"That garden is Lucas's responsibility, not yours."

"I know, Mama, but he shares with us."

"All right." Lucy was surprised she didn't argue more. She knew
from experience that when Papa wasn't well, Mama seemed more
temperamental and preoccupied, so Papa must be doing poorly.

"Papa wants to see you. Go right upstairs and clean yourself up
before you go to his room."

In her room, Lucy climbed out of her dress and grabbed the first clean dress she found in her armoire. Unlike her mother, she had plenty of dresses, all ones that had belonged to her mother, but Mama could no longer fasten them.

Before leaving her room, she unraveled her braids and ran her brush through the curls left behind. Without taking time to plait her hair again, she swept it back with a ribbon and hurried down the stairs. She took a deep breath before entering Papa's room. She wished she'd taken time to say a prayer for Papa. She firmly believed in praying, though she seldom took time to say more than the nursery-rhyme prayer Mama had taught her when she was so young she could barely lisp the words.

"Papa?" She pushed the door open and peeked inside the room behind the kitchen that had once been Lucas's home. Since Papa couldn't climb stairs, Lucas had moved his sparse belongings to one of the cabins used for slaves before the war. Mama had hung curtains in the room, and Lucas had hauled the bed his old master had slept in down the stairs piece by piece and reassembled it for her parents.

"Come in." Papa sounded fine. He was sitting up in bed with pillows behind his back. One finger marked his place in one of the thick volumes he loved. Lucy wished she had more time to read and that Papa would soon be well enough to resume her lessons. There had been no lessons since they'd arrived at the big house by the river.

She took a deep breath to calm her racing heart. Sometimes she had bad dreams. In those dreams Papa went away to heaven, leaving her and Mama with no one to care for them. She was happy to see he looked cheerful and much better than he'd been for some time. She'd been foolish to think that just because Papa's legs were bothering him, he might be dying.

Papa patted a spot on the bed beside him. She sat, looking at him expectantly. For several minutes he said nothing, and she began to wonder if her bad dreams weren't so foolish after all. She'd never known Papa to be reluctant to speak, but it was obvious he didn't wish to say whatever he'd called her to his room to tell her.

He reached for her hand, cleared his throat, and then said, "Lucinda, dear, I appreciate how hard you've worked to keep that little patch of cotton growing and that you help old Lucas with his garden, but it isn't enough, and I've been laid up too long. The time has come to sell the horses."

"No, Papa! Not Duke and Dandy. We won't be able to plant any cotton without our horses."

"I know you love those horses, but we need the money they'll bring in for food."

"Oh, Papa, I'll work harder. I promise." A tear found its way down her cheek.

"Please don't cry." He reached out a hand to brush the tear from her face. "I gave my word. A farmer from the next county will be here in the morning to collect Duke. I won't sell Dandy until I must."

CHAPTER FOUR

1886

TRAVIS SEEMED TO BE HAPPY as long as he was surrounded by horses, but Clayton tired of the thick dust that clung to his clothes and skin, sleeping on the ground, the stench of livestock, and the relentless sun and wind. He didn't complain, but after the first drive, he'd reserved some of his pay from each subsequent drive to purchase dime novels and any other reading material he found for sale in the railroad towns where the trail drives ended. He didn't find much time to read, but he savored any odd moments that came his way.

Between cattle drives, the trio picked up short-term jobs in the towns and ranches across Texas. For a while Gavin insisted on the boys attending school if they happened to be in a town for a few months where there was a school, but Clayton didn't like being older and bigger than the other students. His haphazard education and his own determination to learn often placed him far in advance of the teachers found in the little one-room schools. He longed to attend an academy or college.

Clayton was approaching his twentieth birthday when they joined Mr. Sorensen for the cattle drive the trail boss announced would be his last. Fences were going up across the prairie, causing contention between farmers and those anxious to get the cattle to market. Few small towns on the trail to the railhead still welcomed the cowboys trailing the great herds. The towns were becoming more civilized and were catering to the farmers who were moving to the Great Plains and becoming permanent residents. Tracks were being laid, bringing the trains closer to the ranches where cattle were being raised. Ranchers and cowhands alike recognized the end of an era.

Clayton figured this would be his last drive too. He was a man now and could make his own decisions. He'd debated whether to ride with Pa and Travis one more time, finally deciding he couldn't leave his pa and brother until he knew what plans they had for the future, but this would be his last cattle drive. If he didn't attend school soon, he'd be too old to enroll. Pa and Travis sometimes talked about going farther west, perhaps finding a ranch they could buy where they could raise horses, but that life didn't appeal to Clayton. He had a desire to go east and explore other opportunities, but he didn't relish being separated from Pa and Travis.

Clayton hadn't worked with the remuda since that first drive—not since Mr. Sorensen had put Travis in charge and assigned whatever new cowboy who came along to assist him. Still, they pushed their bedrolls together at night whenever possible and shared their thoughts as they'd done as long as either could remember.

"You think Pa'll ever settle down someplace where we can keep our horses?" Travis asked one night as he and Clayton lay on their backs looking up at the stars near the horses Travis was guarding. Clayton knew Travis was mourning the sale of two promising colts for which Gavin had received a good price. Travis was long past crying over colts that were sold, but he made no secret of the fact he'd like to have the chance to raise and train their colts.

"I'm thinking it won't be long now," Clayton answered. "He told me he's got enough cash hidden in his gear that it's making him nervous. He's been asking some of the other drovers about California, and I figure he's thinking about settling there. Besides, he's getting too old for this business; I've noticed he's slowed down, and sometimes I catch him grimacing like it pains him to throw a rope."

"It'd be good for the horses if we had our own place." Travis's voice was wistful.

"You suppose it's too late to go to school?" Clayton wondered aloud. After a few minutes of silence, Travis spoke again. His voice sounded troubled.

"Clayton, you know that new man Mr. Sorensen hired on?"

"Is he giving you trouble?" Occasionally a new rider objected to taking orders from Travis until Clayton set him straight.

"Mark does what I tell him, but I don't trust him. I saw him going through some of the men's things while they were eating their supper last night."

"I'll keep an eye on him. Best you give Mr. Sorensen a heads-up."

"I don't want to get him in trouble if he was just looking for something he lost."

"Not likely he lost anything in another man's gear."

* * *

With the coming of spring, Mama was insistent that the house be cleaned from top to bottom. Papa's health was improving with the advent of warmer weather, and he was spending more time in the library or sitting on the verandah. Occasionally he found time to continue his daughter's schooling. When Lucy was convinced there wasn't a spot left to clean, Mama told her to clean the bedroom where Mama and Papa slept while they made one of their infrequent trips to town.

"I've already changed the bedding and swept the floor, so you'll only need to wash the windows, dust, and tidy up the wardrobe." Her mother pulled gloves over her hands, straightened her bonnet, and made certain Papa had his cane.

Lucy followed her parents to the verandah and watched as Mama and Lucas helped Papa climb onto the buggy seat and take up Dandy's reins. She watched until the buggy disappeared down the tree-lined lane.

Returning to the house, Lucy gathered up a bucket of soapy water and a supply of rags. She would prefer to be outdoors helping Lucas plant his garden. She could see his stooped figure already moving slowly down a row as she wiped at the window.

As she worked, she wondered at Mama and Papa's trip to town. She'd checked, so she knew the larder was nearly bare and she suspected the money from selling Duke was gone. Their small cotton crop had only produced enough to purchase a couple barrels of flour. The situation made her nervous that Papa might be planning to sell Dandy. They could make it through the summer and into the fall by eating vegetables from Lucas's garden and the field greens she'd learned to gather, but she feared it wasn't enough. Only if their small patch of cotton did well would there be funds to purchase a supply of flour for next winter.

Even if Papa sold Dandy, the sale wouldn't be immediate. There would be no way for Papa to return to the farm without Dandy to pull the wagon. She made up her mind to put the thought out of her head. Instead, she'd try to find a way to earn the coins to buy the supplies they needed.

When the window was clean enough to pass even Mama's inspection, Lucy opened the doors to the wardrobe. There were few items to straighten, but she worked diligently at straightening the hanging ones and neatly folding the others.

Next came the dusting. Mama was adamant that feather dusters only scattered dust around and insisted that she use a soft cloth, rubbing each piece of wood with a bit of tallow until it gleamed. Lucy started with the elaborately carved headboard of the bed, taking care to remove every speck of dust from each swirl and loop of the intricate pattern. The matching table came next, its flat top requiring little effort. She stopped to survey the wardrobe before starting on it. Its fancy pattern matched that of the bed, but it was so tall she doubted she could reach the top without standing on something.

She pushed the only chair in the room closer to the large piece of furniture. Even standing on her toes atop the chair, she still couldn't quite see over the top edge. Raising her arms and starting at the edge, she daubed her cloth across the part she could reach. Instead of being smooth like the tabletop, the top of the wardrobe was rough. When she had dusted all she could reach there, she slid the chair to the middle of the wardrobe. As she began to run the cloth along the wood, her hand bumped into something hard lying on the surface. When her best efforts to grasp the object failed to satisfy her curiosity, she climbed down from the chair and went in search of something taller to stand on.

Her eyes lit on the bucket she'd used to hold water for washing the windows. She lost no time dumping it outside on a scraggly rosebush. Giving its wooden sides a cursory swipe inside and out to remove any water that might remain, she hurried back inside. Turning the bucket upside down on the chair, she climbed back up and balanced atop the makeshift step.

Grasping the sides of the wardrobe to maintain her balance, she gazed at the object lying before her. Her eyes widened, and a soft gasp escaped her lips. It was a gun—a rifle or maybe a shotgun. She didn't know much about guns. As far as she knew, her Papa hadn't owned one since he was discharged from the army, and she couldn't remember whether he'd gone hunting before the condition of his legs limited his actions.

Extending one tentative finger toward the weapon, she brushed the side of the long barrel. Too late she noticed it was covered in a thick layer of dust. In disgust she wiped her finger on her apron.

She gazed at the gun for a long time. Gradually an idea began to take shape. If she could learn to shoot that gun, there would be squirrels and rabbits and maybe larger animals to add to the family's meager diet. She was probably just dreaming. She hadn't the faintest idea how to load a gun or shoot one. And if she could, could she really kill an animal? Of course she could. It might make enough difference that they could keep Dandy.

After some hesitation, she reached for the gun and carefully lowered it to the floor. Mama said to clean everything, and she supposed that included the top of the wardrobe and anything she found there. She ran her cloth over the gun, dreaming of the possibilities it represented.

As she scrubbed at the thick layer of dust atop the tall cabinet, she discovered a small leather bag and a long slender metal rod. She felt certain they had a connection to the gun, and she carefully placed them beside it. Once the wardrobe was as polished as she could make it, she stood, contemplating her discovery. Mama wouldn't let her keep the gun. She was certain of that. But what if she really could learn to use it to help them subsist? Was she obliged to let Mama and Papa know about her discovery? If she chose to keep the gun, where would she put it? Finally she made up her mind. She gathered up the items she'd discovered and went in search of Lucas.

* * *

Clayton watched a rider approach, moving easy to avoid startling the cattle that were settled for the night. It had been an uneventful night, and he and Pa had even had an opportunity to talk for a few minutes when they passed each other while slowly circling the herd. The rider coming toward him wasn't Pa or one of the other night riders taking the long shift during the night. He tensed and one hand dropped with practiced ease toward the repeater resting against his hip. He'd heard tales of whole herds being stolen by bandits.

As the rider moved closer, Clayton recognized Joe Horrocks, the man who was to replace him in another hour.

"You're early." A glance at the bright moon convinced him he hadn't miscalculated the time.

"Couldn't sleep, so I figured you might as well." Joe grinned an almost toothless smile. In the nearly four years Clayton had been trailing cattle from Texas to Kansas, he'd gotten to know the older man well and knew the man suffered from pain in his joints and was a restless sleeper. He was also a good man, who hadn't hazed him and Travis too much when they'd started with the outfit.

"What are you going to do when Mr. Sorenson retires from driving cattle north?" It was hard to imagine the half-crippled cowboy finding work with anyone else.

"Sorensen said he's got enough put aside to buy his own place. I figure I'll take him up on his offer to go on working for him. Now you get on back to camp and get some shut-eye. Young fella like you needs to sleep while you can."

"Thanks, Joe." Clayton nudged his horse away from the cattle and toward the bedroll he knew Travis would have waiting for him. Approaching the remuda corral, he was surprised to not see his brother or Mark, the cowboy who had been assigned to work with Travis, anywhere near the horses. Alarm bells sounded in his head. It only took a minute to remove his saddle and turn his horse into the corral before going to look for Travis.

Travis hadn't gone far from his beloved horses. Clayton easily spotted three bedrolls near a clump of brush. Only one was occupied since he and Pa had both pulled night-rider duty.

"Travis," he whispered, kneeling beside his sleeping brother. He reached out to shake his shoulder. "Where's Mark? There isn't anyone watching the horses."

Travis sat straight up, reaching for his hat as he attempted to untangle himself from his blanket. He cursed under his breath as he staggered to his feet. "That no-good jerk! If anything happens to those horses . . ." He started toward the corral, but Clayton clasped his arm, holding him back.

"Watch your horses, but stay out of sight. I'll see what Mark is up to."

Travis nodded his head, indicating he understood. Clayton let him go and moved in the opposite direction of his brother, taking care to keep his steps soundless. The full moon cooperated by sliding behind a stream of thin clouds. He paused to scan the area before moving closer to the chuck wagon, where he could hear the cook snoring loudly. His gaze moved a short distance away to where a fire had burned down to red coals.

Most of the cowboys had spread their bedrolls near the campfire. Two were a little distance apart from the others. Clayton knew they belonged to Mr. Sorenson and Joe. They were with the herd, so why was there a hunched form beside the empty bedrolls?

Taking silent, careful steps, Clayton circled the camp, working his way toward the crouched figure, examining each clump of brush and sleeping form on his way. An occasional cough and varying levels of snores were the only sounds he heard.

He paused when he noticed the shape he'd been moving toward was gone. He continued to stand motionless until a faint click caught his ears, seeming out of place. A dark shadow separated from the cook wagon, carrying something that looked like a box. Clayton waited until the figure started toward the place where he stood.

Stepping from the brush, he pointed his six-shooter at the man. "Empty your pockets and hand over that box," he ordered.

Mark let loose a startled yelp, then began to swear. "Mind your own business," he snarled. He made a move to push past Clayton. The clicking of the gun's hammer as Clayton drew it back caused Mark to hesitate, but only for a moment.

"You ain't going to shoot me and stampede the herd." The moon slipped from behind the clouds and revealed the triumphant sneer on Mark's face. White-hot fury filled Clayton, and for a moment he considered risking a stampede. His left hand clenched into a tight fist, and he let it fly straight for the smirking mouth. The box clattered to the ground, and Mark retaliated with a blow that sent Clayton's gun flying toward some sagebrush.

Mark had at least forty pounds on Clayton, but it wasn't the first time Clayton had fought an unmatched fight. He staggered under the larger man's blows, but he hooked a leg behind Mark's knees, knocking his assailant to the ground. They fell and rolled together, each delivering a ferocious pummeling on the other.

A blow to his temple sent Clayton's senses reeling, and he barely escaped the knife that suddenly appeared in his opponent's hand.

"What the thunder is going on here?" A hand jerked Clayton backward. He clawed at the hand, attempting to free himself, before he realized it was Mr. Sorenson dragging him away from Mark. Four cowboys held Mark immobilized.

"He jumped me! I was only defending myself!" Mark shouted.

"That's a lie! I caught him sneaking—"

"Enough!" Mr. Sorenson roared. "Both of you get to bed, and we'll sort this out in the morning."

"But . . ." Sorensen made it clear he wouldn't listen to anything Clayton had to say. Clayton feared Mark would ditch whatever he stole from the cook wagon before morning, but he limped away. When he reached the corral, he told Travis what had happened and cautioned him to wake the whole camp if Mark tried to take a horse before morning.

Dawn was just beginning to break when he remembered his pistol. It had gone flying into the brush and grass when he'd fought with Mark. Pulling himself out of his blankets, he made his way to where the previous night's altercation had taken place. He searched around until he caught a gleam of silver in the long grass. Once he found the six-shooter and dusted it off, he made his way to the campfire, where several men sat cradling cups of coffee between their hands to warm their cold fingers. He joined them, but there weren't the usual jovial greetings. Several of the men looked away, clearly ill at ease. He understood. Mr. Sorensen didn't tolerate fighting. It was the fastest way for a man to be sent packing. Sorensen was a good boss, but he ran a tight crew with no favorites and no allowance for violating the rules he set down. Clayton might be on his own sooner than expected.

The men set down their cups far more quickly than was usual and, with a few sympathetic glances, began making their way to the horses. They'd relieve the night riders and start the herd moving. As soon as the night riders finished their breakfast, they'd catch up to the herd, and the chuck wagon would follow. Clayton waited, hoping for a chance to clear himself with the boss.

When the trail boss arrived, Clayton saw Pa walking beside him. The worried expression on Pa's face, along with the scowl Mr. Sorensen wore, didn't bode well for Clayton. Setting his plate down, Clayton rose to his feet to meet whatever fate was coming. Before any of the men could say a word, a wild yell, followed by pounding hooves, came from the direction of the remuda corral. Gavin and Mr. Sorenson turned and began to run. Clayton passed them both.

When he reached the corral, he found Travis lying crumpled in the grass and only one horse in what was left of the corral. Mark was on one end of a rope fastened around the neck of Gavin's stallion.

"Let him go!" Clayton shouted. "No one but Pa rides that stallion!"

"Says you!" Mark dropped the rope and reached for a gun prominently displayed on his hip.

He was too late. Clayton's gun left its holster, and he fired before the big man could bring his gun to a level.

CHAPTER FIVE

Mark dropped to the dirt as Zeus reared, front hooves pawing the air. The stallion tore across the trampled ground toward the open prairie. Clayton walked slowly toward Mark, his six-shooter cocked and unwavering. He stood beside the fallen man for just a moment before kicking the man's gun across the trampled ground and well out of reach of grasping fingers should the thief come to. Mr. Sorensen came forward to kneel beside the bleeding body. Clayton returned his gun to its holster and stood watching.

"He ain't dead, but I'm not sure he's going to make it," Sorensen said.

"I'll see what I can do." The camp cook bustled forward. He was as close as the crew came to having a doctor and had proved his ability several times with cuts and broken bones. The crowd that had gathered gave way for him to approach the injured man.

Clayton turned his back and with long strides joined Gavin and several other men who were kneeling beside Travis.

"Is he breathing?"

"Yes, but he has a nasty lump on his head. He was hit awfully hard with something."

"It's my fault. I shouldn't have left him to guard the horses alone. I knew Mark would attempt to steal one before I could tell Mr. Sorensen what he was up to."

"And what was Mark up to?" He hadn't heard the boss arrive behind him. Clayton straightened to look the trail boss in the eye.

"Travis saw him rifling through some of the men's packs a few nights ago, then last night I caught him sneaking out of the cook wagon. His pockets were bulging, and he carried a box of some kind in one hand. He tossed it aside when I confronted him, but I didn't find it when I went looking for my gun this morning."

Mr. Sorensen didn't speak for what seemed a long time, then he stepped briskly toward a pile of blankets and a saddlebag lying beside a fancy tooled saddle on the ground. He merely grunted when he unearthed the small metal box. His eyes narrowed, and he reached for the saddlebag. Opening it, he pulled out more cash than Clayton had seen in his whole life. Mr. Sorensen rose to his feet, a grim expression on his face.

"Men, check your saddlebags. If anything is missing, I want to hear about it."

Travis made a choking sound, and Clayton dropped to his knees beside his brother. Someone handed Gavin a wet rag, and he placed it over the lump on his son's head. Travis moaned and opened his eyes. He appeared confused, and then his eyes widened.

"Mark stole your horse, Pa."

"It's okay. Zeus got away, but Mark didn't. We'll catch Zeus soon enough."

Over Gavin's protests, Travis struggled to his feet. He gave a piercing whistle. In minutes the big stallion came galloping toward him, followed by half a dozen mares. The men clapped and cheered. It didn't take long to put ropes on the mares and get them saddled. Gavin saddled the stallion that stood patiently waiting for him to complete the task.

"Clayton! Jones! Butterfield! Go after the rest of those horses!" Clayton glanced back at Travis, who once again sat on the ground, with his head resting against his knees. Clayton didn't dare disobey Mr. Sorensen, and in minutes he joined the other two men in a mad dash across the prairie.

When they returned with the horses, they learned that the cook's team of draft horses had wandered back into camp on their own and that Mr. Sorensen had sent the cook and one outrider ahead to a small settlement with orders to leave a badly wounded Mark there. Travis was insistent he could ride, and Gavin was assigned to stay with him and help with the remuda. It was time to get the restless herd moving. They were fortunate the morning's excitement hadn't started a stampede. With no more setbacks, they'd make Wichita in a week.

* * *

Gavin leaned against the corral to watch as the train wound its way through the hills, carrying cattle east from Kansas and then north before it disappeared altogether. A sense of melancholy filled him, adding to the persistent ache that had slowed his steps much of the past year. The ache in his shoulder had intensified during the last days of the cattle drive, leaving him longing for a real bed. He glanced toward the hotel where he'd sent Clayton and Travis to book rooms for the night. It seemed much farther away than he remembered.

He continued to linger beside the stock corral, knowing some decisions needed to be made. The long drives were at an end. The railroads were moving deeper into cattle country, leaving even Wichita turning its attention to farmers more than to the few herds still being driven north. It was time to bring this phase of his life to an end too. Clayton and Travis both nearly matched him in height, and the past weeks had proven them more than capable of shouldering a man's responsibilities. Yet his sons were still boys and should have the security of a home to call their own.

He stared down the dusty street lined with saloons. A gust of wind sent tumbleweeds scuttling from one side of the street to the other.

He regretted the nomadic life his sons had been forced to lead. He'd never meant for it to be this way. In the back of his mind, there had always been a plan to acquire land and raise his sons and the horses he and Kathryn had dreamed about. Gleaming white fences, not dirty cattle towns, should have been their lot.

He'd heard some of the other drovers urging Clayton to join them in one of the saloons. Knowing his son was old enough to choose for himself whether to join them for a drink didn't ease his concern. He knew that many of the men now looked up to Clayton for his skill in handling horses and cattle and for his quickness with a gun. The story of Clayton's altercation with Mark was making the rounds, spreading beyond their own crew. He didn't want his son to become known as a fast draw. That wasn't the life he and Kathryn had dreamed of for either of their sons.

His eyes lingered on the rolling hills to the east. His sense of remorse intensified. The Southbridge plantation was Clayton's by right. The boy should have been groomed to take his place as the master of the finest farm in Alabama instead of eating dust, trailing cattle, and gaining a reputation as a fast gun. Still, no matter how many times Gavin had regretted tearing his son away from his heritage, Gavin believed he'd had no choice about leaving. Without Kathryn he couldn't have stayed, and he couldn't have walked away from Desmond's hate and fury without taking both of his sons. They could go back; the old man was probably long dead. But could he claim the land? Not likely. By now it had surely been sold for taxes or taken over by unscrupulous carpetbaggers. It was time he and his sons started for California. He glanced toward the setting sun and noted the lengthening shadows. Just a few more minutes and he'd start the long walk toward the hotel.

His thoughts turned from the plantation to memories of Kathryn's vibrancy and the love they'd shared. In his mind, he saw her as surely as though she stood before him with her chestnut curls tangling in the wind and her ever-present riding crop slapping softly against the palm of one hand. For just a moment he thought he heard her voice. He turned, facing into the wind to search the rolling hills.

"Kathryn," he whispered as a blinding pain burned in his chest. His knees sagged, and he dropped to his knees beside the holding pen gate. "God willing, we shall be together again."

* * *

Clayton lay atop the sagging bed beside Travis, who sprawled in exhausted abandon across the shabby bedspread. Travis's deep breathing testified that his brother didn't share Clayton's difficulty falling asleep.

Something didn't feel right. He couldn't put his finger on what troubled him, but he couldn't deny the restless uneasiness that filled him. He rose to his feet and walked to the window, pushing aside a dusty rag that sufficed for a curtain.

Sometimes when all was quiet, he thought about Mark and wondered if the man was dead or alive. Had he killed Mark? He hadn't had a choice, he argued with himself. He couldn't let the man steal the stallion, and he had to protect himself. Still, he found some comfort in thinking the thief might have survived. It wasn't the first time he might have killed a man, but some part of him didn't want to know for certain that he was responsible for another man's death. He wasn't concerned about the cowboy coming after him someday. If Mark did survive, there was little chance they'd ever cross paths again since the cattle drive was over and in a few days Clayton would be headed east to school.

Tinny music and loud laughter spilled from a nearby saloon. Perhaps he should have joined the other men in their celebration of the trail's end, but knowing this was the last cattle drive he'd participate in, he'd opted to keep his pay. He'd need every cent he'd managed to save to pay his admission to the school he hoped would accept him in a few months. Peering out the window, he noted there was still no sign of Pa returning to the hotel.

He was just reaching for his hat when a heavy pounding rattled the door of the room he shared with Travis.

"Open up! Your pa needs help." Clayton recognized the voice of the trail boss he'd bid farewell a few hours earlier.

"What is it?" He flung open the door to see two men holding Pa between them. Seeing the gray, unmoving form, he motioned them toward the bed beside which Travis was now standing, looking bewildered.

A man carrying a black bag bustled into the room behind the cowboys. He went straight to the bed, where he leaned over Gavin. Clayton and Travis moved closer, almost forgetting to breathe as they watched the doctor examine Pa.

After a few moments the doctor stood, slowly shaking his head.

"Doc?" Clayton didn't know what to ask.

"He's going to be all right, isn't he?" Travis dropped to his knees beside the bed.

"I'm sorry, son." The gray-haired doctor met Clayton's eyes. "He's gone. There's nothing I can do."

Clayton nodded his head, indicating he understood, but he didn't understand. How could Pa be dead? Pa was the one constant in his and Travis's lives.

"Wasn't anything anyone could have done. His heart just plain wore out. That happens more often than most folks suppose." Clayton wasn't listening anymore. Turning his back to the doctor, he joined his brother beside their father. Travis wasn't crying; he was almost a grown man now, but Clayton knew Travis shared the crushing pain that filled his own heart. He rested a hand on his brother's shoulder and was aware of Travis's lips moving as though in silent prayer.

His own lips were still, and he felt unable to put together two coherent words of comfort or prayer.

A sound behind him reminded him there were others in the room. Some inner prompting told him that he had responsibilities now. He needed to see to Pa's burial, and it was up to him to look out for Travis. He stood to face the men who had brought Pa to their room and was surprised to see that only Mr. Sorensen remained.

The trail boss cleared his throat and began. "There are things we have to discuss."

"I noticed a clapboard church when we rode into town."

"Your Pa was a good man and he deserves a few church words said over him. The sooner you find the preacher and make arrangements, the better. Most of the men will want to pay their respects before heading back to Texas."

"Pa wasn't a churchgoing man, but he carried a Bible in his saddlebags and believed in a heaven where Mama would be waiting for him."

"That wasn't all your Pa carried in his saddlebags." He swung a heavy leather pouch onto a small table. "You already know the cowboy, Mark, was a lowdown crook. You and the other men assumed the box you saw him carry away belonged to the cook and that various small items and amounts of money were the property of several different cowhands. What he stole from the cook wagon that night was a small strongbox containing funds belonging to me that I stored in the wagon to cover emergencies. His most serious theft went unannounced. Your Pa didn't want anyone to know. While Travis tended to the horses and you were out riding night herd earlier that night, he took this from your Pa's gear." Sorensen handed Clayton a thick stack of large bills.

"I didn't count it, but Gavin said it contained several thousand dollars, enough to buy the ranch he'd been saving for. I figure he'd want the two of you to split it between you now."

CHAPTER SIX

1887

THE PREACHER STOOD AT THE head of Pa's grave to deliver a short sermon, then Mr. Sorensen took his place and said a few more words, mostly pointing out that Gavin Telford had been a hardworking, honest man who treated his horses and his fellow men with respect. He finished with the twenty-third Psalm. A hot wind blew across the prairie, and Clayton's mind drifted back to that day eight years earlier when Mama had been buried beneath the willow tree at the edge of the path leading down to the river on the Southbridge plantation. He regretted being unable to bury Pa beside Mama, but he hoped they'd find each other up in heaven.

Travis stood ramrod straight beside Clayton as the box was lowered into the ground. Travis had said little to Clayton since the previous day when Mr. Sorensen had brought Pa's body to the hotel. He was extremely young to be orphaned. Travis didn't do a lot of talking, but his feelings ran deep. He needed to have a good talk with his brother when they got back to the hotel.

When the burial was finished, the brothers walked back to their room together. Clayton was conscious for the first time that Travis towered a head taller than him. His shoulders were broader too. Though still a boy by age, Travis had been taking on a man's responsibilities for years. It occurred to Clayton that Travis might not want to fall in with the tentative plans he had begun making in his head for the two of them. He began considering ways to broach the subject of their future.

On reaching their room, Travis began packing his few possessions in his saddlebags. Clayton watched for a few minutes before speaking. "Travis we need to talk, make some plans for where to go and what to do next." He indicated one of the two chairs in the room. He seated himself on one while Travis sat down on the other.

"I ain't going to that fancy school you been talking about ever since we left Alabama. Pa taught me to read and write and do a little arithmetic. That's enough for me. Mr. Sorensen said I could go back to Texas and work for him on his new ranch. I already told him I would."

Clayton felt as though he'd been punched. He shook his head, trying to think.

"You should have talked to me. You know I don't want—"

"I know you don't want to work on a ranch, but I don't want anything else. I'd most die cooped up in a school room. You can go to that school in Boston, and I'll go to Texas with Mr. Sorensen."

"That's not what I meant to say. I don't want us to be separated. Mama said I was to look after you, and you know Pa wanted us to stay together."

"I don't need anyone looking after me. I'm almost eighteen now, and out here that's a man."

Clayton was tempted to agree to Travis's plan, though his claim of being almost eighteen was a bit of an exaggeration. It had been no more than a month since Travis had marked his seventeenth birthday. His little brother was a good six inches taller than he was and had developed broad shoulders. He'd handled a man's job for a long time. Mr. Sorensen was a good man, and he knew and respected the other cowboys who planned to follow the trail boss to his new ranch. He just hadn't imagined a day when Pa would be gone and he and Travis would go their separate ways.

"Can't we think about this for a few days?" Clayton hoped to change his brother's mind.

"You can't talk me out of it. Mr. Sorensen and the rest of the boys are pulling out of town in two hours. I'm going with them. The next train east will be through here in two days; I already asked about it. With the money Pa saved, you'll have plenty to buy your ticket and pay your way at that school."

"Half that money is yours."

"I'm taking the horses—the stallion and all five mares. I don't figure you'll be needing a horse for a bit."

"You'll need some cash too." The minute the words left his mouth, Clayton knew he was consenting to Travis's plan and it was too late to back out.

"I've got my pay. I haven't spent any of it yet."

Clayton leaned forward, his elbows on his knees, his head hung in resignation.

"You ain't—" Travis began.

"No, I'm not going to try to talk you out of going to Texas, but there are a few things we need to talk about. For beginners, Pa would have insisted you buy a few new shirts while we're in town. I can see you don't have much time, but you should take Pa's extra suit of clothes and my spare shirt with you. My pants wouldn't fit you or you could have them too. I'll need different clothes for school. Take all three saddles and gear. Cook will let you stow them in the cook wagon."

"I'd kind of like to have Pa's canteen, the one he carried through the war, but I think you ought to keep his Bible." Travis spoke in a tentative voice as though he wasn't sure his brother was sincere in agreeing to his plan.

Clayton nodded his agreement as he reached for the bag that held Pa's savings. "We best count this." This time it was Travis's turn to nod his head. When they finished counting, they stared at each other without speaking for several minutes.

"I can't believe Pa carried all this money around with him." Clayton shook his head. He pursed his lips and coughed a couple of times before finding his voice.

"Even if you take the horses, I can't take all this." Clayton waved his hands over the piles of bills and coins on the table. "It isn't safe for either of us to walk around with so much cash. Mark isn't the only dishonest man just waiting for a chance to relieve an unwary man of all of his hard-earned savings. Mr. Sorensen always has the cattle buyers send money by wire to the bank here in Wichita to pay the crew; then he sends the rest by wire to Fort Stockton. He keeps his own money in a bank here too. Before you leave, I think we should visit the bank he uses and open two accounts. If you decide someday that you want your own ranch, your share of the money will help you get started."

"All right, but you keep most of it." Travis's concern touched Clayton, revealing that his brother, too, had some misgivings about the separate paths they were about to take.

* * *

Finding the bank wasn't difficult. It was the only brick building on the dusty cow-town street. With the large number of cattle being shipped from that part of Kansas, it seemed to do a brisk business. One man sat at a desk off to one side, while another stood at a counter where a short wall and bars half hid him. The man at the counter directed Clayton and Travis to Mr. Long, who was seated at the desk, and advised them that he was the one who owned the bank and took charge of new accounts.

Clayton liked Mr. Long at once and felt he could trust the owner when Mr. Long advised Clayton and Travis to put both their names on both accounts to keep their money safe should one of them die before the other. Clayton didn't want to consider the possibility of either of them dying young, but he figured it was good advice. Before they left, Mr. Long instructed them in how to compose a wire to the bank should they need access to their money when they were in faraway places. Clayton shook Mr. Long's hand, and Travis did the same.

"Good luck, boys." Mr. Long followed them to the door.

In too short a time, Clayton stood in the dusty street, watching his brother and the men he'd ridden with for the past four years ride out of town. Travis turned once and touched the brim of his hat in a gesture of farewell. Clayton returned the gesture, then watched until the riders were just a dusty speck on the vast prairie. He hadn't felt such a strong urge to cry since that day many years before when his mother was buried beneath the old willow tree.

Before making his way back to his room, he crossed the street to the mercantile, where he purchased a valise and two shirts. He considered buying a pair of britches but decided to wait until he reached Boston. He added some hardtack, jerky, a chunk of cheese, and a few sweet peppermints to his order. Mr. Sorensen had warned him there wouldn't be many opportunities to obtain food during his trip, so he should carry a few cold rations with him. Seeing some dusty dime novels on the shelf behind the counter beside a McGuffey Reader, he decided to purchase one to read while he waited for the next eastbound train. As an afterthought, he asked for the reader too.

The next evening, after eating his supper in the hotel dining room, he trudged down the street to the churchyard to say his last farewell to Pa. He stood beside the fresh mound of dirt, with his hat in his hands. His mind drifted back over all the trail drives, farther back to dodging bandits in Mexico, and the long string of ranch bunkhouses where the three of them had signed on for a few weeks or maybe a season. He reached into his pocket and withdrew the grimy handkerchief that still held a few grains of dirt from the plantation where he'd been born. Not for the first time, he felt a wave of homesickness. He carefully sprinkled the few grains of dirt over the grave.

"Pa, I had to let Travis go. I know you wanted us to stay together, but he's wanting a different life than the one I need. I won't forget him, and I'll write letters and send them care of Mr. Sorensen. If one day he needs me, I'll go wherever he is. I won't ever forget you either, and I'll think about you and Mama together somewhere where the grass grows tall, raising those horses you always dreamed about. I reckon there's horses in heaven 'cause Mama set a lot of store by horses and she believed in heaven, which she wouldn't have done if there were no horses there."

He stood for several minutes, then swiped the back of his sleeve across his eyes, set his hat back on his head, and turned toward the hotel.

* * *

Clayton slouched in his seat, with his hat pulled low across his eyes. Sleep was impossible, and he felt like he'd been traveling most of his life. At first it had been exciting to roll across the prairie at such a remarkable speed. After a while he became bored with the monotony of the endless prairie punctuated by an occasional farm, a soddy, or a water tower. The past and memories of his early childhood seemed to haunt him until even when he dozed he saw the cool green of trees leaning over water, rows of cotton, and the lush green of pastures dotted with his mama's horses. He longed to feel the cool rush of spring water closing over his head as he and Pa dived into the swimming hole behind the barn.

On reaching St. Louis, he'd decided that since he was in no particular hurry and he'd never had the pleasure of riding a riverboat, he'd detour to see his childhood home. The steamboat went to New Orleans, and he could catch a northbound train from there to Boston. He couldn't get thoughts of the old plantation off his mind. It wasn't that he regretted the last eight years with Pa and Travis, but something about the rich, black dirt and beckoning shade trees that grew thick along the riverbanks of Alabama seemed to call to him.

His memories of New Orleans were vague, and there was little that stirred memories from when Pa, Clayton, and Travis stopped there briefly when they fled from Grandpa. Clayton found the colors and sounds fascinating, but he'd heard stories about the city and thought it best to keep his money well guarded.

As he wandered about, he discovered a restaurant where he could purchase the first real meal he'd eaten since St. Louis. He wished Travis were with him to enjoy buttery crab cakes like Dulce used to make. After filling his stomach, he made his way to the train station, which was a longer walk than he'd anticipated.

On arriving at the train station, he found it closed, so he spent the night on a hard wooden bench. His feet ached far too much to wander about looking for a hotel. Besides, he wanted to be certain he didn't miss the train. Before dawn, he was awakened by a black man wearing a railroad uniform. "Best be on your way," the man warned. "De stationmaster don't allow no one on dese benches less they be waitin' for a train, so if you ain't plannin' to buy a ticket, you be movin' on."

"I'm riding all the way to Boston." He tried to look affronted as he blinked to come fully awake. "Is there some place I can freshen up a bit?"

The man pointed out a nearby outhouse where he could refresh himself and don his extra shirt. "There be a pump at the edge of the platform," the man added, pointing.

Clayton did his best to make himself look presentable. When he was satisfied he'd done his best, he returned to the bench to wait. The morning was almost gone when he heard the shrill whistle of the train. It ground to a halt in a cloud of steam and cinders.

As the train wound its way north, Clayton subsided into a drowsy state, neither asleep nor quite awake. On the train's arrival in a small town that afternoon, he made his way to the station platform, where he paced while the train took on fuel and water. He sniffed the air, and memories from his half-forgotten childhood stirred his senses once more.

When the train resumed its journey, it angled more toward the east. The terrain they were passing through brought memories of his childhood on his grandfather's plantation, and he wondered if his grandfather might still be alive. He really wanted to see the place again, and since he was now an adult, his grandfather could have no hold on him. He wasn't sure he would announce himself at the plantation, but he meant to see it.

As the miles ticked by, he listened for the conductor to say the names of towns he remembered and fretted over the possibility of passing by the closest town to the plantation and missing his opportunity. With each clacking mile, his excitement grew and his attention remained focused on the window beside him.

A long wail from the steam engine's whistle sounded as the train slowed following its descent into a long river valley just as the day was drawing to a close. He felt a sense of nervous energy as he recognized once-familiar landmarks. The train was passing through what he felt certain had once been fields of cotton and tobacco surrounding the house where he'd been born. On his left was the river. He craned his neck for a better view and became aware that the train was almost at a standstill.

The view from his window was achingly familiar. Surely the train was stopping right near the spot he'd once considered his favorite fishing hole. His heart pounded at this opportunity to visit his former home and pay his respects at his mother's grave. He felt certain Grandpa would welcome him, and if Grandpa had passed on and a new family lived in the house, he could make his way into the village and stay at the boardinghouse.

When the car came to a full stop, he jumped to his feet and made his way to the back of the train, where he gazed over the caboose rail. After a moment he jumped to the ground. Through the trees he caught a glimpse of white. He wasn't mistaken! A sense of destiny filled him, and he remembered his bag resting beneath his seat. He hurried back for it, and, with the valise in hand, he paused to inform the conductor he was leaving the train and enquired when the next train would pass through the valley.

With eager strides he made his way toward the long, grassy slope he'd last traversed as a twelve-year-old boy. He was disappointed to find that more weeds than grass grew on the hillside and that the little grass that remained was unkempt and shaggy. A familiar willow tree came into view, and he slowed his steps to approach the spot where he'd knelt so long ago. A second marker stood beside the one he remembered his father hammering into the ground to mark his mother's resting place until a suitable stone could be obtained. Both markers were gray, but one was more weathered from storm and the ravages of time than the other. There was no trace of the words Gavin had carved into the first, nor any indication of who lay in the second, though Clayton conjectured it might be his grandfather.

A short distance away was a rough stone marker. Chiseled into it in uneven letters was a single word: "DULCE."

Clayton removed his hat and dropped to one knee. His head bowed, and his mind filled with memories of that long ago time when his mother was the center of his world. How he had missed her during the long years since he last knelt at that spot.

"Are you praying?" He hadn't heard footsteps approaching. He jumped to his feet to find himself facing a young woman dressed in overalls. It took a moment for him to realize she was pointing a shotgun at him, one that looked suspiciously like his grandfather's old squirrel gun.

CHAPTER SEVEN

NEVER TAKING HIS EYES FROM the girl, Clayton noted that a long, yellow plait swung over her shoulder and a squashed felt hat partially hid her features. She was only about five feet tall and skinny. Her stance was wide, and though she looked young, she appeared quite accustomed to handling a shotgun. He bent to brush the dirt and grass from his pants in an effort to appear unconcerned and to gather his thoughts. As he rose, he quickly grasped the gun barrel with one hand, swinging it up and away from the girl. With the shotgun in Clayton's hand, she turned to run, but Clayton grabbed her wrist, turning her so that she faced him. He was shocked to see her wide blue eyes so full of defiance, without a trace of fear. He guessed her age to be somewhere around fourteen or fifteen, though not having had much experience with girls, he couldn't be certain.

"Let me go!" She kicked at his shins, though her bare feet had little impact against his boots. She likely hurt herself more than him.

"Who are you?" he demanded to know. "And what's the meaning of sneaking up on me with a shotgun?"

"I wasn't sneaking, and you've no right to be trespassing or asking questions." She glared back at him.

"I have more right than you know," Clayton said in a firm voice while he retained his grip on the struggling girl. "Perhaps you'd care to tell me what you're doing on Desmond Southbridge's property and why you're carrying a shotgun."

"This farm don't belong to old Southbridge anymore. He sold off some of it to the railroad before he drank himself to death. The rest belongs to my papa, seeing as he's the old man's closest kin." Her words caused Clayton to almost lose his grip on her arm.

"Where's your pa? I'd like to have a word with him." Clayton felt a surge of anger. As far as he knew, he and Travis were the only Southbridge relatives with a legitimate claim to the property. Aunt Caroline didn't have any children, and Clayton's mama was Desmond's only child. Desmond had told Clayton many times of how Desmond's father had been an orphan who worked his way to America on a sailing vessel and then worked along the waterfront until he had acquired the means to purchase a small tract of bottomland along the river. He'd married an indentured servant, Elizabeth Palmer, also an orphan, from a neighboring tract, and the two of them had acquired more land, bought slaves, and built a big house. Next came a daughter, Caroline, and a son, Desmond. Elizabeth died giving birth to Desmond. Years after Desmond's mother died, his father remarried, and though his new wife was young, she never gave him any children. She ran off as soon as Desmond was old enough to take control of the plantation. Everyone was accounted for; the girl's pa was no relative. Maybe Grandpa's drinking habits had run up bills, meaning a creditor might have a claim to the property. If the state thought Clayton and Travis were dead, government bureaucrats might lay claim to the plantation.

"He'll shoot you if you don't let me go," the girl threatened.

"We'll just walk up to the house and see about that." Clayton had no intention of letting some carpetbagger get away with claiming the home promised to Clayton since the day of his birth. Faced with the prospect of a thief profiting from four generations of his family's labor incensed him. He walked the girl toward the house.

Clayton took care to stay alert as he marched toward the once stately mansion, which now appeared to be in sad repair. He didn't want anyone taking him by surprise. The girl was no longer fighting him, but he didn't trust her. He couldn't risk the chance she was biding her time, waiting for a chance to catch him off guard. He hadn't forgotten any of the training Pa had given him while they wandered west nor their struggle to keep banditos and Apaches from stealing their horses.

Once on the verandah, he ordered the girl to open the door. Before she could act, the door was flung open, revealing a slender, middle-aged woman attired in a neat but faded gown, her pale hair carefully wound in a coil atop her head. She frowned on seeing the pair standing on the verandah. She glanced at the girl and then at Clayton. Her eyes widened, and her glance went back to the girl, whom he assumed was the woman's daughter.

"Lucy!" she gasped. "Why are you dressed like that, and who is this man?"

"He was trespassing!" the girl yelled.

The woman looked to Clayton as if seeking an explanation while keeping a wary eye on the gun he held. She seemed to recognize it. Her mouth tightened, and her features turned stern. She held out her hand. "I'll take that now." Clayton had the distinct impression the woman had commandeered the gun from her daughter multiple times in the past.

Clayton hesitated, uncertain whether he should turn the gun over to her or not. Releasing his hold on his prisoner, he checked to see if the shotgun was loaded. After finding it empty, he handed it to the woman. He stood, feeling awkward and a little foolish as he faced her. The girl darted past the woman and fled up the stairs, which he noted were polished to a high sheen, though they appeared more chipped than they'd been when he and Travis had played on them. Over the woman's shoulder he could see familiar rugs covering the floor, but they were now faded and shabby.

"Well?" The woman stood with her hands on her hips.

He hesitated a moment, then remembered he was the one who had a right to an explanation.

"Ma'am, I didn't mean to frighten you or your daughter, but it seemed prudent to disarm her when she approached me with that shotgun as I knelt at my mother's grave." A frightened look appeared in the woman's eyes. Ignoring it, he went on. "I'm Clayton Southbridge Telford, and I'd like to speak to your husband about how you happen to be living in my grandfather's house."

A spectrum of emotions flickered across the woman's face, ranging from fear to weary acceptance. "Come inside." She motioned toward the open door with a tired, nervous gesture. "It isn't my practice to discuss family matters on the verandah." Clayton raised an eyebrow at the reference to family, and the woman blushed.

Keeping his eyes open for some sort of ambush, Clayton stepped across the threshold. Memories came rushing back from where he'd buried them long ago, and he saw his mother graciously inviting guests into the large parlor, Dulce bearing tall glasses of cool lemon tea toward them, and old Lucas coming to carry away the gentlemen's hats and walking sticks.

It took just a moment to realize the grizzled, stooped figure coming toward him really was Lucas. His shoulders were slumped, and his hair had turned a gritty white. He stopped midway, staring with the same shocked expression Clayton was feeling.

"Lucas?" Clayton took a step toward the elderly servant.

"Mastah Clayton?"

Not knowing how it happened, Clayton found himself with his arms wrapped around Lucas. It wasn't that he'd given Lucas a lot of thought or even felt a particular closeness to him in those years when his mother was alive, but the black man was a part of his childhood, someone who had shown his mother deference and who had stood up for him when Grandfather's obsession sent Clayton fleeing his home beside his father and brother.

Lucas stepped back, swiping a hand across the tears flowing down his usually stoic face. "I think you never come home, though I keep hoping. Your grandfather be dead. He sell 'nuff land to a railroad man to keep himself most de time he wait for you to come back. He not plant cotton after you boys and your papa go away. Three years he be gone now."

With unexpected swiftness, Clayton felt a twinge of regret. Was it possible some part of him had cared for the irascible old man? "He's buried beside Mama?"

"Yes, sir." Lucas hung his head.

The black man was old and had worked hard all his life without compensation. He appeared to be crippled with joint pain, but he seemed to still persevere in caring for Grandpa's big house.

"We kept him on though there was no money for wages. He had nowhere else to go." How could he have forgotten the woman who stood nearby, twisting her hands together in the folds of her faded dress? Her words sounded odd. They were spoken as though she were preparing a defense.

"Who are you, and what are you doing here?" Clayton turned to the woman, his temper somewhat cooled, though his mind was still grappling with confusion and perplexity.

"I can answer that." A gray-haired man leaning heavily on a cane hobbled into the room. Even though he was bent and moved with great difficulty, Clayton sensed an element of dignity in the man's bearing.

"Won't you be seated?" the woman indicated a blanket-draped settee as though suddenly reminded of her manners. Her fluttering attempts at hospitality saddened Clayton, though he couldn't have explained why.

The man, who appeared to be much older than the woman, settled heavily on the nearest chair facing the settee. Clayton sat on the edge of the indicated seat without taking his eyes from the gaunt figure before him. He didn't waste time apologizing or erecting a defense. He looked him in the eye.

"My name is Elliot Southbridge, though I'm not sure I have a legitimate claim to the name," he began with a weary sigh. "It was never my intention to cheat you of your claim to Desmond's property." His statement was explanation, not apology, but there was a kind of sadness to his words. Elliot closed his eyes, and several minutes passed before he spoke again. Clayton held his tongue, not wishing to antagonize the old man before he'd spoken his piece.

At long last, Elliot spoke again. "I would like you to know the full story, and though I might ask for proof of your identity, I think there's little doubt you are the grandson named in the old man's will." His pause this time was brief.

"Desmond's mother died when Desmond was born and his sister Caroline was only three. When his father remarried twelve years later, taking a much younger wife, Desmond objected to the marriage and never accepted the woman as his mother. Desmond's father died too, before Desmond reached his majority. And even though Desmond made his stepmother's life miserable, she stayed until Desmond came of age, to preserve the property and to prevent the children from being turned over to an orphanage. When he came of age and could assume legal ownership of the plantation and guardianship of his sister, his stepmother ran off with a riverboat gambler. They never married and soon separated. She returned to the plantation, but Desmond refused to let her stay. She was with child, but her desperate situation didn't deter Desmond. That woman was my mother, and when she eventually married again to an upstanding merchant in Georgia, she passed me off as her first husband's child.

"Following the war, I married and then fell on hard times as I was struck by a crippling disease. About the time I learned my family was to be evicted from our farm, I read a notice in a newspaper that the estate of Desmond Southbridge was to be placed on the auction block due to a failure of any heirs to step forward to claim it. I had no problem convincing the local authorities that I was your grandfather's younger brother."

Clayton stared at the man, aghast. How could the man possibly think his odd relationship to Desmond Southbridge entitled him to claim the plantation?

As the man took up his story again, Clayton could see he wasn't as old as he'd first thought, though his hair was gray and he appeared to be severely crippled. He guessed the man was somewhere near the same age as Pa had been when he died.

"I know I have no legal claim to this land and house other than it was my mother's generosity in remaining with her husband's children following his death that preserved the property for Desmond. Without her, Desmond and Caroline would have been sent to an orphanage, and the state would have laid claim to the property since they had no kin to serve as guardian."

Clayton remembered his grandfather had similarly refused to acknowledge Pa's role in saving the plantation.

"I never meant to take what is rightfully yours. I only claimed the farm when I saw a notice that it was to default to the state since no heirs had been found—and because my family was facing desperate circumstances. We were in need of a home since I'm no longer able to work to support my wife and daughter."

"How did you pay the taxes, or are they in arrears?" Clayton wasn't sure how much of the man's story to accept. If the man meant to play on Clayton's sympathy, the man would soon discover his ploy wouldn't work.

"Your grandfather was paid a great deal by the railroad for the right-of-way along the river. There was enough left after his death to pay the taxes, and, by being careful, I expected to continue to keep up the taxes until Lucinda is of an age to marry." Clayton thought back to the shotgun-wielding young woman who had caught him so off guard. She probably seemed younger than she truly was.

"What are you going to do now that I am here?" He didn't know why he asked the question. This family of imposters was no concern of his. Perhaps it was because he'd never expected that he might return one day to claim his grandfather's plantation and hadn't quite taken in the reality yet. Now that he was there, he acknowledged the strong pull to remain.

* * *

Lucy covered her mouth with her hands. Why hadn't Papa and Mama told her the truth about how they came to be living in the run-down old mansion? She'd thought a time or two that it was strange Papa's brother had left his property to him but had never communicated or made an effort to help them during the years they'd struggled to stay on their farm. She leaned against the wall beside the sitting room door that never fully closed anymore. They would have to leave. But where would they go?

For just a moment she wished she had shot the young man who had come to take away another home from her family. No, that wasn't true. She'd been so caught off guard when she had confronted the handsome young man that she'd forgotten all about the wild turkey she'd shot and stuffed into her game bag. She'd been so busy gaping at him that he'd gotten a jump on her. What she really wished was that he wasn't the real owner of her home and they'd met at one of those fancy balls Mama was always talking about.

She hadn't planned to eavesdrop on the stranger's talk with Papa, but she hadn't been able to resist when she passed the sitting-room door on the way back from delivering the game to the kitchen. She'd be in big trouble if Mama caught her listening to a private conversation, but she'd discovered a long time ago that it was the only way she ever learned anything of interest. She'd really come down stairs to discover where Mama had hidden the old gun. The last time she'd caught Lucy with the gun, she'd hidden it on the top shelf of the pantry. Mama thought Lucas was the one keeping a steady supply of small game animals ready for her to cook. She'd be sure to faint if she learned it was Lucy.

Lucy was startled by a figure appearing at the end of the hall. Seeing it was Lucas, she relaxed. He smiled and winked. In his hand was the squirrel gun. It would be all right. Mama had returned the gun to him. She returned the smile before darting up the back stairs to her room. She'd collect her gun later.

CHAPTER EIGHT

"Dinner is served." Lucas announced, making Clayton reminisce about the good memories of Travis and him running for the kitchen. Clayton had spent most of the day with the Southbridge family, discussing options and their history and what he had done over the years after fleeing the Southbridge plantation with Pa and Travis. He hadn't realized what an appetite he'd worked up from just talking.

"You'll take dinner with us?" Mary Beth Southbridge asked as she stepped into the parlor from the direction of the kitchen. The polite invitation took him by surprise. He hadn't noticed she'd left the room while her husband was telling his story. Clayton had been so intent on Elliot's explanation of his family's presence in the house that he hadn't noticed her absence. Now he wondered if she'd prepared the meal herself. There didn't seem to be any servants about other than old Lucas. His first inclination was to decline the invitation, but instead he found himself nodding his head in acceptance.

Stepping into the great hall, his eyes turned to the grand staircase that wound its way to the upper floor. He watched in amazement as Lucinda descended the stairs. She was careful to avoid meeting his eyes. She looked so different from earlier that day. Her wide skirt and fashionable curls revealed a complete opposite to the Lucy he'd encountered beneath the willow tree. The gown was a little large for her; doubtless it had been borrowed from her mother as her earlier attire had likely been liberated from her father's wardrobe. On second thought, there had been something familiar about the boy's attire she'd worn. Had she perhaps discovered some of his old clothing that had been left behind when he'd made his hasty departure all those years ago?

Already Lucy showed promise of being a great beauty. He scoffed at his own thoughts. He'd never paid women much attention, and he wasn't going to start by admiring a woman so young.

Elliot, with his wife's support, made his way to the head of the table, and Clayton found himself seated opposite young Lucy, who gave him one haughty glance, then studiously ignored him for the duration of the meal. A pang of sympathy touched him for the girl caught up in a situation not of her own making, and he couldn't help admiring the courage it took for her to come down to dinner. He found himself feeling sympathetic toward Mrs. Southbridge too, who revealed with small nervous mannerisms her fear of what might happen to her family and what the future would bring.

Lucas passed a platter with one small turkey followed by a bowl of baked sweet potatoes and one of fresh peas. Conscious that the servings were meant to feed five, he helped himself to small amounts, though he was famished. There was little conversation, and it was all Clayton could do to avoid a childish urge to squirm.

He didn't know what to think of Elliot, who openly admitted he had no real claim to the property but didn't show concern over the matter. So it was with relief that he accepted the other man's invitation for a private discussion in the library following the awkward and meager meal.

Elliot settled himself in a chair opposite Clayton and waited for the younger man to take the proffered seat before speaking.

"Are you ready to assume management of this property?" Elliot's question was blunt and wasted no time on pleasantries.

"I suppose I must," Clayton revealed more reluctance than he had intended. "It is legally mine. I have papers to prove my identity, and Grandfather left his will with a local judge naming me his heir. Unless he changed his will after I left with my father and brother, this property is mine."

"I am aware of that will. It was never replaced." Elliot seemed to brush Clayton's remarks aside without any attempt to dispute Clayton's claim.

"You arrived without knowledge concerning your grandfather's passing or the present situation here. It appears that your arrival is the result of a whim, a chance occurrence, and not the result of advance planning. From that I can only conclude you have other interests and another destination awaiting you. Am I right?"

"Yes, but . . ." Clayton couldn't guess where the man was headed with his questions and seeming lack of concern for his certain eviction.

"I know your father took you and your brother away from here after an altercation following your mother's death and that the three of you successfully eluded your grandfather's determined search for many years. I'm also aware that the plantation only remained in your grandfather's name following the war because your father chose not to change the title to his own name when he paid off the heavy tax penalties placed on the land by the government. Still you are not yet twenty, and I wonder if you are ready to assume the responsibility of managing such a large estate."

Clayton felt a jolt. Accustomed to the West, where a boy of sixteen often shouldered a man's responsibilities and could prove up on a homestead, he hadn't considered that in Alabama he might not yet be considered an adult. Elliot Southbridge clearly had done his homework and knew an awful lot about Clayton and his family. Obviously he'd prepared himself for the possible arrival of a legitimate heir. Clayton began to suspect he should have contacted an attorney before making his identity known to this man.

Elliott continued to watch him, waiting for an answer. Clayton felt uncomfortable, but honesty compelled him to admit he wasn't ready to assume responsibility for the plantation. He'd set his heart on obtaining an education at the academy in Boston. Yet he didn't wish to relinquish claim to the land that had been his grandfather's life either. Clayton's collar felt uncomfortably tight as he considered being forced to choose between the education he'd dreamed of for as long as he could remember and the plantation that felt like a piece of his being. He recognized a need within him for a home.

Elliot seemed to almost read his thoughts. "I have no intention of taking this house or the fields that surround it from you," he said, and Clayton believed him. "But I have a proposal to make."

Clayton leaned back in his chair, narrowing his eyes, as he wondered if he was being gullible in listening to the man's proposition. He'd never felt so unsure of himself and at the mercy of someone older and more astute since the day he'd left here eight years earlier.

Grandfather had been a master manipulator, and Clayton had sworn long ago to never fall prey to his or anyone else's manipulations.

"My family is in a bad way." Clayton could see the older man's admission wasn't easy for him to make. "I returned from the war determined to marry my sweetheart, who had waited for me in spite of her family being of greater consequence than I could ever hope for. I dreamed of the two of us making something of the small parcel of land my mother's second husband had deeded to me. All went well for some years, and I was able to buy a few more acres. At long last a daughter was born to us, and I thought our future was bright. Then, as I explained earlier, a crippling disease struck and I began to lose the use of my legs along with much of my former strength. Because of the weakness, I fell frequently and was injured further. A dishonest man who wanted my farm turned this weakness to his advantage. Unable to work the fields or pay the taxes on the farm, I lost our land and my means of supporting my family. I faced complete despair. That's when I learned about this property. It appeared to be the answer to my prayers and my last hope of providing a home for Mary Beth and Lucinda."

Clayton once again stifled a desire to squirm. He felt sorry for Elliot, but surely his pity didn't extend to sacrificing his property. He'd been warned by both Pa and Mr. Sorensen numerous times of the disasters that ensued from letting emotions take precedence over common sense, and he wondered if Elliot was only sharing his story as a means of manipulating him into giving up what was rightfully his.

"Surely you don't expect me to walk away from my claim to this property."

"No. Not at all. What I am proposing is that you appear before a judge to establish your claim and then name me as your manager until you're ready to assume management. You will be ensuring that the property remains yours for when you are ready to assume management of it, and I will be able to keep a roof over my daughter's head until she is of marriageable age."

"Excuse me, sir, but it doesn't appear that you're able to manage a property of this size."

For the first time, Elliot appeared unsure of himself. "It's true I cannot manage this property as I understand your father once did or as your grandfather did before the war, but I pledge to use the funds your grandfather hadn't spent to keep up the taxes, thus preventing it from falling into the hands of the state or squatters. With Lucinda's and Mary Beth's help, I have kept up a small patch of cotton, and Lucas keeps us fed from his kitchen garden. I shan't use the railroad money for anything other than payment of taxes."

Clayton could see the advantages to Elliot's proposal, but there were pitfalls too. Fulfilling his dream of attending school and obtaining an education was still his greatest desire, but how could he go to Boston if going meant he might lose the plantation? He wished he could discuss the matter with his father before making a decision. It seemed unfair to throw people off his property when they had kept it from being claimed by the government. Still, with an able-bodied manager, the land could show a profit and pay the manager's wages. Until it did, there was more than enough of the money Pa had saved to pay for his education and a man's salary.

"I'll think on it," he promised, not wishing to make a hasty decision.

The next few days saw Clayton tramping about the plantation, at first accompanied by a reluctant Lucy at the behest of her father, who seemed to think Clayton required a guide. As they walked, Clayton attempted to talk to the girl, who glared at him and refused to answer his questions. Clearly she was no more thrilled to be spending her time in his presence than he was to suffer her reluctant service as a guide. After several futile attempts at conversation, Clayton gave up and turned his attention to the land, ignoring her.

A feeling of sadness touched his heart as he surveyed the fields that once bustled with workers, now lying fallow. Weeds were creeping into fields once kept meticulously free of unwanted growth. The forest was beginning to reclaim the fields. The paths through the wooded areas were overgrown and impassable in many places. Few of his mother's flowers remained near the house, and the barns and stables were in serious need of paint and repair. By the time he finished school, much of the rich, black soil would once again be covered with brambles and trees.

"It's a sinful waste!" He spoke his disapproval aloud.

"Why should you care?" He'd almost forgotten the presence of Lucy and was startled by the anger in her voice.

"Because it was once the most beautiful and profitable plantation along the river," he told her while keeping his eyes on a field. Anger filled him as he observed that the field was now covered with saplings that had sprung up as the forest had begun to reclaim the land. "And it was my home."

"You ran away. It's my home now." Her defiance held a touch of fear that Clayton didn't miss. What was he to do? He didn't want to leave this young woman and her parents homeless, but the land needed to be worked. His grandfather and great-grandfather had devoted their lives to creating the Southbridge plantation. His father, too, had sacrificed greatly to save it from the ravages of war and the aftermath of the conflict. No matter his feelings toward his grandfather, Southbridge blood ran through his veins. Southbridge sweat and blood had built the plantation. How could he betray his heritage by walking away? It would be wrong to even consider such a possibility.

Gradually Lucy's animosity toward him softened as they spent their days tramping over the fields. Perhaps she shared a love for the neglected acres. Toward the end of his stay, she even accompanied him without being ordered to do so by her father, and he discovered that she was largely responsible for the small field of cotton that grew near the creek, clearly the only cash crop under cultivation. She also spent many hours assisting Lucas with both household tasks and the weeding of his garden patch. He found her surprisingly interesting and easy to talk to. Her fierce devotion to her family and her knowledge of farming impressed him, causing him to lean favorably toward her father's proposal.

He'd been at the plantation five days when he once more visited his mother's grave. This time he saw that the grass had been clipped and the weeds pulled. New markers had replaced the old ones with names etched deeply into the wood. He felt ashamed that he hadn't taken responsibility for the task himself.

Hearing a sound behind him, he turned, expecting to see Lucy, but it was Lucas who stood a short distance away. Clayton motioned for him to come closer.

"Thank you." Without being told, he knew it had been Lucas who had tended the graves. He wanted to say more but didn't know how to express his thanks for the years the man had continued to serve Grandpa, to help Clayton and Pa and Travis leave on that night so many years ago, and for still being there long after he might have slipped away to find a better life.

"He was a good man afore the demon whiskey ketched hold a him." Lucas stood before Desmond's marker and seemed to be apologizing for his former master.

"I know. It was the war," Clayton acknowledged. "Some folks suffered too much hurt and loss to ever overcome the pain."

"Your mama was the kindest, prettiest lady I ever know, 'cept my Dulce."

"I never stopped missing Mama," Clayton admitted. "I'm sorry about Dulce too." He paused before adding, "We had to go. You know that."

"Yes, I know. Now dat new Master Southbridge ain't nuthin' like de old one, but he a good man. He do his best and he understan' sometimes folks has no place to go. I remember his mama too. She try hard, but she never could please Desmond's papa or Master Desmond. She good to Desmond and Caroline anyway 'til Master Desmond be grown and he send her away."

Clayton felt a stab of guilt as he recalled never once considering what had become of Lucas and Dulce after he and his brother had ridden away from the plantation with Pa. His respect for Elliot took a leap forward. A lesser man with all of the difficulties Elliot faced would have sent the old man away rather than respect Lucas's claim to the only home he'd ever known or acknowledge Lucas's efforts to help him and his family.

"I'm thinking of letting him stay for a few years," Clayton admitted aloud to his grandfather's old friend and retainer. "He isn't asking much, just to live here until I'm older and ready to settle down. I can't stay here now. I've plans to get the schooling there was no time for when I was younger. Pa died last month, but he left Travis and me his savings. I could send part of it here to hire someone to work the fields if you could help Mr. Elliot find a hardworking, honest man willing to work for a pittance. If there's any profit, I could pay him a little more in the fall. I mean to see that you receive a wage too."

"I know just da man." Lucas smiled his rare smile.

* * *

The last two days of Clayton's visit were spent going over the plantation's books and his grandfather's accounts; making arrangements with the local judge, Judge Martindale, who remembered Clayton as Desmond's grandson; and arranging for permanent markers to be placed on the graves under the sweeping boughs of the willow tree.

Lucy often curled up in a chair in the library while Clayton worked, a thick tome in her lap. Often he found himself speaking his thoughts aloud and was amazed by how easily the girl's opinions melded with his own.

At last he gathered up his small bag and began the walk to the railroad water tower. The train was due through the valley shortly. He'd traveled only a short distance when he spotted Lucy leaning against a thick tree trunk waiting for him. Once more she was attired in overalls, and as was the case last time her long, pale braid was stuffed beneath a felt hat, making her appear more boyish, like she'd seemed when he first saw her.

"Howdy!" He grinned when he saw her. She grinned back, though her smile looked forced.

"Are you coming back someday?" she asked, falling in step beside him.

"I reckon I will," he said.

"When you come back, will we have to go away?"

He stopped and looked at her for a long time, seeing the worry in her eyes, eyes that knew more of sorrow than a young woman's should. The long, drawn-out wail of the approaching train cut through the silence. "Maybe not," he whispered. "Maybe not."

CHAPTER NINE

THE TRAIN WHISTLE BLEW AGAIN, and Clayton stepped rapidly toward the water tower as the giant locomotive ground to a halt with a hiss of steam and the shrill sound of metal scraping against metal. He slowed his pace as he mounted the steps the conductor set on the ground. He lifted his head and took one last look at the ragged fields and the mansion peeking from between overgrown trees, feeling a strange reluctance to leave the place. At last his eyes settled on a stooped, shabby figure in overalls trudging back up the hill. His hand lifted almost of its own volition as though he would call her back.

His hand dropped, and he squared his shoulders before striding down a narrow aisle until he found an empty seat looking out over the platform, where he was surprised to see old Lucas standing. Something in the bearing of the man standing on the empty platform gave him courage. Once again he squared his shoulders; he wouldn't let old Lucas down. He'd be back. He wouldn't let Pa or Travis or even Grandpa down, either. They expected him to make something of himself and he would. He'd make something of the Southbridge plantation too, when the time was right.

The long train ride was filled with stops and starts, poor food, and little sleep. Then, Clayton had a long walk carrying his valise to find the school. His heart pounded and he felt like a naive kid when he at last faced the large brick building. Sweeping lawns and lofty oak trees gave the school a grandeur that satisfied a longing within him. He'd waited so long for this opportunity. In spite of feeling lost and a little out of place, he made his way to the front door and rang the bell. After a few moments a colored servant in a starched apron and cap arrived to escort Clayton to the headmaster's office, where he was greeted by a young man in a neatly tailored suit who gave him a stack of papers and led him on a tour of the school.

After filling out the papers and paying his fees, he was given a list of boardinghouses that accepted students enrolled at the college. He followed the directions on the paper to the first house on the list and learned there were no openings. Still carrying his bag, he visited one house after another with a similar lack of success. He found the city streets baffling, and he felt an uncomfortable rumble in his stomach, but at last he spotted a three-story clapboard house with peeling paint and an unkempt lawn. It appeared a bit run-down, but when he learned there was one bed left in an attic room he would have to share with another student, he lost no time settling an arrangement and paying the charge.

A slovenly maid escorted him to the tiny room in the attic he was to share with an unknown young man. She made it clear Clayton was responsible for making his bed, doing his laundry, and cleaning the room. Her responsibilities didn't extend beyond the main rooms on the first floor. That was fine with him; he'd been doing things for himself for a while.

Standing alone in the center of the small room, Clayton examined the space that was to be his home for the next four years. His perusal took in the one grimy window, the sagging cots, and a none-too-sturdy table with a straight-backed chair on either side of it. A narrow, rickety wardrobe awaited his and the stranger's clothing. Beside the wardrobe stood an equally shabby bureau. His shoulders sagged, and he wished himself back in Texas, riding and laughing with Travis or, better yet, back at the plantation. The journey had been long and hot and dusty, and he was filled with trepidation. He longed for a long soak in a cool stream, a steaming plate of familiar food, and his bedroll laid out beside that of his brother. Or maybe the feather comforter that covered his boyhood bed.

After setting his bag at the foot of one of the cots, he stretched out to test the cot's length. Though not as tall as Travis, Clayton had grown considerably over the past year and found his feet hanging over the end of the cot. He stared up at the pitched ceiling and felt a quick spike of moisture in his eyes. Angrily he dashed his fists against the offending moisture. He was nineteen, almost twenty, and much too old for tears.

A stillness crept over him, and he closed his eyes, beginning to doze off.

"Well, if this ain't a fine how-de-do!"

Clayton jerked awake to find himself staring into bright blue eyes surrounded by a cheerful, round face liberally sprinkled with freckles. The young man, studying Clayton with equal curiosity, had his blonde hair plastered tightly against his head. He wasn't as tall as Clayton nor as broad in the shoulders, but there was a hint around his middle of being a little too well fed.

Clayton stood and was met with a jovial slap on the back by Arthur Bennington. Arthur then extended a soft, pink hand—a sharp contrast to the leathery, work-worn hand Clayton extended in return. Arthur seemed to be a few years younger than Clayton, but his youthful appearance may have been due to an easier life than Clayton had known. Clayton soon learned that Arthur was nothing like Travis, but the two young men struck up a liking for each other that cheered Clayton immensely and revived his enthusiasm for attending the academy.

Arthur produced a packet of sandwiches and invited Clayton to join him at the wobbly table, where Clayton learned that Arthur, too, came from a Southern family but was much more conscious of social manners and the dictates of fashion than Clayton. Arthur was affronted by their shabby accommodations and expressed frustration with his inability to procure better housing, going so far as to state his intention of complaining to his father.

After a week's futile searching, Arthur had conceded that there was nothing he could do about moving to a better boardinghouse until his first year of college was behind him. In the meantime, he'd set about making friends and entering into activities, in which he assumed Clayton would wish to join him. Clayton preferred to concentrate on his studies but succumbed to Arthur's determination to include him in his many exploits. Before long, Clayton found himself in a world totally unfamiliar to him. Without quite knowing how it happened, he became the owner of several new suits of clothing and was spending his spare time playing games on the large green square behind the school. He showed interest in a rowboat on the nearby river and soon found himself, along with Arthur, a member of the rowing club.

Attending lectures occupied the greatest portion of Clayton's time and interests. He was frequently the first to arrive and the last to leave the spacious rooms where the classes were held, and he never begrudged a dime spent on the thick volumes he was expected to study. He struggled at first with the papers he was required to write, but once he learned the proper form, he found he enjoyed expressing his newfound knowledge in copious essays.

In many ways, attending school was all he'd once dreamed it would be, but he was often conscious that he was older than the other students, even older than some of the lofty upperclassmen. Some of the first-year students were no older than Lucy. He and Arthur were fortunate to escape much of the hazing other first-year students were subjected to. He thought it might be due to his age, but Arthur insisted it was something more, something in Clayton's bearing that made upperclassmen bent on mischief shy away from him and, luckily for Arthur, his roommate.

Clayton continued to miss Pa and Travis and made it a point to write frequent letters to his brother, though he received few in reply. He also kept up a regular correspondence with Elliot concerning the workings of the plantation. Elliot sent Clayton frequent missives, informing him that Lucas had found help to work the fields and updating him on the field preparations and the crops' progress. Clayton composed pages of instructions and directions for bringing the land back into productivity.

In commiserating about the deprivations of their first lodging and the rigorous hours of study demanded by their professors, Clayton and Arthur were determined to not spend another winter in the shabby boardinghouse, studying at the rickety table and blowing on their fingers to keep them from freezing. They'd grown accustomed to being together and had become firm friends, making it an easy decision to continue rooming together. The fact that they were both from the South and away from their families for the first time added another dimension to their relationship. It also helped that Arthur was not at all shy and that Clayton was particularly adept at solving mathematics problems—Arthur's greatest downfall. Before Arthur left to spend the summer with his family, the two scoured the city for a better room.

Luck was on their side. They found a room that was larger and held sturdier furnishings than their original apartment. It was closer to the school too and was being vacated by two upperclassmen. Clayton particularly liked the large leather chair, where he could sit to read and occasionally glance out the window. It reminded him of Lucy's favorite chair back at the plantation.

As the first year of school ended, Clayton pondered whether or not he should return to the plantation during the summer break. He decided against it, thinking he needed to be careful with his remaining funds and that he could profit from the extra study time. It was a difficult choice, but money he might squander on train fare could be put to better use painting the house and repairing the roof.

Not being the kind of man who could loaf away the summer, he found a job loading cargo on and off the ships at Boston Harbor. Though he found the sailors' tales of far-off places exciting, he never developed a yearning to join the sailors on their voyages.

After hours of poring over his books and working at the docks, Clayton often took long walks along the pier in the evenings. He scoured bookshops looking for any titles that might catch his interest. Once he discovered a novel by a Swiss woman, Johanna Spyri, entitled *Heidi*. The gentleman who owned the shop informed him it was written especially for children but assured him it would be of interest to any young lady, regardless of age. He purchased it and sent it off to Lucy.

On one of his walks toward the end of summer, he noticed a young woman dressed in a sedate calico gown who seemed to be wandering about on her own. She had a pleasant face and wore her hair in a tight roll at the back of her head. Something about her drew his attention— perhaps it was the impression he had that she was as lonely as he was. She walked past him and he lifted his cap, but she paid him no mind, and he failed to muster the courage to approach her.

Arthur returned just a day before classes were to commence, once more filling Clayton's life with noise and excitement. Their new boardinghouse was far more comfortable, and though their studies continued to challenge them, they found time to accept the invitations they received to attend receptions and balls, even an occasional concert or play. Arthur's attempts to teach Clayton to dance led to uproarious laughter. Clayton felt flattered when he and Arthur were invited to join the rowing team again, and together they enjoyed the camaraderie of other young men. His friendship with the jovial young man went a long way toward easing his loneliness for Travis, but sometimes he wished Arthur were more interested in serious matters.

Women were the one area where the two disagreed most. In Clayton's opinion, Arthur spent far too much time squiring young ladies to various popular pursuits and when, at Arthur's insistence, Clayton was persuaded to ask a young miss to dance or to stroll with him in the park, he felt awkward and ill at ease. His tongue seemed to trip over the words he wished to say, and he longed for the ordeal to end.

One young woman, however, did interest him. He was quite certain she was the same young lady he'd noticed strolling along the pier that summer. She sat in front of him in one of his mathematics lectures and was one of only two women he'd encountered in any of his classes at the school. Her name was Lavinia Noble, and she had come to the college from somewhere in one of the western territories. Her brown hair was kept in the same severe bun he'd seen at the pier, and she wore round spectacles, which he hadn't noticed when he'd first seen her. The spectacles exaggerated the size of her brown eyes and made the rest of her face appear small and pinched.

At first he paid her scant attention, but soon she seemed to think it her duty to challenge his position as first in the class. Outside of class, she appeared shy and rushed away immediately following lectures. In class, she seemed as intent on learning as he was and too often refuted his answers if she didn't agree. Not only did she dare to disagree with the young men in the class, but on occasion she disagreed with their professor. Clayton's and her exam marks were usually the same, and sometimes his score was only better by a point. But just as often she surpassed him by a point or two. On several occasions they found themselves locked in fierce battle over the theories of their various mentors, and their competition led to Clayton's ability to overlook her gender and see her only as a brilliant mind that challenged his own. Their professor and several of their classmates dismissed Lavinia in the belittling tone of their voices, but Clayton never did.

One day she showed up to cheer for Clayton and Arthur's rowing team, and when Clayton explained to Arthur who she was, Arthur convinced him it was his duty to thank her for her support. Clayton looked at Lavinia in her plain gown and noticed a breeze had caught a strand of her hair, sending a spiraling curl across her face. Her cheeks were flushed, and she was smiling, appearing to be enjoying her outing. He'd heard several of their classmates mockingly call her homely, but with a start he realized she wasn't plain and that it was only her severe hairstyle and manner of dress that made her appear so.

Feeling a strange reluctance to approach her, he nevertheless let Arthur push him forward.

"Hello, Miss Noble." He hastily removed his hat and stood holding its brim, twirling it between his restless fingers.

"Oh, hello, Mr. Telford. Congratulations on your team's fine showing." Her cheeks were pink, and it seemed to take considerable effort to respond to his greeting.

"Thank you. It's exceptional exercise. Leaves me invigorated and helps me study more productively." Why couldn't he ever think of anything clever to say? Such remarks seemed to roll off Arthur's tongue.

"I quite envy you." She smiled, and he noticed her even white teeth. As he searched for something further to say, Arthur approached.

"Some of us are going to celebrate our victory at the pub across the street. Several ladies will be there," Arthur announced. Then, turning to Lavinia, he added, "Would you care to join us?"

"Oh no." Lavinia appeared flustered as she turned down the invitation. "The race was a delightful diversion, but I have other responsibilities and must return to my lodging." She looked stricken and shuffled her feet uncomfortably for several moments before turning to disappear into the crowd of spectators.

Clayton watched her go and felt a moment's regret that she had refused the invitation.

"So that's the infamous female mathematician." Arthur clapped a hand on Clayton's shoulder. "She doesn't look nearly as formidable as I had expected. In fact, she seemed quite taken with you."

Clayton shrugged off his friend's hand. "She was merely being polite," he muttered. He wouldn't admit it to his friend, but there was something about the young woman that he liked. "Let's catch up to the others." He set a rapid pace toward their teammates, who were gathering across the street.

* * *

On Monday when Clayton stepped into the lecture hall, Lavinia gave him a quick smile. A quiet friendship began to develop between them, and Clayton discovered they shared many views concerning the issues of the day and that they were both more comfortable with numbers than people. They began to share a few words following the lectures they both attended, and Clayton found his thoughts straying to the young woman on a frequent basis.

When summer arrived, he discovered her one day at one of the bookstores he frequented. On learning she was far from her family and alone in the city, save for her elderly landlady, who was an acquaintance of her grandmother, they began taking weekly strolls together on Sunday afternoons. Clayton enjoyed having someone with whom he could share his thoughts and was pleased to have found a friend who knew something of the rigors of the West, someone who seemed to take as much pleasure in trees and sky as did he, and someone with whom he could speak of gentler matters.

His brother had always been his best friend; though he and Arthur had struck up a friendship almost at once, there were certain things Arthur didn't seem to understand. With Lavinia, Clayton developed a friendship that satisfied an ache he hadn't even acknowledged to Arthur. Clayton and Lavinia shared an interest in literature, philosophy, and science. And they both excelled at mathematics.

He learned that Lavinia, too, had lost her mother at an early age, but she'd been fortunate enough to have an aunt who'd stepped in to care for her. They agreed, however, that even a loving aunt wasn't the same as one's mother.

"I thought that as I grew older I would miss Mama less," Clayton confided, "but some days I long for her as much as I did when I was a boy."

"I don't think we ever stop missing those we love who go to heaven before us. But there is consolation in knowing one day we shall be united again."

"Do you really suppose we will be with them again?"

"I know God means for families to be reunited in heaven." She sounded so certain. He wished he could be as sure of seeing Mama and Pa again as she was of being united with her mother. Though not sure he shared her conviction, he found comfort in her words and often found himself entertaining the hope that one day his family would be together again.

By the time Clayton completed his third year at the college, he determined not to spend another summer alone in the city. The few friends he'd made were all returning to their family homes for the summer. Even Lavinia was spending the break with a cousin in Vermont. He considered traveling to Texas to visit Travis, but the distance and the expense were daunting. Instead he accepted Arthur's invitation to spend a few weeks with him, then travel on to Southbridge for the last two weeks before his final year of classes was to begin. It was time he checked on his property in person.

* * *

"Oh, Artie!" Arthur's mother greeted him with a flourish of hugs and kisses when the two friends stepped into the elegant drawing room of the Bennington's South Carolina estate. Clayton felt ill at ease. Not even when he was a boy had he found himself surrounded by so much luxury. He'd known Arthur came from a wealthier background than his own, but he hadn't expected such a distinct contrast.

A servant showed him to a guest room with a high four-poster bed so wide it could accommodate four men his size. He set down his valise and the trunk he'd purchased to hold the suits and additional books he'd acquired since he and Arthur had become roommates and simply stared at the big bed in dismay. He wasn't sure he could muster the courage to sleep in something so fancy. It was so high he feared he might break his neck if he were to fall off of it in his sleep.

Dinner turned into an ordeal when he discovered Mrs. Bennington had invited guests. He felt certain he'd make a fool of himself.

"Uh-oh," Arthur muttered as he descended the stairs with Clayton. "I should have known Mama would invite the Charrington sisters my first night home. She's quite determined that I marry Miss Rachel Ann. Doubtless she sees you as an opportunity to palm off Rebecca Adele."

Clayton raised his eyebrows, unsure what Arnold found objectionable about the young misses. They didn't seem any different from the misses Arthur chased back in Boston. They were certainly pretty enough with their long curls of deep, silky brown hanging down their backs. Their waists were astonishingly narrow, and they were dressed in the latest style. And they both curtsied prettily when introduced.

Clayton found himself seated beside Rebecca Adele. He felt a small catch in his chest when she fluttered her long lashes at him. He wasn't sure he'd ever seen a prettier woman. Just looking at her made him feel large and clumsy.

"I'm so happy you've come to visit with dear Arthur," she cooed.

Clayton reached for his fork. He hadn't eaten a real meal since he and Arthur left Boston, and the steaming piece of ham on his plate had his mouth watering. Rebecca Adele grasped his arm between her two small hands. "It's just so exciting to meet a man who owns his own plantation at such a young age. I so admire a man who makes his mark early. You must tell me all about it."

"It's in Alabama." He attempted to free his arm without creating a scene. The ham was growing cold.

"Oh, I've always wanted to visit Alabama. I've heard such lovely things about that dear state. As a young master, I suppose you entertain frequently. Poor man, it must be hard to keep up your social obligations without a wife at your side." She fluttered her lashes and peeked at him sideways.

Clayton spared a glance for the creamed potatoes on his plate, which he felt certain were growing thick and losing their savor, then sent a desperate look across the table to Arthur, who merely acknowledged his plight with a helpless shrug.

For three weeks, everywhere Clayton turned he seemed to run into Miss Rebecca Adele. Along with Arthur, he found himself promised as an escort to the young ladies for walks in the garden, buggy rides, and various entertainments. Never having been subjected to so much female company before and finding Rebecca Adele's chatter and her maneuvering to be alone with him a little unnerving, he began to doubt the wisdom of his decision to take over the plantation.

His rosy dreams of life as a gentleman planter took on tarnished edges. His dreams of farming and of a comfortable life in the old mansion had never included the social life Arthur and the misses Charrington seemed to take for granted as an essential part of that lifestyle. Sure, he'd supposed he'd have a wife by his side someday, but he'd never considered having one who chattered ceaselessly and would expect him to entertain her and her friends with parties and balls. The only females he'd known to date, other than his mother, were Lavinia and Lucy, neither of whom ever talked so relentlessly as Miss Rebecca Adele. Was he to assume that this provoking malady was common to most women?

On a rare occasion when he and Arthur managed to sneak away for a few hours by themselves, he expressed his concern to his friend. "I can dress like a gentleman, talk like one too, but I'm not sure I'm cut out to be a gentleman. I can't imagine anything worse than listening to Miss Rebecca Adele prattle on every day about fashions and neighborhood trifles. And if I'm expected to entertain guests with parties and dances, well, I just can't do it."

"Living clear off in Alabama, you might not have to do too much entertaining. Lots of folks here don't, but you know my papa is quite set on a political career for me. The South will never regain its glory if young men from the better families do not wrest control from the Northerners who arrived here in legions following the war. There are some who have made up a secret organization to deal with the problems Southerners face, but Papa is quite convinced politics is the only way to bring about needed change and to protect our rights."

"I've heard about the Klan, and I want no part of it."

"My advice is to not make enemies of those who belong to the Klan by stating your views too openly," Arthur cautioned, then returned to their earlier discussion. "I envy you in some ways. With your pa gone, you don't have anyone pressing you to do things you don't like. I just wish Mama would stop pushing Rachel Ann at me.

She doesn't talk as much as her sister, but she's as pushy as Mama and Papa and quite set on marrying me and living in the capital." He sighed and looked downcast. "I was quite hoping you'd take a fancy to Miss Rebecca Adele. Having you as a brother would soften the future my parents have planned for me."

In only a few minutes, Arthur was back to his exuberant self, but Clayton found himself counting the days until he could leave for Southbridge.

CHAPTER TEN

1890

LUCY FELT A FLUTTER NEAR her breastbone each time she heard the long, drawn-out whistle that accompanied the train's descent into the river valley. Papa had announced a month ago that Mr. Telford would be arriving for a brief visit at the end of the summer, and just yesterday Papa had received another wire telling them to expect Mr. Telford by the end of the week. She'd been a mere child when he'd come before, but this time she meant to impress him with the young lady she had become. She was careful to only wear britches and hunt in the woods in the early morning hours before the first train stopped at the nearby water tower, and she'd taken Mama's advice to roll her hair in rags each night so her locks would curl prettily down her back in the daytime.

Of course, she didn't need to hunt every day like she used to. Since Mr. Telford hired Israel and James to work in the fields, there was crop money to buy supplies, and they frequently snared small animals or caught fish they shared with Mama. Lucas had been patient in teaching her many new skills too, and she seldom failed to bring back game when she ventured into the woods along the river.

Selling Dandy didn't worry her anymore. Since James and Israel had brought home three sturdy mules, as Mr. Telford had instructed, to work the fields, Dandy was used mostly to pull Mama's buggy and for tasks that required a single horse. At first Israel had attempted to work Dandy with one of the mules, but both animals had been clear in their objections, and the farm worker ended up picking himself up from across the stable for his efforts.

Some days Papa was strong enough now to walk in the fields and tell the men what they should do. Lucy didn't think she and Mama and Papa had ever been happier. The only thing better would be for Papa to get well. She wished his legs would get stronger, but he'd had periods of better health before, and she'd learned such spells didn't last long.

She looked forward to Mr. Telford's visit with mixed feelings. Part of her wanted to see if the young man was as handsome as she remembered. Her pride wished to show him that his trust in Papa had not been misplaced and that the farm was doing well under his guidance. When she thought of their first meeting, it always brought a blush to her cheeks, and she wanted to show him she could behave like a lady. She was anxious, too, to learn of his plans for the future. With just one more year of schooling ahead of him, his agreement with Papa was nearing its close.

From far in the distance the first shriek of a train whistle floated down the valley. Lucy rushed to the beveled mirror that stood in one corner of her room. Brushing her hands down the length of her pink-and-white striped gown, she twisted to check the fit in back. It was perfect, and she felt a flush of gratitude for Mama's ability to redesign her once-fashionable wardrobe into suitable dresses for her daughter. Mama had been raised with slaves who did the cooking and sewing, but when she married Papa she'd taken on those tasks herself. Lucy took just one more moment to check the curls that fell neatly into place down her back. It wasn't vanity, she assured herself, that compelled her to look her best for Mr. Telford's arrival. Surely if she appeared poised and mature, he'd be more inclined to continue his arrangement with Papa.

* * *

As he made his way up the winding path from the railroad stop, Clayton remembered his grandfather's frequent admonition to hold on to the land at all costs. "Wealth is measured in land," the old man had often reminded Clayton. "All else fades away, but the land remains." It must have cost the old man plenty to sell even a narrow strip of his precious land to the railroad.

The plantation looked much different than when he'd arrived three years earlier. Now, well-tended fields stretched into the distance and the grassy slope leading up to the house was neatly trimmed. A couple of cows grazed in a nearby pasture. He thought his grandfather would be proud of him for the steps he'd taken to save the old place. He also felt a surge of hope that the farm would soon be self-supporting again. He had little money left beyond that needed to finish one more year of school.

As he walked, he felt pride in the marked improvement. Fields were no longer choked with weeds but showed hopeful signs of a coming harvest. The rich abundance of the land pleased him, and for the first time he acknowledged that he and his grandfather were much alike when it came to loving the land that made up the plantation. It was almost as though the rich, black bottomland was part of him.

When he stopped beside his mother's grave, he noted that a scythe had recently been used to trim the grass around all three graves and a cluster of camellia blooms leaned against the marker where "Kathryn Southbridge Telford" had been chiseled in the stone he had ordered to be placed there.

Removing his hat, he bowed his head. As he stood thinking of all that had transpired since that long-ago day when his mother was buried, he couldn't help feeling a touch of melancholy. He wondered if she were really in God's heaven and if she ever thought of him and longed to see him. He no longer missed her with the searing ache that had accompanied him in the months following her passing, but her smile and tenderness flitted into his mind at times, reminding him of how dear they had been to each other. His gaze slid to the space beside his mother, and he felt a wave of sadness that it hadn't been possible to bury Pa beside her. Clayton couldn't help feeling an ache, knowing that his family had been tossed to the far corners of earth and heaven.

After a few minutes, he turned to his grandfather's grave. Because Clayton was Kathryn's firstborn child and for whatever other reasons, the irascible old man had preferred him over Travis and had charged him with continuing the plantation after his grandpa's death. That thought saddened him for both Travis's sake and for the grandfather who had missed the opportunity to know and love his other grandson. As a consequence of Grandpa's bias, Clayton had been treated more kindly and his feelings were softer toward his grandfather than were the feelings of other members of his family, making it easier for him to forgive the old man's behavior and feel compassion for the hard life that had been thrust on his grandfather since early boyhood.

Clayton had spent more time with Desmond than had Travis, listening to his grandpa tell of the grand plantation their home had been before the war. Somehow the old man had instilled in his first grandson a respect for the soil that had once fed the Southbridge family and nearly a hundred slaves. Somewhere deep inside Clayton was a desire to return the plantation to the magnificent farm it had once been. This time it would be accomplished without slave labor. It was his grandfather, too, whom he could thank for his yearning for an education. The old man had been his tutor and had painted glowing pictures of him going away to attend an academy. A smile touched Clayton's lips. Grandpa wanted him to receive formal schooling, but it wasn't a Yankee academy that Grandpa had in mind.

"Grandfather," he spoke the word aloud. "The land is mine now, just as you planned. I'm not ready to leave school yet, but I want you to know I didn't leave you or this land because I wanted to. I needed Pa and Travis, and you made it impossible for them to live here. I'll be back some day to stay, and I'll love these acres just as you did. I hope, too, that one day I'll have sons or grandsons who love this land just as I do. I haven't forgotten any of the things you taught me about taking care of this place."

He started at a small sound behind him. Turning abruptly, he was almost disappointed to see a squirrel scamper up a tree instead of a ragamuffin girl dressed like a boy. Sometimes when his studies were overwhelming or he felt a touch of homesickness during the past three years, he'd found himself smiling as he thought of the tough girl who'd taken so much responsibility on her shoulders.

He returned his hat to his head, ducked beneath the trailing willow fronds, and continued toward the white house farther up the hill. As he neared the door, he noticed two black men sitting on the edge of the wooden platform that covered the well. One held a thick sandwich in his hand, while the other drank deeply from a hollow gourd. Such a drinking dipper had hung beside the well as long as Clayton could remember. He longed to refresh himself the same way.

"Good day!" he greeted the pair. He couldn't help feeling curious about them, wondering if they were the workers Elliot had hired.

"Good day, sir." The two men hastily set down their lunches and doffed their hats like schoolboys, though they were each at least a dozen years older than Clayton.

Clayton continued past them to the front door and then knocked to announce his arrival.

* * *

"Lucinda!" Something in Mama's voice warned her it wasn't the first time she'd called to her.

"Yes, Mama?" She hurried to the top of the stairs.

"I need you to polish the furniture in the parlor. It won't do for the mansion to look less than its best when Mr. Telford arrives. Papa said his last communication suggested he would arrive by the end of the week."

Lucy nearly tripped in her haste to descend the stairs. How could she have forgotten to dust the parlor? She quickly donned the cap and apron her mother held out to her. She usually protested the necessity of wearing such items, but since she didn't wish to soil her new dress she lost no time tying the voluminous apron at her waist and settling the too-large cap over her curls.

Dusting the furniture wasn't Lucy's favorite task, but it was better than some chores Mama thought she should learn. Her rag flew over the heavy pieces in what she considered a silly task, since tomorrow they would require dusting again. Her mind wandered to fanciful daydreams, and she longed to be clad in trousers, enjoying an outdoor adventure. Mama didn't approve of her wearing trousers, but Lucy found them far more suitable than skirts and petticoats for her early-morning forays into the woods. They were more comfortable too, and she wished there wasn't such a wide discrepancy between suitable attire for young men and young ladies.

A sharp rap on the door interrupted the best part of her dream. Sighing with annoyance, she stepped into the hall and flung open the door.

* * *

The door was opened after what seemed a long wait. Clayton found himself staring at a young maid in a frilly apron, her hair tied up in an old-fashioned cap. She carried a cloth that smelled of beeswax. It was odd that Elliot had never mentioned hiring a maid.

"Good day!" He removed his hat. "Mr. Southbridge is expecting me." He'd sent a telegram several days previous, notifying Elliot of his expected arrival date, but Clayton had been fortunate to find passage on an earlier train. Possibly the maid had been hired to prepare for his arrival.

With a startled exclamation, the maid dropped her cloth and turned to flee toward the staircase. He debated whether he should step across the threshold or wait for the maid to advise Elliot of his arrival. Several minutes later Mrs. Southbridge appeared, wearing a long apron that covered her gown from neck to toe. She brushed a damp tendril of hair behind her ear and seemed uncertain whether she should extend her hand to invite him in or curtsy.

Clayton decided the matter by stepping through the door and into the hall. "I'm pleased to see you again," he addressed her. "I assume my wire was delivered, informing you of my arrival."

"Yes, yes." She fluttered about him, taking his hat and ushering him toward the parlor. "Lucy and I were just straightening the house in anticipation of your arrival." Blushing, she quickly peeled her apron off and then stood balling it in her hands, clearly uncertain what she should do with it.

Clayton remembered the maid who had met him at the door. He struggled to keep a grin from surfacing. He should have recognized the little hoyden.

"My dear boy!" Elliot Southbridge entered the room, leaning heavily on a cane, though he appeared more robust than he had during Clayton's previous visit. Mrs. Southbridge's welcoming smile revealed her gratitude for her husband's arrival, granting her a reprieve from hostess duties.

"Come, sit down." Elliot pointed to a seat with his cane. As soon as Clayton sat, the older man sank into a seat opposite him. Though he was obviously stronger than when they first met, Clayton noticed a slight tremor to the older man's hands.

"I see more fields are planted than when I was here before," Clayton began. "And it appears the house has been painted."

Elliot puffed out his chest a bit. "I expect, if cotton prices hold, to show a small profit this year. Last year we met expenses and kept ourselves fed, but there was nothing to spare."

"I intend to inspect everything with an eye toward further improvements," Clayton said before changing the subject. "Your health seems much improved." He hoped he wasn't being too personal, but the state of Elliot's health was of concern to him because a man who was ill would find managing the large estate difficult and could undo the progress made.

"Yes, I am able to make my way about with greater ease, though unfortunately, I shall never be able to walk again without assistance. Old Lucas brought his sons to me shortly after your departure two summers ago, and they have proved to be able workmen, asking only a small wage and to be allowed the use of a couple of the slave cottages for their families. They had fallen on desperate times and were hard-pressed for means to care for their young families."

"Lucas's sons?" Clayton hadn't known the old slave had a family. With a sense of chagrin, he acknowledged that, as a boy, he'd been oblivious to the black man as a person, and though he'd known Lucas and Dulce were married, he'd never given a thought to whether they had children. He recalled the two men he'd seen sitting beside the well. Were they Lucas's sons?

"And is Lucas well?" he asked.

Elliot seemed pleased to turn the conversation to the old former slave. "Yes, he doesn't see as well as he once did and his steps are slow, but he does what he can. He moved out of the house and into a cabin after we arrived. Jacob's and Israel's wives have made the cabin comfortable for him. He enjoys fussing over their little ones, and his sons' wives seem to dote on him. He asked permission for the women to raise their own gardens near their shacks. I hope I wasn't amiss in granting them leave to do so. He keeps the children occupied helping with the gardens."

Clayton couldn't imagine Lucas as a grandfather or playing with children. He'd been a strong, formidable figure during Clayton's early childhood who tolerated no disobedience or boyish pranks from Clayton or Travis. Everything that happened on the plantation was reported to Grandfather. Lucas looked after Grandfather and only ever smiled at Clayton's mother.

"The funds I sent to build up the plantation—have they been sufficient?" he asked.

"Yes, I have kept a meticulous record," Elliot was quick, perhaps too quick, to assure him. "We've relied on the funds you sent to bring the fields back into production, but this year we used some to paint and repair both this house and the workers' quarters. Of course, two men cannot accomplish what a hundred slaves once did, but I think you will be pleased with the results of this year's harvest. Before your arrival, I set the books on the library desk for your convenience."

"I shall look them over this evening following dinner," Clayton promised. "Now I think I should like to retire to my room until dinner." He'd traveled by train for two days since his last stop and felt much in need of refreshing himself.

"I think you will find everything in readiness," Elliot said with a quick glance toward the stairs.

As Clayton mounted the stairs, he wondered at Elliot Southbridge's nervousness. The man had tried to hide his edginess, but Clayton was certain there was something on the man's mind. What Clayton had seen of the farm as he'd walked up the hill looked to be well cared for, and he'd noticed several improvements to the house in addition to the new coat of paint. He'd taken a chance on the man; he hoped he wasn't about to learn he'd been mistaken in his judgment of Elliot's character.

Finding a pitcher of fresh water in the room where he'd slept as a boy, he removed his coat, pushed up his shirtsleeves, and commenced to scrub himself and shave his face. There had been few opportunities for proper grooming since leaving Arthur's home.

From the mirror above the basin, he caught a reflection of movement beyond his window. Curious, he stepped closer to the window. A highly agitated woman was running toward a massive oak tree with branches hanging over a pool of water where he and Travis had learned to swim as boys and where they'd drawn water for the horses confined to the stable. A small creek meandered aimlessly across the farm and along the north side of the lawn, forming a deep pool where it rounded the oak before picking up speed on its way to the river.

Faint screaming reached his ears. Several children ran after the woman, and an older child danced up and down near the swimming hole.

Clayton tossed his razor aside and flung himself toward the stairway that led down the back of the house, his long strides carrying him across the lawn. Just before reaching the pool, he heard a loud splash, followed by more screaming. Crashing through the shrubs that hid the pool from the house, he barely managed to skid to a stop before sliding into the water. The path that had once led gently to the edge of the water was now a mudslide.

He made a hasty survey of the scene before him. In the pool, a slim feminine form rose out of the water, holding an unmoving, dark bundle in her arms. Lucy! On the bank, the woman he'd seen running toward the pool held out her arms, sobbing and begging for her baby. A girl of about seven or eight floundered wildly in the water near the mudslide's drop-off point. Clayton held out his hand, and the child clutched it. He drew her to the edge of the pool, where she clambered out of the water and, without really seeing him, ran sobbing to the frantic woman he suspected was her mother.

Ripping off his boots, Clayton jumped into the water and began swimming toward Lucy as she made her way with awkward, cautious steps toward the shore. The water was little more than five feet deep, but it rose above her shoulders, and whenever she stepped in a hole, she and the child she held received a dunking. Stopping beside her, Clayton held out an arm to assist her with the toddler she held above her head. The muddy creek bottom made movement difficult and dangerous. She slid again, almost losing her hold on the child.

On seeing his outstretched arm, she hesitated only a moment and then allowed him to steady her, though she didn't relinquish her burden to him. With great care he guided her toward the shore, securing her whenever her feet slipped and lifting her when the water threatened to rise above her chin. When the sloping sides of the pond brought them to where the water was only three feet deep, he gently grabbed her waist, swinging her and the child up into his arms, and moved swiftly toward the shore. When he reached the bank, he set them down in the long grass at the sobbing woman's feet. Then Clayton began pounding on the toddler's back, pushing at the boy's small chest and shaking it in a desperate effort to get him to breathe. Clayton's efforts were rewarded when a stream of water spewed from the child's mouth and he began to whimper. The mother scooped the boy into her arms, holding and hugging him while tears streamed down her face.

Lucy had moved to stand and was anxiously watching the mother alternate between tears and laughter as she hugged her child and wiped at his eyes and mouth with her apron. At some point, Lucy clearly became conscious of the wet muslin dress clinging to her skin and of her hair plastered against her head. She took a self-conscious step backward, and one foot landed on the mudslide. For several seconds she teetered, trying to regain her balance. It was no use; her feet flew out from under her, and she slid with a resounding splash back into the pool.

Clayton hesitated but a moment before plunging back into the water in what he suspected was a totally unnecessary attempt to rescue her. He hit the water as she surfaced, showering them both in a deluge of water that sent her flying backward. He reached to steady her, but to his surprise she attempted to elude him. The slippery mud at the bottom of the pond sent them both sprawling. Clayton struggled to regain his footing while flailing about in search of Lucy.

He rose to his feet, scraping mud and water from his eyes and mouth, in time to see the girl clutching at grass and roots to pull herself from the water. He considered giving her a boost but decided chivalry demanded he look the other way. However, what his conscience told him was the gentlemanly thing to do and his ability to look away were two different things. The sight of Lucy's drenched form held him mesmerized. She was no longer a child. Even as he reached to offer her a hand, she pulled her sagging skirts from the water, turned, and with one foot kicked with all the force she could muster, sending him backward, his arms windmilling, the water closing over his head once more.

There was no time to prepare for the shock of water covering his head and filling his mouth. Seconds later he rose to his feet, spitting and spluttering. This time as he wiped muddy water from his eyes, he caught a glimpse of Lucy, with her wet skirts clasped above her knees, running at full speed toward the house. He decided to let her have her little victory and, with a grin, knelt beside the woman cradling her child to assure himself that the child was truly safe. When he felt confident the toddler was behaving in a normal fashion, he helped the mother shepherd the children back to the cabins that had once housed the plantation's slave families.

He took advantage of the opportunity to view the cabins and was pleased to see how comfortable they looked, though they appeared a mite small to house the number of children he saw running about. Perhaps he could suggest to Lucas that his sons make use of some of the unused cabins by dismantling them and using the lumber to build additions onto their homes.

At dinner that night, Clayton found his attention straying toward the grand staircase he could barely see from his place at the table. He wasn't surprised when Lucy didn't make an appearance at dinner, but he was surprised by the twinge of disappointment he felt at her absence.

Over the following days he gave little thought to his tenant's daughter as he surveyed the crops growing on the plantation, paid his respects to Lucas and his sons, and checked on the child who'd nearly drowned. He also devoted time to studying the books Elliot had kept of his expenditures. He rarely caught sight of Lucy. Much to his amusement, Lucy was avoiding him, though at times he thought he could feel her eyes upon him. Once he happened upon her curled up in her favorite chair in the library.

She rose to her feet, appearing anxious to hurry away.

"Wait!" He held out a hand as if to physically prevent her from leaving. "I've wanted to tell you how much I admired your actions in rescuing that child."

"I only . . ."

"Don't say that anyone would have done it, because that isn't true. Most of the young ladies I've become acquainted with in Boston would have hesitated to get their gowns wet, and I doubt many of them know how to swim."

"I never really learned to swim, but Papa taught me to dog paddle before his legs began to limit what he can do. I just couldn't bear to let that child drown when I might be able to save him. I didn't know you were close by and could aid him better than I."

"I'm not certain I would have reached him in time."

She looked down for a moment, then lifted her chin to face him. "I've been remiss in not thanking you for the book you sent."

"Did you like it?"

"Yes. At first I thought I wouldn't because it is about a very young girl, but I found I enjoyed it nonetheless." She went on to explain how much she liked learning about a distant land and how much she admired the little girl's attachment to her grandfather. As she spoke, Clayton settled himself in a broad window seat nearby.

The afternoon slipped away as the conversation turned to his own longings for his family, her concern for her papa, and the happenings in each of their worlds. Clayton marveled at how easily they fell back into the camaraderie they'd shared three years earlier.

His visit to the plantation passed much too quickly, and the day before his departure he found himself in the library seated across from Elliot once more. "I'm pleased with all that has been accomplished since I was here last," Clayton said as he closed the ledger he had been poring over. He stared into space for several minutes, deep in thought, and then added, "Would you be willing to continue our arrangement for another year? I have one more year of schooling before I complete my course, and I would like to see it through to completion." Clayton felt torn between his desire to assume management of the plantation and his desire to graduate from Boston College. His visit had convinced him that the plantation and its management were the future he desired most.

The relief on Elliot's face revealed the reason for his seeming nervousness, and Clayton felt shame for not realizing sooner that the man had feared he would be without a home or means of supporting his wife and daughter again.

Clayton's smile matched that of his tenant as it occurred to Clayton that he didn't want Elliot and his family to leave the plantation. With Travis so far away, they were the closest thing he had to a family. On an impulse, Clayton added, "In the coming months I think we should work out a more permanent arrangement so that even after I come here to live, I will have the security of knowing my property is being properly cared for should I choose to travel or be absent for a period of time. As quickly as profits allow, I intend to hire more workers. There will be more than enough work for both myself and an overseer. Would you be agreeable to such an arrangement?"

As Elliot gave his fervent approval, something crashed in the hall, and though it only took Clayton a few seconds to reach the door, the hallway was empty when he jerked it open. When he glanced both ways, though, he thought he might have caught the swirl of a skirt disappearing around a corner at the far end of the passageway.

CHAPTER ELEVEN

1891

CLAYTON'S FINAL YEAR AT BOSTON COLLEGE passed quickly, with time away from his studies devoted to the rowing club. Clayton loved both the competition and the chance to be outdoors, testing his strength against the river and other teams. Arthur began paying particular attention to a pretty, dark-haired girl who often appeared on the riverbank to watch their races and cheer for him. Once, Clayton accompanied his friend to a dance at a nearby girls' school, where Arthur's pretty friend was enrolled. Clayton no longer felt awkward and out of place at parties and dances, but he felt no enthusiasm for any of the giggling young misses he met there, and when his friend invited him a second time, he declined. "I'm not much for society," he tried to explain. "Those young ladies are all much too young for me anyway."

"A man of your property and standing will be expected to take a wife before long," Arthur reminded him. "The young ladies at this school are taught the social skills needed to enhance your social standing." It was useless to try to explain to Arthur that Clayton wished to be respected by others but possessed no interest in what Arthur and many of the young men he encountered at the college referred to as "society."

Clayton had a feeling the pampered young ladies at the girls' school would flee if they knew his real background. Sure, Grandpa had been a Southern property owner of considerable standing before the war, but Clayton hadn't grown up with the manners expected of a Southern gentleman. The gentility that seemed second nature to Arthur seemed silly and useless to Clayton. He'd never shared the details of his earlier exploits and his gun skills with Arthur. He hadn't even confided such matters to Lavinia. Even though Clayton had become good friends with both Arthur and Lavinia, he'd always known he could never share with either of them the kind of open relationship he'd had with Travis.

After Arthur left to attend the dance, Clayton lay on his bed, the book he had been reading forgotten, staring at the ceiling. He couldn't get Arthur's words out of his mind about his need for a wife. Perhaps he was being unrealistic, but he didn't want a wife from whom he'd have to keep certain aspects of his life. He was pretty sure neither of his parents kept secrets from the other. He remembered his parents had almost always been together, talking, laughing, and making plans. Their closeness had made him feel secure and was one of the many things he'd missed since his mother's death. When he married, he wanted someone with whom he could share the important things in his life, the way he'd once shared his thoughts and dreams with his brother. He was as drawn to a pretty face and a trim figure as any man, but he wanted more. Was he being unrealistic to want to spend his life with a woman whose interests were as diverse as his own and who wouldn't condemn him for the things he'd done? His thoughts turned to his mother. He sure could use her advice. It didn't seem fair that he and Travis had grown up without her influence in their lives.

Thinking of Travis, Clayton felt a heaviness in his heart. His brother didn't write often enough. Though Travis wasn't as interested in academic matters as he was, he could write and had a good head for figures. It just didn't occur to Travis to keep his brother apprised of his life. Of course, opportunities to mail letters came less frequently for Travis, living on a remote ranch on Texas's frontier, than for Clayton, living in the heart of one of America's first cities.

One day as spring approached and the trees lining the paths of the school were beginning to provide an overhead canopy of leaves, Clayton and Arthur came upon several young men who had gathered around a young lady. The young men, all lowerclassmen, seemed bent on teasing her unmercifully, and she appeared close to tears. The sight stirred protective feelings inside Clayton. When he realized the object of the young men's teasing was Lavinia, his anger erupted.

"Here, now." Clayton waded into the group with Arthur close behind. "The lady doesn't appreciate your wit. Be off with you." He threatened to punch anyone who defied his order. Being close to six feet tall, with heavy shoulders and arms kept strong from rowing, neither Clayton nor Arthur inspired the hecklers to challenge their right to intervene. Most of the hecklers lost no time finding other pursuits demanding their attention.

"She ain't a lady; she's a Mormon," one of Lavinia's tormentors added, taking one last jab before hurrying off.

"I'm sorry you had to experience such rudeness." Arthur doffed his hat, and Clayton quickly followed suit.

"Did they hurt you?" Clayton extended his hand as though about to check for injuries but then withdrew it, unsure how to approach the situation. He knew some of the men attending the college objected to females being enrolled.

"No, they didn't hurt me. I shall be fine." She tossed her head in an attempt to brush off the incident, though the moisture gleaming in her eyes said she wasn't as unaffected as she claimed.

"I do hope they aren't students at this college," Arthur asserted. "My papa was assured that attendance here would provide the polish a gentleman requires to move about in the business and political world and that the young men here were all from the best families and of the finest caliber. No gentleman would tease a lady in such a disgusting manner, calling her names and rendering insults upon her character."

"But I am a Mormon." Lavinia faced them with her chin held high as though daring them to say anything disparaging about Mormons.

"You're what?" Arthur gulped and seemed to turn pale.

"What's a Mormon?" Clayton looked between his two companions, puzzled by Arthur's shock and Lavinia's defiance. In all their discussions, Clayton didn't recall Lavinia mentioning Mormons. Even so, he wasn't sure whether he'd been mistaken in his assumption that Lavinia was being harassed for being a female studying at a college generally attended by males or if there was another cause.

"I'll explain," Arthur nudged him with his elbow, indicating they should leave.

"Not until after I escort the lady to her room." Clayton extended his arm, and, after a moment's hesitation, Lavinia took it. Arthur appeared about to say something but held his tongue. He didn't join them in the walk to Lavinia's boardinghouse but appeared agitated as he hurried away.

As they walked, Clayton could feel the hand resting on his arm shake and knew Lavinia was more upset than she'd admitted. He was also aware of her frequent glances at his face. After walking a few blocks, she asked a question.

"You really don't know anything about the Mormons?"

"No, should I?"

"'Mormon' is a slang term used for members of the Church of Jesus Christ of Latter-day Saints. We're a religious group who were forced out of our homes in Missouri, then again in Illinois, where our prophet was murdered by a mob. Our people traveled west a decade before the war and built thriving communities in the western states, but mostly in Utah Territory. Mormons are hated and despised by many because our religious beliefs aren't like those of other churches."

"I don't go to church, really," Clayton admitted. "So I don't know a whole lot about religion. My Pa never seemed to think listening to preaching was too important, but he attended church a couple of times each year when we happened to be in a town with a church, and he often read from a Bible he carried with him during the war. My mother used to attend mass regularly, and sometimes she insisted on my accompanying her, but that was a long time ago and I don't remember much about it. Occasionally preachers came to some of the ranches where Pa, my brother, and I worked, and we'd go listen to them. It was kind of exciting to see how worked up some of them got, but nothing they said stuck with me for long. I guess what I'm trying to say is that my religious training has been limited enough that I don't understand why anyone would hate someone else over religion." He glanced sideways to judge how his words were received. He noticed how pretty she was with her face flushed and wisps of hair curling against the damp spots on her cheeks.

"I don't think I'll ever understand hate. We're Christians, but unlike most religions we believe there is a prophet on earth today and that God communicates with him through revelation just as He did with the ancient prophets." Her bottom lip trembled, and Clayton wished there was something he could say to comfort her. He wished, too, that he'd spent more time reading Pa's Bible. If he had, he might be better able to understand what had upset Lavinia so.

"I can see where it might come in handy to have a prophet to set us straight, but I don't see why anyone should hate you for believing in one." So far she hadn't said anything he could see a reasonable man objecting to.

"It gets complicated. Some of the hatred sprang up from ministers who feared that our prophet would lead away their congregations and that they'd lose their livelihood. Some of it began over poorly written homesteading laws that allowed others to take over land settled and improved by our people by merely preventing them from filing papers at the conclusion of the homesteading period. Since large numbers of Mormons who settled in Missouri and Illinois were opposed to slavery, they became pretty unpopular in those territories where most of the other people were hoping to enter the Union as slave states."

"I can see where those issues might lead to trouble. My grandfather and father were always at odds over slavery and politics. Grandpa owned a large plantation, and my pa was a Yankee officer. I don't recall them ever fussing over religion, though."

Lavinia looked like she might say something more, then changed her mind. After a few minutes of silence she asked, "Why are you being so nice to me?"

Clayton thought for a moment and then said, "I figure we Westerners need to stick together."

"I remember you said your pa took you west and you spent several years in Texas, but I thought your home was a big plantation in Alabama." She stopped and looked at him, obviously puzzled.

"The plantation belonged to my grandfather. He passed away a few years ago, and I fell heir to it. I wasn't raised there, except for when I was a little tad. When my mother died, Pa and my grandfather parted ways. That's when Pa took my brother and me west to Texas. Travis and I were just boys, but we grew up fast during the years we spent working on ranches and trailing cattle herds to Kansas."

After a moment's silence, they continued walking. Lavinia seemed as deep in thought as he was. As they approached the big house where she boarded, she asked in a low voice, "Now that you know I'm a Mormon, will it change our friendship?"

"I don't see why it would." The question puzzled him and hurt some too. It seemed she ought to trust him by now not to pay too much attention to other people's opinions.

At the door of her boardinghouse, he tipped his hat and bid her farewell. He puzzled over their odd conversation all the way to his and Arthur's room, where Arthur proceeded to tell him, "You'd best steer clear of that woman. Mormons aren't socially acceptable. Besides, their men marry dozens of women, and Reverend Charrington says they're all going straight to hell."

Clayton kept his thoughts on the subject to himself, but he wasn't about to take Reverend Charrington's pronouncements too seriously, and he couldn't see why a bright, pretty young lady deserved to be ostracized for her religion any more than she should be criticized because she was smarter than most of the men in her classes. Instead of severing their friendship, he found himself looking for opportunities to talk to her and escort her to her boardinghouse following classes over the next few weeks.

* * *

"A letter came for you," Arthur greeted him when he returned to their room after his last lecture one day. He didn't look up from his book. There had been a coolness in their relationship since Clayton had refused to end his friendship with Lavinia. Clayton ignored the petulant look on his friend's face and picked up the letter Arthur had left on the table. Clayton recognized his brother's scrawl across the front of the packet and immediately slit it open. Though he wrote to Travis every month, he'd received only a handful of letters in almost five years. He pulled out a single sheet of foolscap, smoothed the rumpled page, and began to read.

Dear Clayton,

I hope you are well. I am fine. I am partnering with a man who has done a lot of traveling. We signed on to deliver a herd of cattle to a new ranch in Montana. Leave tomorrow. Sorensen, good man, will take care of my horses till I get back. Thinking about buying my own spread if I find a good place. Montana sounds good. Send letters care of Francine Butler in Salt Lake City, Utah Territory. Claude and me will stop there on our way back to Texas.

Your brother,
Travis

Clayton sat down and reread the letter. He shook his head, feeling a twinge of melancholy. He missed Travis and wished his younger brother would write more often and fill pages full of the kind of talk they'd shared as boys. He couldn't help feeling concern over learning Travis was leaving the Sorensen ranch to strike out with an unknown companion on another cattle drive, this one of far greater distance than those they'd undertaken with Pa.

"Well, I'm glad to see you've come to your senses. There's no future in following after a Mormon." Clayton had forgotten all about Arthur.

"What?"

"Oh, maybe you're not mooning over ending things with that Mormon girl. Did you get bad news in your letter?" Arthur waved a casual hand toward the letter Clayton still held in his hand.

"No, nothing like that. My brother is setting out on a new adventure, and I was just thinking how much I miss him."

"You're not going to see Lavinia anymore, are you?"

Clayton felt a rush of irritation. "There's nothing to break off with her. We're friends and I don't see any reason to change that."

"You can't be serious!" Arthur jumped to his feet. "If word gets out that you're hobnobbing with a Mormon, you won't have any standing anywhere. If you marry her, you'll be completely ruined!" Arthur grabbed his hat and stomped out of the room.

Clayton couldn't see what all the fuss was for. He wasn't planning to marry Lavinia. But now that the possibility had been planted in his mind, he found he couldn't stop thinking about it.

* * *

As graduation grew nearer, Clayton's hours spent studying increased and he sweated over exams. He found himself thinking about what awaited him at the plantation with mixed feelings. He was anxious to take over the management of the farm, but he wasn't sure he was ready for the responsibility. So far his arrangement with Elliot was working well, but would everything be different when he returned to his childhood home to stay?

The morning he was to listen to a final address from the college president and receive his diploma, he was packing his trunk to leave in the hall of the boardinghouse, ready for transport to the rail station. He was surprised by the amount of clothing and books he had accumulated over four years. His oldest clothing was in the bottom, still wrapped around the fancy Browning rifle he'd purchased during his first lonely summer and hidden away. He still wasn't certain whether he would keep it or find a way to present it to his brother, who would have far more need of it in the wilds of Montana than he would in Alabama. He'd been toying with the idea of going West for a visit with Travis before taking up the reins on the plantation, but with Travis off to Montana, there would be no use. Clayton had no idea where they might meet up.

Arthur, packed his bags and a large trunk, but he was unusually quiet.

"Why the long face?" Clayton asked. "I thought you'd be bubbling over with happiness and confiding your engagement to Miss Phyllis Madsen by now." His roommate had been seeing the dark-haired Louisiana beauty at every opportunity for several months now.

"There won't be an engagement."

"What? You two have been inseparable since Christmas. Surely her papa has no objections." Clayton stuffed the last of his books in his trunk and sat on it to struggle with the straps.

Arthur slumped onto his bed, now stripped of blankets. "I can't marry Phyllis. My family would disown me, and I would never be accepted anywhere."

"Your parents are that set on you marrying that girl back home—what was her name? Rachel Ann? Come on, you're a man now. You reached your majority some time back and have every right to choose your own bride."

"I wish it were that simple." Arthur was uncharacteristically somber. "When I knelt to do the pretty deed last night, Phyllis confessed to me that her mother is a light-skinned mulatto, her papa's New Orleans mistress. Phyllis said her papa loved her and wanted her to have all the advantages he could give her, so he'd sent her to school here in Boston and lied about her mother's identity, claiming his deceased wife was her mother. She knows she can never return to the South and is thinking of going to France after graduating from the school for young ladies. She says people like her are more accepted in France."

Clayton watched his friend struggle to hold back tears. "You love her, don't you?" he asked.

Arthur nodded his head. "Why didn't she tell me sooner?" Then he seemed to grow angry. "How could I have not known? For one mad moment, I considered asking her to be my wife anyway, but I couldn't do it. My parents would disown me, and there would be no chance of a political career. I'd even be stripped of my membership in the church."

"But what would all that matter if you were with the woman you love?" Clayton colored with embarrassment and wondered what had possessed him to make such a silly, romantic statement.

"Sometimes I despair that you'll ever understand what it means to be a Southern gentleman." Arthur shook his head. "There are certain things society just won't stand for."

* * *

Fearing he might arrive late, Clayton ran almost the entire way to the auditorium for the last time. As he took his place, he found himself searching for Lavinia. He knew she should be the class valedictorian or spokesman, but that honor had gone to a young man since it wasn't proper for a woman to be given such a high academic honor. At last he spotted her, but she was a considerable distance away, and there was no chance he could reach her before the procession began. Their eyes met and he felt cheered by the smile they exchanged.

The speaker droned on, and Clayton found his mind drifting. He was anxious to begin the day-to-day management of the plantation, yet it scared him. Could reality measure up to the dream? For a fleeting moment his thoughts went to Arthur, and he felt a stab of pity for his friend. Disappointment, too, that Arthur placed his social standing above his love for Miss Phyllis.

The speaker's voice faded in the background, and Clayton drifted toward sleep. As he jerked awake, he caught a glimpse of amusement on Lavinia's face. He was both embarrassed and pleased that she was watching him. He was going to miss Lavinia. She was as pretty as any miss he'd seen at the nearby school for young ladies, and he enjoyed their spirited discussions. It occurred to him that Lavinia would make a lovely mistress of Southbridge and that he didn't relish the thought of never seeing her again. Had he settled for friendship when he could have had much more? He couldn't get the thought out of his mind. Perspiration trickled down his back beneath the heavy wool suit he wore. The morning had grown excessively warm. Did he dare propose to Lavinia? Where had that thought come from? It wasn't like him to be rash, but time was running out. He might never see her again.

Honesty compelled him to admit that the idea of proposing to Lavinia wasn't really so sudden. It had been at the back of his mind for some time. He could use a familiar friend at his side as he took over building the plantation into a grand estate. Like him, she didn't seem to be drawn to society's social whirl, and she was easy to be with and intelligent.

At the conclusion of the ceremony, Clayton joined in the jubilant shouts of the other graduates and found himself swallowed up in a crowd of well-wishers. With hearty handshakes and comradely slaps on the back, farewells to students and professors rang through the hall. He made up his mind. Tearing himself away from the well-wishers surrounding him, he began pushing his way through the crowd. Time was short and he needed to act fast or he'd miss his train and his chance to ask Lavinia to marry him.

CHAPTER TWELVE

"Lavinia!" He called her name once he'd managed to work his way through the throng of people crowding the hall and was within a few feet of her. She turned her head and smiled across a gap that opened between them.

At least a dozen people separated them. He maneuvered his way between them, and then, squirming his way between two large men with a quick apology, he at last reached her side.

"I feared I would be too late," he said.

"Too late for what?" Startled, he glanced around and was surprised to see she was flanked by two gentlemen in outdated, worn, dark suits and stiff collars. Both looked at him with suspicion.

"Clayton, I'd like you to meet two missionaries from Salt Lake City. They're on their way home and have done me the courtesy of offering to escort me home. This is Elder Thackery." She turned to indicate one of the gentlemen, then turned to the other. "And this is Elder Morton. He is a longtime friend of my family." The adoring blush that lit her face when she took Elder Morton's arm surprised Clayton.

Clayton eyed the men with a degree of wariness. It was quite evident they weren't any more pleased to make his acquaintance than he was to make theirs. Nonetheless, he extended a hand, and the men took turns shaking it. Elder Morton squeezed his hand a bit harder than necessary—as though he were making some sort of point.

"Lavinia, might I have a word with you?" He wondered how he might separate her from the gentlemen for a stroll in the rose garden. He couldn't propose in the crowded hall in front of them.

"I'm afraid we're out of time. We have a carriage waiting and the remainder of our party will be growing restless." Elder Morton pulled a timepiece from his pocket and looked at it pointedly.

"I'm sorry, Clayton, but I really must go. Don't think I don't appreciate all the times you championed me or the times you challenged me to excel in our classes. I truly shall miss your friendship." She reached to deliver a sisterly hug, and then, with an arm looped through Elder Morton's, the trio disappeared into the crowd.

Clayton stared at the spot where Lavinia had stood. He seemed to be having trouble catching his breath. Suddenly he wasn't certain that if he had the opportunity to propose, she would accept. He'd never imagined that he wouldn't have a chance to ask the young lady of his choice to be his bride, nor considered that she might refuse him. By the time he thought to run after her to plead his case, there was little chance of finding her again. The many times they'd discussed their favorite books, the lectures they attended, philosophical views, and even religion, somehow they'd never gotten around to discussing anything so personal as their feelings toward each other. Over the din of the crowd, he heard the deep bong of the clock on the square. It seemed to be telling him he was too late. It was also telling him the time had come for a wild dash to the train station.

Neither Clayton nor Arthur had much to say when they met on the train platform. They ensured their trunks were loaded properly and then made their way through the crowded car to two window seats where they could sit facing each other. Stowing their valises under their seats, they settled down for the long journey. Miles passed with the two young men staring sightlessly through their respective windows, each absorbed in his own sorrow.

"I'm sorry," Arthur said, hours after their journey began. Clayton turned questioning eyes toward him. Did Arthur somehow know about his failed proposal?

Arthur continued as though he'd rehearsed a speech and was determined to deliver it.

"I didn't understand how you could care for someone so unsuitable. Then I discovered that my feelings for Phyllis were not acceptable. I believe my mistake was greater than yours." He spoke in a low voice, showing his concern for being overheard by the other passengers.

Clayton didn't think much of the apology and refused to think his friendship with Lavinia was either a mistake or unsuitable. His mistake was in not seeing Lavinia as a desirable wife soon enough, or in not caring enough to go after her in spite of the obstacles. Nor did he see what made Phyllis an unsuitable bride for Arthur. Clayton chose to say nothing, hoping their friendship could be rescued. He suspected his friend would be married to the elder Miss Charrington before the summer was over. As for himself, he wasn't certain how much of the pain he felt stemmed from a broken heart and how much from a blow to his pride. He was accustomed to winning whatever he set out to win. One thing was certain, if he fixed his attention on another young lady one day, he'd make certain his heart was engaged and that she was of the same mind as he was before he offered a proposal.

He nodded his head in silent acceptance of Arthur's lame apology, and the two continued to travel in silence.

Clayton leaned his head against the sooty, smudged window of the railcar, experiencing mixed emotions. He thought about his distant childhood, his years spent roaming Mexico and Texas with Travis and their father, and his student years at Boston College. His life seemed to have been partitioned into three distinct segments, none completely of his own choosing, though he didn't regret any of them. It was his future he was unsure of. Though he was anxious to return to the plantation, he wondered if he'd made a huge mistake by not pursuing Lavinia more vigorously. Why hadn't he recognized he had feelings for her sooner? A moment of introspective honesty had him questioning whether it was Lavinia he was reluctant to give up or the safe though challenging environment of the school he regretted leaving behind. An ache filled his heart, along with a wave of something much like homesickness. Once again he was leaving people and a place dear to him to begin a new life. Not for the first time, he wished Travis were beside him sharing this new adventure.

* * *

The miles clicked by, and eventually the porter lit flickering lanterns, which provided minimal light in the car he shared with Arthur. Clayton stretched out the best he could on the narrow bench and bunched up his coat to use as a pillow. He was too tired to worry much about his uncomfortable position and was soon sleeping soundly.

"Psst!" Arthur woke him just as the first rays of light were beginning to illuminate the inside of their railcar. "Something's not right."

"What do you mean?" Clayton asked, his annoyance at the early wake-up showing. About the same time his head began to clear, he became aware that the train wasn't moving. "We've just stopped to take on water or wood, haven't we?" He'd learned long ago that the steam engines had voracious appetites, requiring frequent stops for water or fuel.

"I don't think so. I can't see a water tower or a platform, and we've been stopped for some time. I thought I heard gun shots."

Clayton eased his way back to a sitting position and looked around. First he pressed his nose to the window but could see nothing more than a few shadowy shapes moving about outside the car. Unless he was mistaken, some of the shapes were men on horseback. Inside the car, a number of people were still sleeping, but a few were looking around in confusion. He noticed a finely dressed man looking out the window on the opposite side of their car. After a moment, the dandy ducked his head and pulled a gun from beneath his coat. His right hand, holding the revolver, disappeared beneath the hat that rested on his lap. Something was definitely wrong.

Clayton reached for the valise he'd tucked under his seat. It took no fumbling to find the six-shooter he'd tucked into an inside pocket. Taking care not to draw attention to himself, he concealed the weapon in his boot. If there was trouble, he wished to be armed.

He looked up to find Arthur staring at him with round, scared eyes. He supposed he hadn't been as careful as he'd thought. "Where did you get that?" Arthur gave a stiff nod toward the gun Clayton had hidden in his boot.

"I've always had it. There just wasn't a need for it in Boston, so I left it in my valise."

"It was in our room all the time?" Clayton wasn't certain it was admiration or alarm he heard in Arthur's voice.

Clayton nodded his head. He didn't know why Arthur was so surprised. He'd told his roommate he'd grown up in the West and had participated in half a dozen cattle drives and become adept at handling a rifle and a six-shooter. Didn't it stand to reason he would have kept the firearm he'd learned to depend on?

A door opened at one end of the railcar, and a rough-looking man stepped inside brandishing a pistol. He was a big man with unkempt hair and yellow teeth, what few he had left. A woman screamed, and bedlam broke loose as those sleeping awoke. Several ducked behind the high backs of the benches before them. Women pushed children into the narrow spaces between benches and then joined them, their arms hovering protectively, like hens guarding their chicks.

"Quiet!" the intruder shouted, thrusting a flour sack toward a young woman sitting on the first bench, who looked disoriented and confused. "You! Collect everyone's valuables." He shoved her toward the aisle. "Watches, rings, money. No exceptions. All valuables go in the bag, and don't try to hold out. I'll shoot anyone who doesn't move fast enough."

The woman began to inch her way down the aisle. Passengers hastily complied with the robber's demands, thrusting jewelry and cash toward the bag she held. Tears streamed down her face, and her hands trembled so much that the passengers had difficulty dropping their valuables into the shaking sack.

Clayton fumed. Ever since he'd pursued the horse thief as a boy, he'd had no tolerance for crooks. He weighed his chances of getting a clear shot at the bandit and decided not to risk it. If a gun battle erupted, some of the passengers were likely to get hurt. Though it angered him to have to allow the robber to steal from his fellow passengers, he reasoned the loss of a few rings and watches was better than the loss of lives.

"Hurry up!" the robber shouted. "Move faster or I'll start shooting!"

From the corner of his eye, Clayton saw a stout woman slip something under the cushion she sat on. The thief caught the movement too, and his gun blazed. The woman fell into the aisle and blood spattered in every direction. Gasps and screams sounded throughout the railcar. The thief stepped to the place where the woman had been sitting and snatched an ornate jeweled brooch from under the cushion.

"Emma, oh, Emma!" a slightly built man knelt beside the woman. He fumbled with his handkerchief in a futile effort to stanch the blood that poured from the wound in her chest.

"Leave her!" the shooter shouted. "Get back to your seat!"

"She's my wife. I must help her!" the man pleaded. He continued to kneel at her side.

The gunman's response was a shot fired at close range into the pleading man's face. Clayton felt sick inside as he watched the slender man topple without a sound onto his wife's motionless form, his blood mingling with hers.

Clayton inched his hand down the side of his pants toward the boot that concealed his weapon. Something spattered near his boot, and he heard a retching sound he assumed came from Arthur. His eyes narrowed, and he forced himself to ignore the sounds of crying and people made sick by being forced to witness cold-blooded murder. His hand closed around the gun.

Another shot rang out. This one much closer than the previous shots. A quick glance confirmed that the dandy he'd noticed earlier had fired his pistol and was getting ready to fire again. Before the would-be hero could squeeze the trigger, return fire sent him sprawling backward. Pandemonium reigned as people ducked behind benches, screaming.

It was time to act. Rising to his feet, Clayton took hurried aim and fired. Years of practice sped the bullet to its target. The bandit's gun barked once more as he crumpled toward the aisle. His gun fell, clattering against the planking of the floor.

Clayton felt nothing—neither satisfaction that his bullet had found its mark nor sorrow for taking a life. Though there was a cacophony of sound, he heard only a distant roar. With slow precision he lowered his gun and attempted to return it to the holster at his hip, but there was no holster. Over the sound of a roaring waterfall he remembered the gun had been in his boot and not in its holster. As he puzzled over what to do with it, the gun fell from his useless fingers. He stared at it and noticed his pants; there was something strange about them. He didn't remember what they should look like, but surely they shouldn't feel warm and sticky. His knees refused to hold him upright, and he pitched toward the seat where he'd been sleeping a short time earlier, blackness rushing toward him.

"You're bleeding!" It was Arthur's voice, but he couldn't make sense of what he was saying. Someone had blown out the lamps, and he was cold and tired—so terribly cold and tired.

* * *

"Come, Mama. You must eat." Lucy urged her mother to take a few sips of the broth she'd carried to Papa's room.

"I can't," her mother murmured, turning away from the spoon Lucy held. "You must coax your dear papa to take just a sip. He hasn't eaten for days. I can scarce get a drop of water between his lips. Perhaps you'll have better luck."

"I will try," Lucy promised, "but I made plenty for both of you. You are as much in need of nourishment as Papa. And rest. You should go lie on my bed for an hour while I try to press a bit of broth between his lips."

"I shan't leave his side." Mary Beth shook her weary head, her untended, graying locks falling about her face.

Feeling helpless, Lucy stood watching her parents. This argument had repeated itself over and over for so many days she'd lost count. Papa was often ill, but he'd never been so ill as this. She'd sent James for the doctor a week ago. That gentleman had arrived promptly enough but had held out little hope. He'd been back twice, each time with a new elixir for Papa to try, but there had been no improvement.

Now she feared almost as greatly for Mama as for Papa. Mama, who was always so fastidious about her appearance, no longer bothered to brush her hair or put on a fresh apron. Neither could she be coaxed to eat more than a few mouthfuls of food.

"Miss Lucy." She hadn't heard Lucas enter the room. "Israel's Hannah be comin' to do the cookin' and cleanin'. I'll stay wif Mastah Elliot. You and Miz Mary Beth need to sleep."

Lucy knew the old man was right. She needed sleep as badly as poor Mama. Neither of them could bear to leave Papa for fear he would slip away from life while they were asleep. Through the cloud of fatigue that surrounded her, Lucy acknowledged that she was useless to Papa in her current state. She reluctantly relinquished the bowl and spoon she held.

"Come, Mama. You cannot care for Papa if you become ill. I shall bring you a blanket and a pillow, and you can rest on the settee just beyond the door. Lucas will wake you if there is a change."

Mary Beth was finally persuaded to go with her daughter, and Lucy saw her settled in the small lounge. She couldn't help wondering if her mother would be back in Papa's room before she even reached her own bedroom on the second floor. She thought fleetingly of the kitchen piled high with dishes and pans, but her guilt over leaving the mess to Hannah was quickly superseded by her need for rest.

It seemed she'd just closed her eyes when a soft tap at her door awakened her. She stumbled to open it and found Hannah wringing her hands and looking apologetic. "Lucas say you best come."

Leaving her shoes behind, Lucy fled down the stairs. A sense of foreboding wrapped the house in silence, and she found herself tiptoeing to Papa's doorway. She could see Mama kneeling beside the bed with her face pressed to Papa's chest, her scattered hair falling across her face and spreading across Papa's nightshirt. Lucas stood back, the shock and dread on his face clear.

"Papa?" Lucy crept forward until her hand rested on Mama's trembling back. "Mama, is he . . ."

There was no answer, but she saw Papa take a shallow breath, then no more.

In the days following Papa's death, Lucy found herself trying to comfort her mother and handle the business of the estate. She made careful entries in the ledgers the way Papa had taught her. She sent one of the older children to town with a message to be wired to Mr. Telford, and she arranged for the local minister to conduct a brief service for Papa. Receiving no answer to her telegram, she instructed James and Israel to dig a grave beside Desmond's for her papa.

A small number gathered for the service, and Lucy was grateful to Hannah and Ruth for preparing the luncheon that followed. There was thinly sliced ham and a nice array of side dishes, many made from their own garden produce, though neither Lucy nor Mary Beth could bring themselves to swallow a bite. Lucy felt a stab of hurt when Mr. Telford didn't arrive, but she consoled herself with a reminder that there might not have been time for him to travel such a great distance.

Mama rallied slowly following the funeral, and as her sorrow abated somewhat, she seemed to be filled with worry and her actions revealed a great deal of nervousness. She reacted with fright at each knock on the door.

Fatigue became Lucy's constant companion as she struggled with the household tasks, directing and assisting James and Israel with picking the cotton and attempting to keep the farm records up-to-date. Lucas did his best to help, but his movements were slow and uncertain. As the days passed into weeks, Lucy wondered why Mr. Telford had not contacted her or Mama. Surely he had long since finished his studies. In order to keep herself calm, she closed her mind to speculating about her and Mama's future.

One morning when rain forced her inside, Lucy was searching through a pile of correspondence and papers that had accumulated on Papa's desk. She happened on a yellow envelope, and at first she glanced at it with casual interest. Then, realizing it was a telegram, she opened it, pulling the single page free. It was addressed to Papa and signed by a man who called himself Clayton Telford's friend, Arthur Bennington. Mama was so absentminded that she could have accepted it and left it on the desk a month ago.

A loud hammering on the front door interrupted her before she could read the telegram. She rose with a sigh. Mama couldn't be counted on to answer the door, and Lucas was probably taking advantage of the rain to take a nap in his cabin. Her mind was still on the unread telegram when she swung the front door open.

A stranger bearing a heavy portmanteau stood on the verandah. He smiled and doffed his hat. "Hello, miss. I'm your Papa's cousin, Maxfield Mason. I've come to inspect my inheritance."

CHAPTER THIRTEEN

AT FIRST THERE WAS A humming sound. No, it wasn't exactly a hum he heard but a more high-pitched sound, almost like voices. Children's voices. He struggled to open his eyes, but there seemed to be a weight on his eyelids and they wouldn't move. He lay still, listening, trying to remember. Slowly he drifted back to sleep, seeing his little brother giggle as they raced from the creek to the barn, a heavy bucket swinging between them, sloshing its contents over their clothes and across their feet. The dream changed to a nightmare. His little brother was running away, but Clayton was stuck in a quagmire and couldn't reach him. Lucy kept trying to help him, but she was sinking too.

He couldn't say if minutes or days passed before he became aware of his surroundings again. There was silence around him, but he sensed he wasn't alone. There was something he should remember. The train robbery! The man pointing his gun toward him! It came to him in a flash, and his hand moved toward his hip, searching for the gun he'd once worn as easily as his boots. His fingers encountered some kind of heavy cloth, but no gun. He forced his eyes open the barest sliver. He could see nothing but darkness.

His panic brought an audible gasp. Was he blind? Wait! He could see just a pinprick of light. It was something! Forcing himself to become calm, he opened his eyes wider, and shadows began to take shape. He was in a room, and the first speck of light he'd seen was a star glimpsed through an uncurtained window at the foot of the bed where he lay. That thought brought another realization—he was lying in an unfamiliar bed in an unfamiliar room with no idea how he'd gotten there. He attempted to sit up and found he could barely lift his head and shoulders. Crashing pain in his head and leg nearly caused him to black out. Before lowering himself again, he noted that a rope crossed his chest, anchoring him to the bed. Somehow he'd been injured and was being held prisoner.

He didn't waste time wondering if he were dead. If that were the case, he suspected he wouldn't be hog-tied to a bed, nor would he be expecting his head to explode any minute. He lay still for several minutes, attempting to calm himself and to think clearly. If he was going to get out of the mess he found himself in, he had to have a plan. He had to force himself to think, to remember.

He remembered the train robbery and the man shot for attempting to go to his wife's aid. He remembered looking at the robber and squeezing the trigger. He hoped he'd hit the murdering thief. Had the other gang members discovered what he'd done and brought him here to torture him? He thought that if his head didn't ache so badly, he could break free of the rope that held him. The rope didn't prevent him from moving his hands.

"Clayton? Are you awake?" He recognized Arthur's voice. Had the robbers captured him too?

"I'm awake," he mumbled.

"You sure had me scared!" A shape he recognized as Arthur came closer. "When you fell, I thought you were dead, but there was no time to check. I had to help barricade the doors so the other outlaws couldn't get inside our car. Ladies and children were screaming and crying. We grabbed everything we could get our hands on to block the door. It was awful, I tell you."

"Are we prisoners?"

"What? Oh no. A troop of soldiers came along and gave chase to the gang of outlaws. A few soldiers stayed behind to help the passengers. I went back to check on you and found a lady holding your head in her lap. She'd wrapped a piece of her petticoat around your leg to stop the bleeding, and I could see you were breathing. Never been so happy to see your mug before in my life."

"Why tied . . . ?"

"Oh, that. You were doing a lot of thrashing about, and Mrs. Macintosh—the lady who stopped you from bleeding to death on the train—feared you might hurt yourself or fall off the bed, so she had me put a rope around you."

"Where are we?" Clayton found his mind drifting toward blackness. He resisted the urge to close his eyes. There were things he needed to know.

"The soldiers said it was the Henry Gooding Gang that held up the train. They killed the fireman and knocked out the engineer, but he came around and someone bandaged his head. He said he thought he could get us to the next town, so some of the passengers helped the soldiers clear the tracks and we got this far before he passed out again."

Clayton still had no idea where he might be, but it appeared they were safe, and he was too tired to fight the lethargy creeping over him.

The sun was shining through the window when he awoke again. Children's voices came from somewhere nearby, and he had a vague feeling he'd heard them before. He turned his head and noticed a chair filled with a rumpled quilt and a pillow as though someone had slept in it.

"Ah, I see you are awake." He turned his head so sharply that a stabbing pain shot through his head. Arthur had mentioned his leg, but he wondered if he'd been shot in the head too.

"I warned you about moving too quickly," the cheerful voice continued. He didn't remember seeing or hearing the woman before. She moved into his range of vision, and he was surprised to see that she was younger than he'd assumed, though not really young. She appeared to be in her late thirties, more than a decade older than he was. She was tall and large-boned, and several strands of pale reddish brown hair escaped from what appeared to be a hastily fashioned bun at the back of her head.

He eyed her warily.

She chuckled. "I reckon you don't remember. We weren't exactly introduced proper, seeing as how you were already unconscious when you toppled onto my lap after that outlaw shot you. I'm Martha Macintosh, and that young scamp who arrived here with you said your name be Clayton Telford. Right pleased to meet you." She laughed again as though she'd said something clever.

"Ma'am." He didn't know why she'd remained with him, wherever he was, but the least he could do was be civil.

"I 'spect you've got questions," she went on. "I'll see if I can tell you what you're wantin' to know without you wearin' yourself out none askin' questions."

"Obliged," he managed to murmur.

"First off, you was shot by some no good thievin' outlaw, but I'm happy to say you're the better shot. He's dead. The bullet went clean through your thigh, but it's healin' nicely. You been out most of two days, and I had some doubts you'd come out of it. You lost a lot of blood, but I 'spect bein' unconscious is from the nasty lump you got on the back of your head when you fell down after you was shot. Your head smashed into the back of the bench on your way to landin' in my lap. The soldiers and that friend of yours brought you here. I ain't a doctor, but I've been deliverin' babies and patching up folks in these hills most o' my life."

"Thank you." There wasn't much else he could say. He wasn't thrilled to be in the hands of a midwife, but she probably knew as much about doctoring as Mr. Sorenson's trail cook did. Since he didn't feel pain anywhere other than in his head, he figured the wound might not be too bad. The midwife soon corrected him.

"It's time you tried sittin' up a bit." She put her arms around his chest and tugged him into a near-sitting position. Pain exploded through his lower body, and blackness swirled around him for several seconds, but he didn't resist as she pushed him forward and stuffed pillows behind him. The pain in his leg was a sure indication that Mrs. Macintosh was right about where the outlaw's bullet had got him.

While he fought to stay conscious and clear his head, she stepped away but went on talking. "My man and that friend of yours went off on the train to town to send a wire to your folks and his'n. 'Spect they'll be back afore dark." She moved closer again and set herself down on a stool he hadn't noticed before beside his bed. She held a bowl and a spoon in one hand.

"I reckon you're a mite hungry by now," she said. "Best you start out easy with a bit of broth. If that don't upset your belly none, I'll bring you some real vittles for your supper." She gently eased a spoon toward his mouth.

The broth tasted good, and he was hungrier than he realized. He supposed he could have pulled an arm free of the rope and taken over feeding himself—the rope was plenty loose—but swallowing the broth consumed all of his energy. By the time the spoon scraped the bottom of the bowl, he was nodding off again.

He wasn't certain what woke him some time later. He found himself slumped sideways, almost off the pile of pillows Mrs. Macintosh had heaped behind him. Before he could make an effort to straighten himself, his eyes widened at the sight of a row of children standing at the foot of his bed, staring at him with solemn eyes. Either he was seeing double or there were six tow-headed boys staring back at him. A burst of activity near the door heralded a little girl of about four, followed by what appeared to be an older version of the child, both sporting long red braids and bangs that nearly covered their green eyes.

"Mam said we should bring you your supper." The older girl hurried forward, lugging a wooden tray.

Clayton winced as he moved with caution to straighten himself to a sitting position. He felt the pull to his leg, but the pain in his head had lessened considerably. The girl set the tray across his lap. He looked down, noticing a bowl of stew with thick chunks of meat and vegetables. Beside the bowl sat a large slab of dark bread generously smeared with butter and some sort of preserves.

He noticed something else; the rope that had secured him to the bed was gone. Clayton glanced up, and, as though reading his mind, the largest of the boys at the foot of his bed held up the long length of cord and flashed him a mischievous grin—after which all six boys scrambled for the door in a rush of flying feet and triumphant giggles.

His attention returned to his two remaining visitors. The older girl fussed about straightening the contents of the tray while the little one handed him a spoon. He thanked her and asked, "What is your name?"

"I'm Jessica Elizabeth Macintosh, and that's Mary Susannah Macintosh." She pointed to her sister, who appeared to be around ten or twelve. "I'm four an' I have a doll. Papa made it, but Mam sewed her dress. Pa said you better get well fast 'cause he's tired of sleepin' in the loft. He's getting too old for climbing ladders, he said."

Clearly little Jessica wasn't shy, but before she could say more, her sister told her to hush. "Mr. Telford is supposed to rest. Mam said." Then, turning to Clayton, she added, "She'll tell ya everthin' she knows, which ain't much, but it takes a long time if you encourage her. Mam said you should eat those vittles, then sleep some more." She took her sister's hand and led her from the room, closing the door behind her.

Clayton ate the stew but lacked the energy to chew the bread. He didn't fall asleep after he finished but lay back against the pillows, trying to make sense of what he'd learned so far. He wished Arthur would return. He wanted answers. He wondered how serious his wound was, where he was, and how soon he could be on his way.

It was a struggle, but he managed to move the tray from the bed to a nearby table. Since his head no longer throbbed, he decided to attempt getting to his feet. He swung his legs over the side of the bed, stopping several times as he grimaced in pain. Slowly he straightened until he was sitting with his feet dangling over the side of what he suspected was a corn-husk mattress. From this position he could see that his right leg was swathed in bandages from his thigh to his knee. He sat there for several minutes, feeling weak and dizzy. Perhaps tomorrow would be soon enough to try standing, he thought, sinking back against the pillows.

Over time Clayton's strength improved and the pain diminished. By the end of the second week, he and Arthur were taking short, stumbling walks around the Macintosh farm, sometimes wandering onto the paths that led into the West Virginia hills. Arthur filled him in on all that had happened, and learning that four people had died in the holdup filled Clayton with sorrow and anger even though he hadn't known the people who died.

On frequent occasions a few of the children accompanied Clayton and Arthur on their walks. By now, Clayton had learned there were nine children: the eight he'd met and a toddler who crawled more than he walked. Clayton felt an affinity for the baby's efforts to take a few steps as he struggled to regain the use of his leg and faced the possibility that he might never walk with the ease he once had.

The Macintosh boys' enthusiasm and escapades brought a hint of nostalgia to Clayton, and his thoughts often strayed to Travis, though such thoughts reminded him of how alone he was.

He didn't regret his years at Boston College. Going there was something he had to do, just as raising horses was something Travis had to do. When Clayton got thinking about how he and Travis and Pa *should* have been together on the plantation, he conceded that leaving was something Pa had to do. Folks didn't always get to choose to stay together, but it seemed to him there ought to be some assurance they'd meet up again somewhere. Sometimes he thought about Grandpa too and wondered if Grandpa had felt as alone after Pa left with Clayton and his brother as Clayton now felt.

"How soon do you think you'll be able to travel?" Arthur interrupted his thoughts. He was showing signs of being anxious to leave the Macintosh family and return to the life he'd been groomed to lead. References to Rachel Ann peppered his speech now, and he spoke of her in a more approving manner than he'd previously done. It appeared he was reconciling himself to the plan his parents had outlined for him. Clayton expected it wouldn't be long until he'd receive notice of Arthur and Miss Rachel Ann's approaching nuptials.

"Mrs. Macintosh says I shouldn't bump or jar my leg too much for a couple more weeks, but I can see each time she dresses the wound that it's healing, and I don't need you to keep me upright when we walk anymore. I can dress myself now and take care of my needs, so you shouldn't feel obligated to stay here to look after me. I appreciate all you've done. Without you I likely would have bled to death. You even notified my farm manager of my late arrival, so he's not expecting me right away. However, your family is anxious for your arrival, and there's really no reason for you to stay longer."

Arthur didn't immediately protest, and Clayton knew his friend was considering his words. Clayton would miss Arthur, but it really was time for Arthur to get on with his life. It was time, too, for Clayton to make some decisions.

* * *

Ev Macintosh pushed his meat and gravy onto his spoon with a thick chunk of bread, chewed for a few minutes, then spoke. "Met them soldiers when I was in town takin' your friend to the train. They tol' me them robbers held up another train west o' here last week, over near Louisville. Shot the engineer dead and half a dozen other folks.

Two of 'em was a farmer and his wife, plannin' to take up farming some o' that prairie land. Left four little ones orphans. Week before that, the robbers held up another train east of Lexington. Someone said he heard the robbers was headin' for Missouri. They been leavin' a trail of misery and puttin' folks out fer way too long." Clayton knew the words were meant for him as a kind of hint that he should be moving on.

He nodded his head. He'd been listening to reports concerning the Gooding Gang ever since he began to mend. Each holdup occurred a little farther west than the one before.

One of the boys used his knife as a catapult to launch peas across the table at one of his brothers.

"Stop teasin' your brother!" Martha confiscated the knife and admonished her son to eat or she'd give his supper to the hogs. She snapped a towel at the troublemaker to emphasize her words. She never joined the family at the table but kept busy refilling dishes and cups; she filled her own plate after the others had finished their meal. The rascal's target smirked and aimed a kick under the table at the brother who had been reprimanded.

Usually the boys' antics brought a smile to Clayton's face, but today he paid them little attention. Ev's words filled his mind, and he felt a burning rage for the callous robbers who had caused him and so many others so much pain. They'd killed at least four people on the train he'd been on. One could have just as easily been Martha Macintosh, leaving Ev alone to raise his large brood of children. Now the gang had murdered another six. Someone had to stop them, and it didn't seem the army was having much success.

Clayton had benefitted from the Macintoshes' hospitality long enough. It was time Ev got his bed back and Clayton took hold of the plan that had been growing in his mind for weeks.

CHAPTER FOURTEEN

SHE WASN'T EXACTLY HIDING, BUT she'd had about all of Mr. Mason she could tolerate, and she hoped he wouldn't think to look for her in the little cemetery. She leaned against old Desmond Southbridge's marker, not caring whether her dress became soiled. Mama said she had to be nice to Papa's cousin, but she had her doubts that the man was truly any kin of her beloved Papa.

Maxwell Mason had moved into Papa's room, leaving Mama to claim one of the upstairs bedrooms. He'd forbidden Lucy access to Papa's library. He'd even snooped in her room and ordered her trousers burned. Fortunately Lucas had helped her find a hiding place for her shotgun to keep Mama from finding it, so Maxwell didn't know of its existence and hadn't been able to take it.

Lucy couldn't help wondering why Clayton didn't come or send her word if he'd changed his mind. Of course, if he had sent a wire, Maxwell probably kept it. She fingered the scrap of yellow paper she'd kept in her pocket since the day she'd discovered it. It merely said Clayton had been injured and would be delayed. It advised Papa to continue on as per their agreement until Clayton arrived. His continued silence made her uneasy. Had he been injured far more seriously than his friend implied? Was he dead? The man who signed the telegram, Arthur Bennington, hadn't even said how Clayton was injured.

She wished there was a way to contact Clayton's friend, but she knew the two had left Boston College, so even if she managed to sneak into the library to search the addresses Papa had kept in his desk drawer, it would be of no use.

Hearing Mama call her name, she cringed. Sometimes she didn't understand Mama at all. She knew her mother didn't like Maxwell nor trust him, yet her mother followed his every order, even his directive to withdraw almost all of the money deposited in the bank for the farm's expenses and employee wages and to turn the money over to him. Lucas and his sons hadn't been paid all summer.

Thinking of the bank sent an idea to her mind. She'd overheard Clayton tell Papa he had funds in a bank in Kansas that he could draw on to pay for his school. He'd had funds transferred to the local bank until the farm began paying its own way. Perhaps Clayton still had money in that bank and could be contacted through that institution. She'd write him a letter and sneak away in the morning to obtain the address of the Kansas bank from Gil Willis at the local bank. Though Gil was too bashful to say anything, she'd suspected for some time that he was sweet on her and would be eager to supply her with the information she needed.

"Lucinda!" Again she heard her mother call. Rising to her feet, she didn't bother to wipe away the soil that clung to her skirt.

Leaving the protected bower provided by the towering willow tree, she made her way toward her mother. She was halfway across the lawn before she was noticed. When instead of scolding her, her mother threw her arms around her and began to sob, Lucy felt a wave of guilt.

"What is it? Has something happened?" She couldn't help suspecting Maxwell Mason had something to do with Mama's agitated state.

Mary Beth looked around as though afraid to speak. Lowering her voice, she whispered, "You'll have to say yes. I wouldn't ask it of you, but if you refuse, he'll ruin us."

She had no idea what her mother was talking about. She was more concerned about her obvious fear. What was it about Maxwell Mason that caused her mother to be afraid?

"Come, Mama. You need to rest. You're still grieving for Papa."

"That's right, dear cousin. You should rest while I speak with Lucinda." Lucy whirled about to confront Maxwell. She hadn't heard him sneak up on them. She made a mental note to be more aware. Taking each woman by an arm, he escorted them inside the house. Then, in a voice that sounded more threatening than solicitous, he sent Mama up to her room.

Mama glanced back once, and the look she gave Lucy revealed sheer terror.

"In the library, my dear." Maxwell gestured toward the open door that was usually firmly closed. Shaking off his arm, she flounced into the library. In an act of defiance, she ignored his gesture toward a small settee and sat in Papa's chair.

Maxwell appeared amused by her rebellious act, and instead of taking a chair he perched on the corner of the desk, where he towered over her threateningly. He smiled in a way some people might consider charming, but she knew better.

"Now, Miss Southbridge, I think it is time we came to an understanding." Again the smile. "Early next month, matters will be finalized in establishing my claim to the plantation. And in order to establish myself as the leading citizen of this county, I shall need a wife. You will do nicely. We shall make the formal announcement following the settlement of your Papa's estate and the formal recording of the deed in my name."

"You must be joking!" Lucy rose to her feet so suddenly that her head cracked against Maxwell's nose. "I've no intention of marrying you, and even if you can claim to be Papa's heir, the Southbridge plantation never belonged to him so you can't inherit it. Every acre of this farm belongs to Clayton Telford!"

With a handkerchief pressed to his bleeding nose, Maxwell's voice was muffled, but his anger was unmistakable. "Young Telford is a fool if he thinks to claim anything. I've made arrangements to have his claim set aside. As for you, we *will* wed. I think a few words of enlightenment from your mother will persuade you to accept my proposal."

* * *

Clayton wasn't a lawman. Sure he'd gone after horse thieves once when he was still a boy, but that was more tracking horses than men. There was just something about the gang of train robbers that riled Clayton deep inside. He didn't suppose they'd had any rougher time growing up than he had, but even if they had, they had no call frightening passengers and killing people who were just going about their business. He shifted in his seat and resisted the urge to rub the thigh that still ached from the train robber's bullet.

Clayton couldn't have explained, if he'd been asked, why he felt compelled to go after the outlaws himself. He was anxious to return to Southbridge and had considered that a priority for four long years, but this was something he had to do. It wasn't mere revenge for his injuries. He supposed it might have something to do with the protective streak that ran deep within him. He'd taken to heart his mother's admonition to protect Travis, and he'd never had any tolerance for people who took advantage of those who were smaller or weaker. It was tied somehow to his defense of his brother, and of Lavinia, and his admiration for Elliot's daughter. He smiled, remembering the plucky girl who'd threatened him with a shotgun and plunged into the swimming hole to save a worker's child. He didn't think he had an obsession with being a hero, yet there was something within him that couldn't tolerate seeing injustice continue unchecked.

He'd sent a letter to Elliot, explaining he was taking a side trip to Wichita to see about transferring his funds to the bank in the little village named for his great-grandfather. If Southbridge was going to be his home for the rest of his life, it made sense to have an account there rather than in far-off Kansas. He could have taken care of the matter by wire, but he'd used the first excuse he could think of for heading West. With the summer well spent, there was little he could do to implement his plans for the farm until the crops were harvested. Elliot, with Lucas's help, could manage that as he'd done in previous years. It was the train robbers who really drew him back to the place he'd left almost four years earlier.

Reports and rumors he'd gleaned confirmed his suspicion that the gang was moving farther west with each holdup. He wasn't sure how, but he would do all he could to stop the heartache and carnage the robbers were leaving in their wake. He meant to make certain there would be no more children crying for their mothers because of the Henry Gooding Gang. If finding the gang meant booking passage on every train just west of the last holdup, he'd do it until he found evidence that would lead him to their hideout.

His trunk had gone on to Montgomery with the train he'd been aboard when the attack happened, and the clothes he'd been wearing that day were ruined, leaving him with only the few items in his valise. Thankfully, Arthur had had the presence of mind to snatch up the valise when they'd disembarked near the Macintosh farm. Clayton had also been able to purchase two sets of clothing in the first town of size he'd come to. He'd considered his mission and opted for business attire. The thieves he followed would be more likely to underestimate a fellow who looked like a banker or an accountant, he reasoned, than one who looked at ease with a six-shooter on his hip. Besides, a suit coat provided several options for concealing a gun. The revolver beneath his coat wasn't the only gun he carried now. A second, smaller revolver was hidden in his boot, along with a thin, sharp blade.

He was amazed by the changes he saw between St. Louis and the Kansas-Missouri border. Sod shanties appeared here and there, but he glimpsed a few real houses and occasional villages or small towns. The farther west he traveled, the fewer traces of civilization appeared and the more the broad prairie dominated the landscape.

From his window seat on the westbound train a full day out of Kansas City, Clayton spotted a couple of riders in the distance near one of the few homesteads he'd seen in several hours. The sharp intake of breath by the lady seated across from him in the half-empty car had him turning toward her, looking for the cause of her alarm.

"Are they outlaws?" she asked, drawing back from the window. He glanced back at the riders, who were rapidly falling behind the faster moving train.

"No, ma'am. They appear to be a couple of kids riding cow ponies."

She leaned forward to peer through the window again. "You're sure they're not outlaws—or Indians?"

He closed his eyes and refrained from scowling. He didn't want to give his fellow passenger the impression that he didn't sympathize with her concerns. He'd been sitting much too long, and his injury was causing him distress. "I'm sure," he muttered, hoping they would soon reach the next small prairie town or water tower, where he could walk about and ease the cramps in his leg. The woman continued to glance toward the window until they were miles beyond the two young riders. Clayton leaned back and attempted to relax. They were crossing open prairie and traveling at a speed that made a holdup unlikely. If the outlaws chose to hold up this train, it would probably be at the next water tower, when the train would have to stop. Still, he kept his senses alert. He had no intention of being taken by surprise again. Experience had taught him that the prairie was deceptive. Land that appeared flat, with no place to conceal men and horses, contained deep gullies and swales that blended in so well they went unnoticed by most observers, and a well-placed obstacle or missing rail could bring the train to an abrupt, unplanned halt.

He was aware of the strongboxes the army had loaded back in St. Louis on a car some distance behind the one in which he sat. The car made a tempting target, and he wondered if the army meant for it to serve as bait. He'd noticed there were fewer soldiers riding away from the train than had been in the escort when it had arrived at the depot. He didn't envy any soldiers who might be riding in a lumbering baggage car.

He'd gotten little sleep the night before, and the steady clack of metal wheels rolling along the rails lured him toward sleep now. But suddenly his eyes flew open, and his hand slipped beneath his coat. He strained to hear what had pulled him from his half-asleep state. The train was still moving at a steady pace; no unusual sound seemed to have disturbed the other passengers, most of whom seemed to be sleeping in the sweltering heat.

Taking care not to awaken or alarm the other passengers, he rose to his feet, wincing at the sharp pain the action sent through his leg, and then sauntered toward the back of the car, where he stepped across the bridge to the next car. There he saw the terrified conductor, his eyes wide in his soot-blackened face, stumbling toward him.

"What is it?" Clayton grabbed the man's arm, but already he could see the cause through the back door of the car, which had been left open. There was nothing behind the car. At least three cars and the caboose were missing. He knew the cars hadn't come uncoupled by accident. He suspected someone had hidden on top of the cars and then crawled down from above to separate the cars carrying luggage and the payroll box from the passenger cars, knowing it would take some time for the engineer to notice that the cars were missing and return for them. The outlaws could plunder the cars at their leisure.

"Got to tell the engineer," the conductor stammered as he pushed past Clayton.

CHAPTER FIFTEEN

"What is it?"

"What happened?"

The passengers in this car were beginning to show their alarm. They too sensed that something wasn't right and surmised the meaning of the missing railcars. He saw more than one man check a hidden firearm beneath his coat. Holdups had occurred with alarming frequency on the line of late, and many men had taken the precaution of arming themselves. Several of the braver men rushed to the rear of the car, crowding onto the narrow platform. There was nothing to see but the undulating prairie stretching on until it met the sky.

Clayton felt the train begin to slow. It ground to a stop, belching black smoke from its stacks. Sparks flew from the friction of the wheels rubbing against the rails. After a couple of sharp jerks, it began to move in reverse.

"Back inside!" a short, bald, bandy-legged man began barking orders. When some of the men hesitated, he shouted, "We're sitting ducks out here if this is the work of the Gooding Gang." Men began moving more quickly back inside the car.

"Get the women and children down." The man continued to shout. "Men with guns, pick your window!" He claimed the nearest window on the right side of the train, and Clayton settled into the one directly opposite him. For now, he reasoned, he'd do as the man who had assumed leadership directed, but when they met the cars that had been detached, he meant to do things his own way.

With squeals and shouts, the women, children, and unarmed men scrambled to the floor, following a reminder to keep their heads below the height of the windows. A few unrestrained sobs reached Clayton's ears, but he shut them out, focusing his attention on the view from the window.

"It might be wise to barricade the doors." He spoke just loud enough to catch the attention of their de facto leader. The man glanced sharply at Clayton, then ordered a couple of the men seated on the floor to barricade the doors with anything they could find, even if they had to form a human barrier to seal the doors against any intruders.

It didn't take long until Clayton spotted the missing cars. Minutes later the engine began to slow. The train lurched to a stop with several hard jerks that nearly threw the men standing at the windows off their feet.

Clayton recovered quickly, and as the silence of the prairie seeped into his senses, he felt a sickness in his stomach. He had a premonition he wouldn't like what he was about to find.

"Move the barricade." The man who had taken charge issued his order in a softer tone, revealing to Clayton that he could feel the eerie silence too. Once the barricade was shoved aside, he took slow steps onto the platform. Clayton was right behind the man, with his hand still clasping the revolver he'd taken from his coat earlier. There was no sign of the outlaws, but he could see the engineer and the conductor hurrying along the track toward the detached cars.

Turning his attention back to the sight before him, he surveyed heaps of luggage, boxes, and parcels scattered on the ground. Many had been broken open, their contents tossed about. Papers fluttered as a whisper of moving air caught at them for a brief moment. Clothing lay in abandoned heaps. Two men lay facedown amid the debris.

From not far away, he heard a horse whinny. He turned toward the sound, his gun at the ready. A buckskin horse with the army brand stamped on its rump came into sight, moving slowly toward the train. It reached the silent boxcar and stood with its head down, reins trailing in the dirt.

Clayton stepped down from the car platform to make his way toward the boxcar where he'd seen the soldiers load their box in Louisville. His heart hammered, knowing he could be walking into an ambush. As he got closer, he could see that the door to the baggage car gaped open. He was aware of footsteps beside him and knew the bandy-legged man trod with equal caution. They paused to check the bodies on the ground. Neither man was a military or railroad employee. Both were dressed for riding, and both were riddled with bullet holes.

Walking away from the dead outlaws, Clayton and the bandy-legged man approached the boxcar. Together they peered inside. At first they could see nothing in the blackness, then slowly the bodies of four men lying sprawled on the floor took shape. Three wore the blue uniforms of Union soldiers, the fourth buckskins. Clayton knelt beside one man after another to ascertain whether any still drew breath, while his cohort stood in the doorway facing the open prairie, a silver pistol in his hand.

Clayton had just finished his examination and turned to report to the man he'd begun to think of as his partner that all were dead when a round of cursing reached his ears. He looked up to see the engineer shouting at a crowd of people who had descended from the train. "I'll need four strong men to load this baggage back on the train. The rest of you get back aboard before the robbers return and kill us all." His words were followed by several toots of the train whistle as someone, supposedly the fireman, backed the train closer to the separated cars.

"Your man?" asked Clayton's partner, who had caught the engineer's eye and nodded his head toward the caboose.

"Dead. Just like the soldiers who were supposed to keep the army payroll and the passengers safe." The conductor, who stood a pace behind the engineer, answered for him. Tears ran openly down his face.

Men were scrambling to toss the scattered luggage and freight into the three boxcars. Instead of helping them, Clayton approached the horse that still stood beside the baggage car. With gentle hands he stroked the horse's withers and lifted the animal's hooves to check for injury. The horse was sound.

"You better get back on board, young man. The train is about to reconnect these cars and then be on its way." The tough little man approached Clayton.

"I don't think I'll be continuing on." Clayton kept his grip on the horse's reins, remembering he'd seen a pile of saddles inside the car with the dead soldiers. "I aim to borrow one of those army saddles.

When I'm finished with it, I'll return it and the horse to the military contingent stationed outside Kansas City."

"You'll *not* be going after those outlaws alone!"

"I don't take orders from you. Those men have to be stopped, and the best place to start trailing them is right here." Clayton stood his ground.

"Don't be a fool! One man can't take on the Gooding Gang alone." He pulled a badge from his coat pocket, identifying himself as a U.S. marshal. "At the train's first stop, I'll get a posse together. You can ride along if you like."

Clayton stubbornly shook his head. He opened his mouth to argue just as a shout came from behind them. "Hello, the train!"

Both men whirled about, guns drawn, and stared in astonishment as a blood-and-dirt-spattered soldier rode into sight on another buckskin gelding. Behind him trailed two more horses on lead ropes. When he drew even with them, the soldier dismounted but leaned heavily against his horse as though hurt or winded.

"I see you caught the other one." He nodded toward the buckskin beside Clayton.

"Walked in on its own." Clayton leaned his head to one side, letting his gaze take in the soldier's appearance from head to toe. He was of average height, with dark hair and hazel eyes. He appeared to be younger than Clayton, probably no more than eighteen or nineteen. Though his ripped uniform and whatever skin was visible were smeared with blood, there were no visible wounds. "Are you hurt?"

"No, the lieutenant fell on top of me when he was shot. I might have gotten more blood on me when I checked the others to see if any of them were still breathing. They weren't." He glanced down and brushed at a spot on his chest in a futile gesture. Clayton chose not to remark on the slight quiver of the boy's chin.

The young soldier straightened and began to speak as though delivering a report to his superior officer. "The lieutenant and me were at the back of the car when we were rushed. He's a big man. Knocked the wind out of me 'til I couldn't breathe, and it was likely too dark for the shooters to see me. There were bullets flying all over the place. Jeb and Clancy got a couple of the robbers before they was hit too. At first I couldn't move, then I played dead until the gang gathered up the strongbox and left. Not much I could do agin six of 'em. I figgered they'd take the hawses, but they just turned 'em loose, 'cept for Mr. Brown's paint. They took him. You got any water on you?"

"Certainly. Just a moment, sir." The conductor, who had edged close enough to hear their conversation, hurried back toward the car behind him. He and the engineer had been recoupling the freight cars when they were distracted by the soldier's arrival. The soldier continued his story.

"We were just kind of dozing in the heat until we felt a jolt, and then the train stopped. After a minute Corporal Mumford opened the door a crack. An outlaw was waitin' on the top of our car. He musta sneaked up there last time we stopped for water. He pried the door open farther with a pole and stuck a wedge in it so it wouldn't close. We couldn't get a clear shot to stop 'im or reach the top of the opening to knock it out. That's when the rest of the outlaws rode right up to the door firin' revolvers and rifles."

"I'll want a full report as soon as we reach the next town." The marshal again displayed his badge.

"Meanin' no disrespect, sir." The soldier shrugged his shoulders. "My orders are to do whatever I must to capture the Gooding Gang. When I saw there was nothing I could do for Mr. Brown or the other soldiers, I set out to recover our horses. I only returned here to see if I could salvage any of our supplies before going after the gang what done this."

The marshal studied the soldier, then gave a curt nod of his head. With a resigned nod toward Clayton, the marshal said, "You won't be riding alone. This gentleman insists on pursuing them at once. I can't let the two of you ride off alone, so I have no choice but to join you."

The three men quickly gathered whatever supplies they thought they could use. The conductor filled army canteens he found in the railroad car with water, and they were joined by a lanky cowboy carrying a saddlebag by its strap over one shoulder. Without saying a word, he saddled one of the army horses, lengthened the stirrups and, with an easy, practiced swing into the saddle, made clear his intention to join their small posse.

"Glad to have you join us." Clayton held out his hand. "I'm Clayton Telford."

The cowboy shook the offered hand. "Pete Sanderson."

Clayton attempted to mount as easily as had the cowboy but found himself clenching his teeth to hold back a groan of pain as he swung with unaccustomed awkwardness into the saddle. Not only had it been some time since he last mounted a horse, but the pain in his thigh was a reminder that he hadn't yet quite healed from his last encounter with the outlaws.

* * *

All four riders reined in their mounts as they reached the top of a long, gradual rise. Clayton looked back the way they'd come, seeing nothing but endless grass that was already turning yellow in the summer sun. The plume of smoke that trailed the train had long since disappeared.

Both Clayton and Pete dismounted to take a closer look at the faint trail they'd been following. Clayton sucked in his breath to hide the sharp pain that radiated up his leg as he freed his boot from the stirrup and stepped to the ground.

"What do you think, Clay? Still heading north?" Pete had shortened his name just as Travis had on occasion. Hearing the abbreviated name left him with an odd mixture of feelings. It both made his brother feel closer and stirred slight resentment to hear the name on another man's tongue. He put the thought out of his mind and answered the question.

"Yes, but the horse carrying the payroll box is tiring. He's slowing down the party." He pointed to the packhorse's shortened tracks.

"That's Mr. Brown's paint. He's a good horse and will keep going," Rafe Jackson, the soldier, put in. "I seen 'em strap that box on that pony just before they took off. The paint's a pony Mr. Brown bought from a couple of Injuns who showed up at Fort Omaha looking to trade last fall. Brown was a good scout; talked to that horse like they was brothers."

"We better keep moving. The gang has a good hour's start on us." The marshal wiped his brow with the sleeve of his shirt. Both Clayton and the marshal had removed their jackets, rolling them neatly behind their saddles and tying them in place with short pigging strings they'd found tied to their borrowed saddles. Clayton had learned that the cocky little marshal's name was Leroy Jacobs and that he'd been trailing the Gooding Gang since Cincinnati. Clayton suspected the marshal was secretly pleased he and Rafe had forced his hand to pursue the outlaws without seeking a posse in some distant town.

Riding two abreast, with Clayton and Pete in front since they had some tracking experience, the group continued to follow the bent grass and scuffed dirt left behind by the outlaws' horses. Comparing notes, Clayton learned that Pete had trailed cattle and hunted strays that wandered off from the herds, much like Clayton had. The shadows were beginning to lengthen when Clayton held up his arm, signaling they should stop. Without speaking, he pointed to a distant speck.

Pete squinted and stared toward the far-off dark spot on the prairie. At last he shook his head. "Ain't nothing but a soddy; few acres plowed around it. It's either just broke out by a new settler or more likely been abandoned."

"I don't know how you can tell all that from this distance, but I think we better check it out. There might be water." The marshal nudged his horse to begin walking.

Clayton reached out to check the marshal's horse. "It might be best to hang back until dark. The tracks we've been following lead straight toward that soddy, and it isn't unoccupied. There's smoke rising from it."

By now both Clayton and Pete had dismounted. Pete plucked a long grass stem and placed it in his mouth to chew on while he continued to stare at the distant soddy. "'Pears to me there's too many horses milling around that corral to be no sod-buster farmer."

Marshal Jacobs looked toward Rafe, clearly seeking the soldier's opinion. Clayton recognized that Jacobs had been drinking far too often from his canteen and was likely out of water and that the homestead represented an enticing opportunity to find relief from the blazing sun and to replenish his water supply. Clayton feared all would be lost if the stubborn man insisted on riding in.

Rafe slipped from the back of the bay he rode. "I had a sergeant once who said to always make the smallest target possible. If Pete and Clayton can make out details, we best figure the folks in that soddy can do the same. Mounted riders bunched together are easy to spot."

The marshal glanced around, then he too dismounted. Clayton sighed in relief. Jacobs was stubborn, but he wasn't a fool.

Clayton pointed. "There's a depression over that way about a quarter of a mile. We'll be out of sight if we hunker down in it. I suggest we make our way there to wait for darkness. Lead your horse and stay low."

The marshal looked as though he wanted to object, but swallowed whatever he'd been about to say and gathered up his horse's reins.

"Spread out," Pete whispered. He waited a couple of minutes, then followed Clayton's limping form, leaving Rafe and Jacobs to fall in behind them.

CHAPTER SIXTEEN

CLAYTON SQUIRMED HIS WAY TO the top of the depression and strained to see the soddy. It was just past dusk, and the first star was showing on the horizon. It was impossible to make out details of the situation at the soddy from more than a mile away, but he felt certain the outlaws were holed up in it.

Something moved between the place where he lay and the rough homestead. It dropped out of sight, then reappeared a few minutes later closer to the soddy. Clayton pinched his bottom lip between his teeth and tightened his grip on the Colt revolver in his hand. After a few minutes, he slowly released the breath he'd been holding, recognizing the furtive movements as that of a coyote. He suspected the farmer kept a few chickens or there was a new calf. It wasn't unusual for the scavengers to be drawn to farmyard scents. He'd known a coyote to approach scraps a farm wife had tossed out for the family dog.

Focusing on the distant soddy again, he caught a glimmer of light. He grinned in grim satisfaction. The door to the rough shelter was open and someone had lit a lamp, something the outlaws wouldn't have done if they knew they were being followed.

Slithering his painful way back to the lower spot where the others waited, he whispered the news and the conclusions he'd drawn.

"We need to get closer." The marshal expressed his dissatisfaction with basing so much on what he considered guesswork. "It's a pretty good walk, but a couple of us need to approach the soddy from the far side and the other two from this side so we can see what's going on. We might be barking up the wrong tree, or there could be civilians in that soddy as well as the outlaws."

This time Clayton agreed with Jacobs. That there might be someone other than the outlaws in the soddy was Clayton's greatest fear. He prepared to speak to the marshal, measuring his words. He was well aware that the man was having difficulty accepting the reality of the other men's independence. Clearly he was accustomed to giving orders and having them obeyed, yet he was intelligent enough to recognize that each of the three other men had more experience than he did in dealing with the circumstances they found themselves in on the wild, windswept prairie.

"Since Pete and I have spent the most time this far west, I suggest the two of us ride our horses in a circuitous path to the far side of the soddy, ground hitch them far enough back to keep the horses down there in the corral from getting excited, and then approach the soddy on foot. The two of you should give us time to get in place on the other side and then ride to within a quarter mile of the house, ground-hitch your horses, and approach from this side."

Discussion was brief, and Clayton and Pete left with a few final instructions from Marshal Jacobs, including not to fire before he signaled to rush the soddy. Clayton refrained from shaking his head at the marshal's persistent determination to take charge. Pete paused to remind the two left behind to keep a low profile.

In less than an hour, Clayton was lying in the deep grass less than fifty yards from the soddy. Pete was nearby but completely invisible to him. From the slight elevation where he lay, he could see a dozen horses milling about in a small corral. No sod farmer kept that many horses. One, a little smaller than the others, was a paint, and two appeared to be draft horses. The draft horses were likely the property of the farmer who was homesteading the tract of land.

A few poles and a thatched roof near the corral formed a shelter of sorts for a cow. Bundles of dry grass formed a low wall, reaching almost to the thatched roof, providing a bit of protection from the wind for the bovine. The cow stomped about and lowed as though she sensed the presence of the coyote. Clayton felt it reasonable to assume that a farmer who kept a cow also had a wife and children. With the thieves and murderers who had been holding up trains across the Midwest holed up inside the soddy, that conclusion brought more complications to any plan they might devise for capturing the outlaws.

Clayton assumed the lumpy shapes atop the straw were the chickens being stalked by the coyote he'd seen earlier. From the soddy came the shouts and accusations of a poker game in progress. Clayton couldn't tell whether the homesteader and his family were inside the low structure, but he couldn't help wishing he didn't feel so certain that the farmer had a wife and children who were caught up in this mess.

A shadow moved, and he squinted to watch a figure disappear behind the makeshift shed. He guessed it was Rafe since the shadow appeared too large to be the marshal. A second shape inched toward the open door of the soddy. The moon had risen, and Clayton easily identified the bandy-legged lawman. He was the only one in their party with a rifle. Clayton's rifle had gone to Montgomery, and he hadn't purchased a replacement. The guns belonging to the slaughtered soldiers had evidently been stolen.

Clayton began a careful crawl, ignoring the pain that had become his steady companion. If gunfire broke out, he wanted to be close enough to Jacobs to back him up. The slightest whisper of sound told him Pete was on the move too.

A furious roar broke the calm of the night. Screaming unintelligible sounds, Rafe charged toward the soddy, a revolver in one fist and a long knife in the other. As he raced inside, confusion erupted from within the structure and gunfire blazed as the outlaws scrambled to take shelter and return fire. Without hesitation the marshal charged in behind the reckless soldier.

Pete was already kicking in the sod roof when Clayton joined him. Both men tore at the chunks of thick grass and soil with their hands and feet. It gave way easily under their onslaught, and the two men were soon taking aim at the outlaws, who were returning the soldier's and marshal's gunfire. In less than a minute, three men lay unmoving on the floor, and Rafe appeared to be staggering about aimlessly with several fresh splotches of blood on his uniform. The marshal had taken shelter behind an overturned table and was pausing to reload. Pete fired, and a man who had been creeping toward the marshal's back sprawled on the dirt floor. That made four, but Clayton was certain he'd counted six in the dugout.

He turned his attention toward one of the outlaws he could see reaching for something in the deep shadows behind an iron cookstove. Angling for a clear shot, Clayton began to press on the trigger, then stopped as he glimpsed what looked like a ragged piece of gingham. His target pulled a young woman from behind the stove, where she'd taken refuge. Using her as a shield, the outlaw began edging toward the door. Light from the lantern that dangled precariously from a hook on the doorpost revealed not a woman but a girl of no more than twelve or thirteen. She stood, stiff and unseeing, neither resisting nor cooperating with the burly man who attempted to drag her toward the door.

The hostage had one blonde braid that lay half unraveled against her back. Her unseeing eyes were blue. She wasn't very tall. Pain clutched at Clayton's gut. She looked so much like Lucy in the dim light that for a moment he shared Rafe's madness. He wanted nothing more than to kill the man who held her prisoner.

Rafe raised his shaking gun toward the fleeing man and his hostage. The look of fury on his face bordered on insanity. The marshal's gun barked behind him, and an outlaw who had been drawing down on Rafe dropped. As though the explosion at his back shook him out of some kind of demented fixation, Rafe shuddered and fell to his knees, retching.

Clayton didn't wait around to see what happened next but jumped toward the door, ignoring the wrenching pain in his leg. He reached the door just as the last outlaw emerged with one hand around the girl and the other gripping a revolver. Clayton judged the distance between them to be no more than six feet. He flung himself forward, knocking the man to the ground and sending his pistol flying. He slammed a hard right to the man's jaw and followed up with a knee to the man's midsection. They rolled on the ground, pummeling each other with desperate blows. Clayton took a hard uppercut to his jaw that made his ears ring.

A sharp sting to his arm warned him his opponent had a knife. A moment later he saw the long blade slash toward his throat. He seized the descending wrist, attempting to ward off the strike, but feared his earlier injury had weakened him too much. Gritting his teeth, he held on, knowing to yield would mean his life and possibly that of the young girl.

A loud blast next to his ear made him wonder if he were losing consciousness. He felt the arm holding the knife go limp and was aware of it falling to the ground. The heavy torso leaning over him collapsed toward him. Rolling to the side with the last of his strength, he tried to avoid being crushed. He lay prone, gasping for breath for what seemed an agonizingly long time before turning to his back. He looked up to see Pete standing over him, a still-smoking revolver in his hand. Clayton glanced to the side and saw the last outlaw facedown, a gaping hole in his head. Turning back to Pete, Clayton accepted his extended hand to help him up. Once upright, he found he couldn't stand and sank back to the ground.

Struggling to make sense of the ringing in his ears and the chaos of his thoughts, he managed to remain sitting upright. After a short time he became aware that the marshal was beside him too, also extending a hand to help him stand. It took several attempts before Clayton could remain on his feet without assistance.

Once he felt steady, he looked around to see if everyone was accounted for. Jacobs jerked a thumb toward the man on the ground. "Henry Gooding won't be holding up any more trains. Too bad Pete had to shoot him. I was looking forward to seeing him hang, all nice and legal."

Clayton looked away. The shot at close range to Gooding's head wasn't a pretty sight, but it explained the explosion in his own head. Pete must have walked right up to them while they struggled on the ground and fired the shot at close range to be certain he didn't hit the wrong target. He swallowed and was glad he hadn't had time for any supper that night.

"What about the girl?" His vision hadn't cleared, and he couldn't see her.

"I don't know. She's kind of funny in the head." Marshal Jacobs shook his head and walked back to where Rafe sat on the ground with his arms around the girl. He hadn't seen her at first because between the dim light and his fuzzy eyesight, he'd only seen Rafe sitting hunched on the ground. Clayton, half supported by Pete, stumbled toward Jacobs.

Someone set a lantern on the ground, and Clayton could see that the girl's blue eyes were wide and staring, seeming unable to focus. At first Clayton wondered if she was blind, but her vacant stare seemed to say there was far more wrong with her than being unable to see.

Her face bore the signs of a battering as severe as the one he'd just experienced. Her gingham dress hung in tatters, and dried blood covered her arms and streaked her once-blonde hair. She looked as though whatever gave a body animation had gone away, leaving an empty shell behind.

Rafe was shaking with great convulsive sobs even as he patted the girl's back and attempted to whisper comforting words to her. She stared ahead, oblivious to him and to his efforts.

The marshal knelt in front of her to ask in a soft voice, "Can you tell me your name, miss?" There was no answer. He tried again. "Miss, those men won't ever bother you again. I'm a U.S. marshal and I'd like to see you safely to your family. Can you give me your name so I can contact them?"

"Leave her be. She has no family. They're all dead, lying over yonder in the cowshed!" Rafe shouted in a hoarse, unrecognizable voice. He shuddered and dropped his head until it rested on the girl's tangled locks.

Clayton's eyes met the marshal's, and understanding passed between them. All that the boy soldier had witnessed in one day was too much for him.

Rafe lifted his head once more, and Clayton could see silvery streaks down his cheeks where the bright moon illuminated the young soldier's tears. "I got a ma and little sisters too," Rafe continued in a hoarse whisper. "I ain't seen 'em for nigh on four years, but as soon as the army will give me leave, I'm goin' home."

"It's all right, boy. I'll talk to your commander, tell him you need to go home for a piece. You stay right here for now and look after this little girl. Me and the other boys have a few things that need tending to." The marshal straightened and looked pointedly at Clayton.

Instead of heading toward the cowshed, Marshal Jacobs led Clayton back inside the soddy. Pete was there ahead of them. "They're dead. I checked 'em all. That soldier kid must've caught 'em off guard. Never expected he'd go off like a prairie tornado that way."

"He stumbled on the girl's murdered family. Something about them was a little too much like his own ma and sisters. After seeing his comrades shot down this morning, something snapped. Drove him plumb loco." He paused to clear his throat before continuing.

"Something drove the girl loco too. She was probably forced to watch what those butchers did to her family. She may have been badly used as well."

"What do we do with this lot? And the girl's family?" Clayton wondered aloud, looking at the bodies scattered about.

Pete offered a practical solution: "Water the horses and fill our canteens, then we can shove these no goods down the well and cave it in." Jacobs winced but nodded his agreement.

"The girl's family needs a proper burial," Clayton insisted.

"They'll get it," the marshal promised, then went on. "Pete and I will start watering the horses and loading the strongbox and other stolen property lying around here. Clayton, you look around, see if you can find any papers with the girl's folks' names on them."

"I already looked around some. Bags over there are stuffed with loot these no accounts stole." Pete pointed toward a pile of saddlebags lying in a corner. I don't think the farmer had much."

The sun was just beginning to rise when the four weary men gathered around five mounds of earth. The girl stood with them, but she appeared oblivious to her surroundings. After Clayton had seen what the outlaws had done to her family, he figured her shocked state was the only defense possible for her. It was probably best if she could shut it out for a time. He suspected he'd have nightmares for the rest of his life remembering the butchered and mutilated bodies of the two little girls who lay in a tangled heap with their parents and infant brother. Even now it was hard to control his empty stomach, recalling the coyote drawn to the stench of blood creeping closer to the slaughtered family.

"Seems someone ought to say a prayer or something." Marshal Jacobs scuffed a line in the dirt beside the fresh graves with the toe of his boot. Usually so determined to take charge and declare his authority, he seemed ill at ease with saying a few words over the family they'd just buried.

"I seen a Bible when I was looking for papers. Thought you might want it so I brung it along." Pete produced the Bible from inside his shirt and handed it to Jacobs.

The marshal fumbled through a few pages before looking around as though seeking help. Clayton reached for the book. He opened it to the passage Mr. Sorensen had read when Pa died. He cleared his throat and began to read. "'The Lord is my shepherd; I shall not want. He maketh me to lie down in green pastures: he leadeth me beside the still waters . . . Yea, though I walk through the valley of the shadow of death, I will fear no evil: for thou art with me . . .'"

CHAPTER SEVENTEEN

CONVERSATION WAS AT A MINIMUM as the four men and the girl picked their way back to the railroad tracks that cut a swath across the desolate landscape. They were in silent agreement that though the day was almost gone and they were suffering from fatigue, they had no desire to stay anywhere near the homestead where so much death had occurred.

Bidding the row of crude crosses an unspoken farewell, they began the long ride. Each seemed preoccupied with his own thoughts. Rafe reigned his horse in close beside the animal he'd chosen for the girl, which happened to be the one Pete had ridden earlier. She'd shown no fear or hesitation in mounting the horse, and the well-trained mount obediently plodded beside the other army horses with little or no direction from its rider. Pete didn't object to cutting out one of the outlaw's horses to ride. He seemed to take pleasure in picking the feistiest one. They trailed the other horses and the cow on ropes behind them. They'd made no effort to catch the few chickens.

It was dusk when they reached the tracks and settled in for a few hours' rest and to eat a meager meal. There was little evidence of the previous day's brutal attack. Clayton suspected he'd be unable to sleep, though his body was exhausted. His leg throbbed with almost unbearable pain. The marshal gave him a number of questioning looks, but as long as he didn't actually ask questions, Clayton made no explanations.

It was one of those times when he knew his mind wasn't ready to shut down. He sat on a small ridge overlooking the temporary camp, and though he didn't expect danger from men or beasts, his ears stayed alert and his eyes slowly scanned the prairie. He visually followed the railroad tracks until they disappeared in the distance. Nothing, not even a rodent, moved. At regular intervals his gaze returned to the small figure lying huddled a respectable distance from Rafe but close enough that he could protect her if the unexpected happened.

From entries in the Bible he'd thumbed through following the brief service for the girl's family, Clayton deduced the girl's name was Svetlana Ostermann, and a badly misspelled letter tucked between the pages of the thick book suggested her mother might have a brother in Pennsylvania. Would the girl's uncle take her in? What would become of her? Would she ever talk or laugh again? Her face bore no real resemblance to Lucy. Still, he couldn't erase from his mind the intense sorrow and anger that had struck him on first seeing the blonde hair and slight form that could have belonged to his young friend.

His heart ached for the child. He knew what it was to be without family, though he had hope that he would someday see Travis again. Loneliness haunted his thoughts as he kept a silent vigil. He wondered if he'd ever stop missing his parents, and though Grandpa had been as contrary as an overworked mule, he'd loved his grandpa in his own way.

If the God Lavinia had occasionally talked about really existed, He must hold in reserve the worst punishments for those such as the Gooding Gang, who tore apart families.

It was the first he'd thought of Lavinia in weeks. He paused to consider his feelings for her. After a few minutes he concluded that he'd always hold a tender spot in his heart for her, but he'd never truly loved her, not the way Pa had loved Mama. Clayton had enjoyed the challenge of competing against Lavinia for academic honors and had taken pleasure in their long discussions. He suspected he'd been drawn to her because he sensed a loneliness in her that he shared, but it just wasn't the same thing as love.

After a few hours Jacobs approached him. "Better get some shut-eye while you can. We've got a long ride ahead of us."

"I figure two days of hard riding, maybe three, will put us in Kansas City."

"I can turn in the army's horses and equipment there, and we can all be on our way to wherever we were headed before the holdup."

"What about the girl?" Clayton asked.

"I'll see that she reaches her uncle. I'm going that way myself." The marshal sighed and sat on his haunches. "Go roll yourself in your blanket until morning."

Sleep came easier than Clayton expected, and first thing he knew, they were trying to saddle the horses and move out. The cow stubbornly refused to follow a lead, bellowing in a forlorn manner and resisting Pete's efforts to attach her lead to a saddle horn. The cow's bawling upset the horses, making them jittery and hard to saddle. Pete swore and threatened to leave her behind.

"That dumb cow needs to be milked," Rafe said.

"Hurry up and get it done," Jacobs growled. "We need to leave."

"I ain't never milked a cow!" Rafe objected.

"Don't look at me!" Pete backed away. "I don't know nothin' about milkin' cows."

Clayton and Jacobs exchanged glances that clearly said milking a cow didn't fall into their range of skills either.

While the men were arguing over who would attempt to milk the cow, Svetlana moved to the cow's side. Clayton saw her first and drew the other men's attention to her. They watched as she whispered soft sounds to the animal, then crouched beside her. To their astonishment, she stroked the cow's swollen udder, then began a rhythmic pull and squeeze that sent milk frothing onto the ground. Pete had the good sense to grab an empty canteen and silently handed it to her.

When she finished milking, the girl handed the canteen back to Pete and tied the cow's lead rope to the saddle horn of the horse Rafe had ready for her to ride. She mounted without assistance. Clayton hoped her attention to the poor cow indicated she was beginning to come out of the shock that had held her in its grip since he first set eyes on her.

If they followed the tracks, they would eventually return to Kansas City, but the journey was taking much too long. The cow was holding them up. Clayton and Jacobs discussed what they could do about it well out of earshot of the others. They agreed they couldn't shoot the animal; young Svetlana had seen too much of gun violence already. Yet at the slow pace the cow set, they'd run out of food before reaching Kansas City. Simply turning the cow loose wouldn't do either. She'd be brought down by wolves or Indians before sunset.

148 JENNIE HANSEN

Their slow, plodding pace brought them to another soddy just before sunset. To their relief, there was evidence of a well a dozen paces from the soddy. A farmer carrying a rifle, with two half-grown boys walking beside him, left the shelter of the dugout to watch them approach. Jacobs reined in some distance back from the trio, and the other riders pulled to a stop behind him.

"Howdy!" the farmer ventured.

Jacobs returned the greeting, then introduced himself as a U.S. marshal. "We tangled with some outlaws back a piece. We're on our way to Kansas City, but we'd be much obliged if you'd allow us to water our horses and fill our canteens from your well."

"Help yourselves." The farmer appeared to relax, but he didn't set aside his rifle as he waved them toward the crude pump near a simple wooden trough. Pete took hold of the handle and began to raise it up and down, sending forth spurts of water. The cow moved faster toward the water than she'd moved all day. In minutes they'd all dismounted and were allowing their horses to drink from the trough. When the horses finished, the men took turns filling their canteens and dousing their heads under the flowing pump.

As Clayton stepped back to give the next man a turn at the water, he noticed a tall, spare woman with long, lank hair join the farmer and the boys. She held a baby in her arms, and two small girls clung to her skirt. The farmer didn't send her back to the soddy, and Clayton took that as a sign he'd decided to trust them.

The woman might have once been pretty, but too much sun and hard work had robbed her of both her youth and her looks. She watched them, her face stoic, until they finished pumping water for their stock and had filled their canteens. From the corner of his eye, Clayton saw her lean toward her husband to speak into his ear. His expression showed reluctance or perhaps wariness of whatever the woman had said. Finally the farmer shrugged his shoulders and stepped toward Rafe, who had assumed his usual stance near Svetlana, who stood with one hand on the cow's broad back.

Clayton sidled closer to listen.

"My wife has her heart set on buying your cow. Is she for sale? I ain't got but two dollars. I could throw in some grub from the missus's garden if you're hungry."

"The cow ain't mine. B'longs to her." Rafe pointed to Svetlana. "But she don't talk none."

The farmer looked helplessly toward Svetlana, then back at his wife. Clayton suspected he had no idea how to bargain with a woman. Thrusting the baby into one of the older boy's arms, the farmer's wife ordered the children back to the soddy. When they'd reluctantly retreated as far as the doorway, she joined her husband, who quickly explained the problem.

The woman looked perplexed for a moment, then she marched up to the young girl. "I need that cow," she said. "It's hard raisin' young'ns without a cow. They need milk. Will you sell your cow to me?"

Svetlana seemed to rouse herself from the stupor that had held her trapped. She appeared puzzled, as though she didn't recall how she had gotten to the farm or didn't understand the woman's question. She looked at the children huddled in the soddy doorway, then at the cow. After what must have seemed a long time to the woman waiting for her answer, she gave an almost imperceptible nod before leaning closer to her and saying something in a voice too low for Clayton to hear.

The woman nodded her head in a vigorous fashion, turned, and almost ran back to the soddy. She returned a few minutes later with her arms full of black gabardine, which she held out to Svetlana. Svetlana looked at the bundle of black cloth, then turned to wrap her arms around the spotted cow. She pressed her face against the cow's face for just a moment, then handed the animal's lead rope to the anxious mother. The woman in turn placed the black dress, probably her only dress other than the one she wore, in Svetlana's arms.

Clayton was glad to be shut of the cow and happy for the family. He turned back once as he and the small posse rode away from the farm. The family was gathered around the cow, laughing and hugging each other and the cow. He wouldn't forget the mother's triumphant smile when she turned back from her exchange with Svetlana to show her treasure to her children. That smile clearly said milk for her children mattered more than her best black dress.

They made better time the next two days and arrived in the city on the third while there was plenty of daylight left. They made their way to the sheriff's office. They found him leaning back in his chair, deep in conversation with the mayor and several of the city's leaders. News of the demise of the Gooding Gang was met with cheers, and it was decided that the lone survivor of the gang's last murderous rampage should collect the thousand-dollar reward offered by the bank several weeks earlier when the Independence to Kansas City train had been held up. A bank note was duly presented to Svetlana, who shied away and clung to Rafe. Marshal Jacobs accepted the reward in her behalf.

Rooms were found for the night, and the following morning they made inquiries concerning trains to take them to their various destinations. Rafe would accompany Jacobs, Svetlana, and the horses as far as Independence, where he would report to the army while the marshal conducted the young girl the remainder of the way to her uncle. Pete had a four-day wait for the Denver train. He spoke of meeting his brother there before going on to Eagle Rock to start a spread of their own. Clayton only had a few hours' wait for the Wichita train.

He purchased his ticket and bid his fellow travelers farewell. He wished Svetlana well. She seemed more alert since her encounter with the woman who traded a dress for her cow. This morning she was dressed in the somber black dress, which was loose on her slender frame, and she'd made an attempt to tame her tangled hair into two braids that appeared almost like silver ropes against the dark fabric. The girl had pluck; she'd be all right.

Jacobs took Clayton aside to caution him to have a doctor take a look at his leg and to rest it as much as possible. Clayton said he'd rest on the train and see a doctor, if need be, when he got back to Alabama.

The train arrived within an hour of its scheduled time, which was pretty good. Clayton settled himself in a seat, shoved his battered valise under his seat, and propped his leg on the opposite seat. Glancing out the window, he waved a final good-bye to the four figures standing on the wooden planks of the station. It seemed his life was always filled with farewells.

CHAPTER EIGHTEEN

CLAYTON TIPPED HIS HAT FORWARD and slept for most of the journey. He was unaware of the light fading, and when he next opened his eyes, the sun was just rising and the cinder- and smoke-belching locomotive sounded three long blasts as it slowed to a rattling, lurching stop in Wichita. Clayton picked up his well-worn valise and stepped down from the train.

He'd expected a moment of déjà vu on returning to the town he'd left nearly four years earlier. Instead he found little that resembled that cow town. There were still cattle yards, but somehow they appeared different, just as the row of saloons had given way to a general store, a cobbler, feed and seed stores, a flour mill, and both a dress shop and a millenary shop. The bank had more than doubled its size. Farmers' wives stood in clusters visiting while children peered in shop windows and chased each other around horse troughs positioned conveniently near hitching rails. More carriage horses than cow ponies dozed in front of the various establishments. The hotel was still standing, but it had a new facade and bore little resemblance to the dingy, clapboard edifice where he and Travis had spent their last night in the town. There were even a few wilting flowers in front of a small café that had curtains at its window, and as he walked down the street, he could see a schoolhouse.

After checking into the hotel, he washed up before making his way to the little church at the edge of town. A neat picket fence now surrounded the small cemetery. There were many more graves now, requiring a longer search to find the simple wooden marker with "Gavin Telford, 1836–1883" deeply etched into the faded wood that marked Pa's final resting place. Clayton knelt beside the marker for some time, then rose to his feet, feeling a heavy loneliness settle onto his shoulders, which slumped as he stared down at the grave.

"Pa, I don't know for certain where Travis is. He doesn't write often, but before I left school I received a brief letter saying he was trailing a herd to Montana and thinking of starting his own ranch where he can raise horses. I know you and Mama always said I should look after him, but his dreams didn't include going east to school, and herding cattle didn't seem right for me anymore. I reckon you always knew our destinies weren't the same. I had some trouble with some outlaws, and one of them shot me. I was laid up for a while, but I'm fine now and if I don't have a letter waiting for me when I get back to Southbridge, I'll go after Travis. If he needs me, I'll go to him."

A hot summer wind swept through the tall grass that partially hid the tombstones and markers in the little church cemetery, and a sense of calmness settled over Clayton. As if they'd materialized beneath the hot Kansas sun, he saw row after row of cotton, deep bottomland, and a young girl dressed in overalls running to meet him. He didn't know if it was the answer he sought or not, but it was enough. He was going home to Southbridge. A sudden urgency overtook him to complete his business and return to the plantation. Perhaps Grandpa was right when he said there was something about the bottomland that called to the souls of Southbridge men. Clayton decided he'd take care of transferring his funds to the Alabama bank nearest the plantation and then catch the first eastbound train.

He felt too impatient to bother with dinner and hurried to his room, only to lie awake watching the small piece of night he could see from his hotel room window. At last he began to drift toward sleep, but suddenly he was jerked awake by a voice. "It be fambly what matter de most."

Why old Lucas's voice came to mind as he drifted to sleep, he didn't know, but he was wide awake again now.

Clasping his hands behind his head, he gazed upward at the blackness of the ceiling somewhere above him. It wasn't the first time thoughts of family had impressed themselves upon his mind in the past few weeks. He wanted no part of family if it meant the kind of total obedience Grandpa had demanded and that was pushing his friend Arthur to marry one young woman when he loved another. Yet Clayton longed for the companionship and shared purpose that he'd enjoyed with Travis and Pa. He smiled remembering the mountain family he'd stayed with after he'd been wounded by a member of the Gooding Gang. He wanted the kind of love he'd seen on Mr. Macintosh's face when the man had thrown himself in front of his wife in a protective gesture during that holdup.

He blinked to keep the moisture that suddenly sprang to the back of his eyes from falling. Alone or not, he wouldn't shame himself by crying. However, there was no holding back the memories. That family who lived in the soddy house when the Gooding Gang arrived had their dreams. He'd seen the careful way the beams supporting the ceiling had been cut, how neatly the small corral had been constructed, and the pride evident in the recording of each child's name in that old Bible. Who knew the sacrifices that father made to build a home where children and corn could grow tall. His stomach churned at the memory of the family's beaten, butchered bodies.

He couldn't help wondering if he might have saved some of them if he'd encouraged the little posse he rode with to approach the soddy when he first spotted it and suspected the gang was inside. Both Pete and Jacobs were convinced the outlaws had been at the house for a couple of days before they held up the train and that the family had been murdered before the holdup, perhaps that morning or the night before.

Clayton's thoughts turned as they often did to the girl Marshal Jacobs was escorting to Pennsylvania. It was time to stop bemoaning his fate. She had far more cause than he did to feel bitter and lonely.

He must've finally drifted to sleep because it was the glare of the sun streaming through the window that woke him. He'd forgotten to pull the shade before crawling into bed. He scrambled into his pants, and since he still had a half hour until the bank opened, he stepped into the dining room for hot biscuits and gravy. Seeing the number of men dining alone, he vowed that someday he'd eat breakfast across from a beautiful woman and between them there'd be a row of children spaced down either side of the old dining room table at the plantation. And when he stabbed the hard biscuit with his fork, he swore he'd find someone who could cook like Dulce to run his kitchen.

His gait was slow and stiff as he made his way to the bank. Sometimes he despaired of ever regaining the full use of his leg.

When Clayton reached the bank and approached a teller, the man appeared excited and beamed as he conducted Clayton to an office that opened from a door off a short hall behind the teller's cage. Looking around the small room, Clayton could see there had been some changes since he and Travis had deposited Pa's money in the two accounts. There was a rug beneath his feet and a solid oak desk with matching chairs. A shelf behind the desk held a row of leather-bound books.

The man who rose to offer a hand in welcome, however, was the same man he'd met with on that long-ago day. He was a little heavier and was dressed more formally in a three-piece suit and crisp shirt with a starched collar and cuffs. A silk tie was knotted at his throat. He had a wide, congenial smile, and Clayton returned the smile as he took the banker's hand in a firm clasp. Not certain whether the banker recognized him, Clayton introduced himself.

"Good to see you again, Mr. Telford. In case you've forgotten, my name is Gerald Long, and I remember you and your brother very well. It's not often we're entrusted with such a large sum of money from someone so young as you or your brother were when you opened your account here. I hope you're satisfied with our service."

Clayton was surprised the banker recognized his name and appeared so pleased to see him. Clayton assured Mr. Long he'd had no reason to complain with the bank's service.

Mr. Long gestured toward a chair placed conveniently in front of his desk and settled himself in a fine leather chair on the opposite side of the desk. He continued in a congenial manner, "I received a couple of letters in the past few days, one inquiring about you and one I was just getting ready to forward to you at your school."

"I've finished with school."

"Congratulations! And may I inquire as to your plans now?"

"That is why I've come. I had some business to attend to north of here and thought to drop in and make arrangements to transfer my funds to the Alabama Central Bank in Southbridge, Alabama, as I plan to make a permanent home there."

"The balance in your account shrank considerably since your initial deposit four years ago . . ."

"I am aware of that," Clayton interrupted. "I suspect there are only a few hundred dollars remaining."

"Actually, there are more funds in your account than you are aware. Your brother stopped in last spring as he has done twice before since you set up his account. He said he'd made a nice profit from selling some of his horses, and he figured you were entitled to half. Each time he has deposited funds in his account, he has transferred some of his beginning balance to your account. He said that since he kept all of the horses and most of the gear that had belonged to you and your father it wasn't fair to divide the cash evenly. Then there's the small matter of a deposit made yesterday by the Wichita Railroad Company."

Clayton stared at the banker, not quite comprehending.

Mr. Long spun a coin between his fingers for several minutes, then chuckled before broaching another topic. "While you think about that, there's another matter I wish to mention. A notice arrived on the train a few days ago from a man who signed himself as Judge Carpenter of Southbridge, Alabama, requesting information concerning whether this bank holds a lien against the Southbridge property. The judge also implied that if you had mortgaged the property, it has no standing and was obtained illegally. He stated that any funds held here in your name legitimately belong to Southbridge's heirs. He also questioned whether you had a legal right to claim any of the property's profits. He ordered this bank to freeze your account. It seems someone else is claiming ownership of the farm in Alabama and all of the assets of one Elliot Southbridge."

"What!" Clayton surged to his feet. "Judge Martindale settled that matter four years ago when he accepted Grandfather's will as valid. And you know my account here receives no money from the plantation."

"I was hoping this might shed some light on the matter." Mr. Long withdrew a wrinkled envelope from a drawer and placed it on the desk before Clayton. "This letter is addressed to you and arrived on the same stage as the missive from Judge Carpenter."

Clayton picked up the envelope. He studied the unfamiliar sloping scrawl someone had made of his name. It wasn't either Travis's or Elliot's handwriting. Disappointment plummeted his hopes when he saw no indication of the sender on the envelope. Picking up the letter opener that lay on the banker's desk, he slid it under the thick wax seal. His eyes made a rapid scan of the single page. Startled, he read the note aloud.

Dear Mr. Telford,

Mother insists it is not proper for me to meddle in your business affairs, but having no other recourse, I have set pen to paper. Mother and I are in dire straits; thus I determined to write to you, informing you that my father passed away in April and is buried in your family plot. It was our assumption that you were informed of his passing, but not receiving instructions, mother and I have continued living in the house and have allowed Lucas to manage the planting of the fields this spring and to supervise his sons in their labors. All seemed to be progressing well until Father's Yankee cousin arrived, claiming ownership of the plantation as Father's only male heir. Since Judge Martindale has been removed from his office and replaced by a Northerner, serious attention is being given to Maxwell Mason's claim, and instructions have been given to Mr. Chalmers at the bank not to advance to mother the funds you left in his care. Mother has taken to her bed, and I daily fear eviction or worse. Please advise.

Sincerely,
Miss Lucinda Southbridge

Stunned silence hung in the air for several seconds, then Clayton surged to his feet. "I need to get there as quickly as possible," Clayton said through clenched teeth as he shoved his hat back on his head.

"Wait a moment." Mr. Long stood, holding up a long, slender hand. "Please sit back down." Reluctantly Clayton sat. The few minutes needed to finish his business would have little impact on how soon he could board a train, though it was hard to think of anything but rushing back to Southbridge.

Before Clayton could speak, Mr. Long assured him of his solvency. "I've done a little checking, and, as near as I can ascertain, the funds you have on deposit in this bank have no connection with the property in Alabama, as you stated. And I don't believe the Alabama court has any jurisdiction in this territory. Your funds are at your disposal."

The banker leaned forward as though sharing a secret. "I'm aware of the service you provided the railroad and the army in recovering funds belonging to them and to several banks by eliminating the Gooding Gang. That gang has been a scourge on business for more than a year. Several banks contributed to a fund for the girl you were instrumental in rescuing. But you should know, the railroad was generous in acknowledging your role in recovering their assets too. I received a complimentary and jubilant wire from an associate in Kansas City yesterday, as well as a visit from a railroad trustee. He deposited a generous reward into your account.

"I have the greatest confidence in your integrity and your ability to fight off this claim. Therefore, it is my belief that between your reputation and my knowledge of the law, we can prevent what appears to be a fraudulent claim from robbing you of your property." Mr. Long seemed to be genuinely pleased to assist in preventing a serious fraud.

Though Clayton had been ready to charge from the room seconds earlier, he hesitated now, wondering how a banker in Kansas could help his situation a thousand miles away in Alabama.

Mr. Long settled more comfortably in his chair. "Ten years ago I was building a successful career for myself as an attorney in Baltimore, but when my father died, it became necessary to take over the management of this bank, which he founded when the railroad first came through this part of the territory back when the big herds were arriving almost every week. I still have connections across the country, and I think you could benefit from a little advice."

"Don't try to talk me out of fighting this. I'm going. I won't allow the Southbridge plantation to fall to some Yankee carpetbagger! Nor will I see Lucy and her mother evicted from their home!" He remembered she'd written "or worse" and hoped she wasn't being threatened with physical harm.

"I'll send a wire instructing the bank in your hometown to accept Mrs. Southbridge as your agent with full rights to access your account there until you arrive and to halt any withdrawals by any other party." Mr. Long's grin reminded Clayton of the way his brother grinned when the two were conspiring to pull some prank on an unsuspecting cowboy.

The banker began drawing up plans to secure the estate. "You'll need to have documentation with you when you appear in court, including your father's discharge papers from the Union army. I can send a wire to the Department of the Army in the nation's capital to have the papers ready for you to pick up in Montgomery. That Yankee judge will have a hard time dismissing the claim of a Yankee hero's son, especially a son the army is calling a modern-day hero. Make it clear to the judge that until you have a son, your heir is your brother. Could save your life for it to be known you have an heir. I'll draw up a will and a few other papers you might find helpful. There isn't a train through here going east until morning, which gives me plenty of time. You can drop by to sign the papers on your way to the depot."

"Do you think that's really necessary?" He felt a touch of panic. Talk of a will suggested he was in some kind of danger. And if he was in danger, what kind of danger were Mrs. Southbridge and Lucy facing? He attempted to close his mind to the recent memory of a woman and her daughters lying in a bloody, fly-infested dung heap. For all of his rough upbringing, he'd never supposed such evil existed. Were outlaws who held up trains any different from the thief who was trying to steal his home? The thought of Mary Beth and Lucy facing such danger sickened him.

"It's just a precaution, and it might prevent further false claims in the future." Mr. Long went on, seemingly unaware of Clayton's sudden loss of color. "Now, Mr. Telford, I know you planned to transfer the funds in your account to a bank in Southbridge, but it might not be the best time to carry out that transaction. We don't want an interloper to have cause to force Mrs. Southbridge to withdraw your funds for his own nefarious purposes. As soon as you get matters cleared up in Alabama, send me a wire, and I'll take care of everything."

CHAPTER NINETEEN

Taking a deep gulp of the hot, humid air laden with the scent of blossoms, Clayton experienced a sense of homecoming that transcended the concern he'd felt for saving his property since receiving Lucy's letter. That sense of coming home was further confirmed when Lucas's dark face came into view through the train car window. Gathering up his old valise in one hand, Clayton limped his way down the steps of the last car with the assistance of a heavy, polished walking stick he'd recently acquired in Montgomery. Lucas's white teeth flashed in a rare, welcoming smile, but the old man maintained a respectful distance, waiting for Clayton to acknowledge him first. Clayton despaired that the former slave would ever completely rid himself of the old servile mannerisms ingrained in him for most of his seventy-five years.

Crushed rock crunched beneath Clayton's boots as he made his way to the trunk the conductor placed on the ground beside the baggage car. Clayton had been relieved to find the trunk waiting for him when he reached Montgomery. The old black man reached the trunk first and swung it to his shoulder. Together they began the slow march up the hill to the house. When they reached the graves beneath the willow tree, they paused, setting down their burdens, and Clayton reached for Lucas's hand, delivering a firm handshake.

Lucas leaned back, eyeing Clayton. His eyes rested on the stick against which the younger man leaned heavily, making it clear he expected an explanation.

"I was headed here after finishing school when a gang of thieves held up the train in West Virginia," Clayton explained in terse words. "One of the bounders put a bullet through my leg, and I spent a month recuperating in the home of some mountain people; then I went on to Kansas to take care of some business. What happened to Elliot?"

"Coughing sickness and the old fever."

"I'm sorry I didn't know in time to be here."

"Nothing nobody could do. Miz Southbridge call in de doctor, but it be too late. She send you a telegram, but you already gone from school."

"Who's this claim jumper who thinks Elliot was the rightful owner of the plantation and that my farm should belong to him now?"

"Miz Southbridge say Mr. Mason be cousin from up North. He didn't come to help none when Mr. Southbridge was shot up by de Yankees den lost his farm. Now he claim dey close as brothers and only kin Miz Southbridge and Miss Lucy have."

"He may be their only kin, but the plantation is mine." Clayton emphasized his words as he stabbed the ground with his cane.

Lucas bowed his head and spoke as though it pained him to say the words. "Dat man say Lucas and Lucas's fambly be gone first thing. He say we steal profits belong to him, so he be hirin' new workers and chargin' rent for de cabins."

"I'll decide who goes and who stays." Clayton narrowed his eyes. "This is your home. I've known you since the day I was born, and never in that time have you taken even a small part of what should rightfully be yours. No one is sending you away."

"Dey be trouble when Mr. Mason see you here. He have paper from judge, saying he boss here now."

"He's staying here?" Clayton couldn't believe the man's audacity. It wouldn't be old Lucas packing up to leave! That would be one of the first matters Clayton would fix.

"Yes, suh."

"Perhaps I should visit the sheriff and that judge before paying my respects to Mrs. Southbridge and Miss Lucinda."

"I 'spect you best hurry. Mr. Mason take de ladies in de carriage to get final papers dis mawnin'."

"Have one of your boys saddle a horse for me."

"Mr. Mason take old Dandy to pull de buggy. Dey jus' be a ole mule down in de stable."

"It'll do! Please get him saddled while I change into something grand enough to face the judge."

* * *

Clayton's first stop was at the sheriff's office, but finding the door closed and no one in attendance, he continued down the single, dusty street of the small town that constituted the county seat and which had been named for his ancestor. He then rode to the old courthouse, which had survived the war with minimal damage, and eased his painful way down from the back of the farm mule Lucas had ordered one of his sons to saddle for Clayton's ride to town. The ride had been jarring, but no more so than the lurching train ride from Montgomery had been earlier that morning and far easier than chasing after outlaws on the open prairie.

After hitching the mule to a post under a broad elm tree and loosening the girth strap, he straightened his best jacket, which Mr. Long had advised him to wear, admonishing Clayton that words carried more weight when delivered by a man who appeared to be a gentleman. Clayton patted his pocket to ensure that his papers were in place before grasping the walking stick tighter to begin making his way up the steps that led to the heavy doors of the stone structure.

He pulled the massive paneled door open and peered inside. First there was a tiny cloakroom, and then, straight ahead, he could see a black-robed figure sitting behind a high desk on a platform. Two smaller desks were in front of and a little lower than the one where the judge sat. The remainder of the room was arranged with benches much like church pews.

There were few people in the courtroom—only two ladies with wide hats and a gentleman dressed like a riverboat gambler sat behind one of the desks, and on the front bench behind them sat a large man with a badge pinned to his vest. A fastidious little man with ink-stained cuffs was seated at the edge of the platform, writing furiously in a ledger. The only other occupant of the courtroom was a man with slicked-back hair and an oily smile who stood with one of his carefully polished shoes resting on the edge of the wooden platform while he spoke in earnest, rolling tones to the judge.

Clayton stood, taking in the scene, just listening for several minutes before placing his stick under his arm as though it merely represented a foppish fad. Schooling his features to hide all signs of stress, he strolled down the aisle to seat himself behind the vacant desk. He crossed one leg over the other and pinched the crease of his pants in a nonchalant gesture.

"Whereas there has been no disputation of Mr. Mason's claim to the Southbridge estate, and since the papers I have presented clearly prove said Mason's sole kinship to the deceased, I ask that Your Honor invalidate any prior claims and award full rights of the property to the claimant," the gentleman speaking to the judge intoned.

"Objection, Your Honor." Clayton rose to his feet.

"And who might you be?" the man who had been speaking asked in a contemptuous voice.

"I'll ask the questions." The judge glared at both men, then turned to Clayton. "Identify yourself and state your interest in this case."

"I am Clayton Southbridge Telford, the late Desmond Southbridge's grandson and heir." He heard a slight gasp from the ladies seated to his right, but he didn't glance their way.

"Do you have proof of your identity?"

"I do, Your Honor." He reached for the papers inside his coat pocket.

"Your Honor," the man seated beside the ladies jumped to his feet. "This won't do. If this gentleman wished to dispute my claim, he should have done so months ago. He is a fraud and has no legitimate claim to my cousin's estate."

"As for disputing this interloper's claim to my property," Clayton's voice was filled with disdain, "I received no notice of my tenant's demise, nor of this hearing, as is required by law. I only learned of Elliot Southbridge's death and the appearance of a counterfeit heir through an inquiry to my banker concerning funds I have on deposit in a Kansas bank—an inquiry put forth by the local bank here since I have, on several occasions, transferred funds to the local bank for Elliot Southbridge's use. I understand the query was prompted by one Maxwell Mason in an attempt to steal my money." He didn't mention Lucy's letter; that was a private matter.

There was a splutter of objections. He was instantly aware of the knowing look that passed between the lawyer and the man he assumed was Mr. Mason, a look that confirmed his suspicion that the two men were working together to defraud him of his property. The clerk merely continued to scribble in his notebook.

The judge hesitated but didn't reprimand either Clayton or the other man for their outbursts. Instead, he extended his hand for the papers Clayton held. Clayton handed them to the judge one by one. "This is my mother's christening certificate, which verifies that Desmond Southbridge was her father. This is my parent's marriage license, my christening certificate, and this is the duly registered will of my late grandfather, Desmond Southbridge, in which he named me his sole heir. And this—" He was cut off.

"Your Honor," the spokesman for Mr. Mason interceded. "As Mr. Southbridge's natural offspring was a daughter and females cannot be burdened with the ownership of property, the property should rightly have passed to his closest surviving male relative, in this case, his younger brother, Elliot, and from thence to Elliot's cousin, Maxwell Mason. Inasmuch as Elliot was the undisputed owner and resident of the property for nearly six years, it is clear his claim to the property superseded that of all others."

"This document with Judge Martindale's signature confirms my claim." Clayton set another paper on Judge Carpenter's desk. "And this one is a contract drawn up between me and Elliot Southbridge who, incidentally, was born seven years after Desmond's father's death to Desmond's stepmother and shared no blood kinship with the Southbridge family. Elliot acknowledged openly that he had no legitimate claim to the Southbridge name. This document establishes that Elliot was my lawfully designated factor for the management of my estate in my absence but in no way shared ownership of the plantation."

Mason and his attorney conferred for several minutes, and Clayton perceived several nervous looks between them and the judge, enough to cause Clayton to suspect the judge was in cahoots with the crooks attempting to steal his property. Clayton stood with his arms folded, waiting for the next salvo. He hadn't fired his biggest gun yet.

"This is highly irregular." The judge pounded his gavel on the desk. "Court is recessed for one hour. I'll need time to study these documents." He rose to his feet as though in a great hurry and fled through a door at the side of the dais. The clerk scurried after him, while the sheriff leaned back in his chair and appeared in no hurry to vacate the room. Mason and his attorney continued their whispered conversation.

Clayton remained standing behind the desk, watching first one, then another of the remaining people across the room. After several minutes his attention turned to the two women who appeared to be arguing. He recognized the older woman in tears as Mary Beth Southbridge. The younger woman took his breath away. Though his mind told him she was Lucy, he couldn't believe this gorgeous creature could be the little terror he first saw in overalls. He'd seen her a couple of times since that first introduction, but somehow he'd failed to really see her. He couldn't believe little Lucy was all grown up and the loveliest vision he could imagine.

Lucy's eyes met his, and she started toward him, but Mr. Mason reached out an arm to clasp her about the waist, drawing her to his side. Something began to burn deep inside Clayton's chest as he saw Lucy caught in the man's embrace. There was a flash in her eyes, reminding him of the young firebrand who'd held him at gunpoint. When Mason said something to her, the spark of rebellion died and she stood as though the life had been drained from her. Somehow that hurt more than the man's previous rough behavior toward her.

Clayton didn't wish to start an altercation, but seeing Lucy cowed and beaten hardened his resolve. He stepped toward the man with a star on his vest. "Evening, Sheriff," he spoke amiably. He remembered a slimmer version of the man and knew from a long-ago conversation with his father that the sheriff had dodged the war and hadn't actually fought on the side of the Yankees or the Rebels. Still, the sheriff had been fair and straightforward with Clayton at the first hearing concerning Desmond Southbridge's will.

The sheriff shifted in his chair, keeping his eyes lowered, indicating his reluctance to talk to Clayton.

"Glad to see you," Clayton said as though he hadn't noticed the man's discomfort. "I checked your office before coming here and was told I'd find you here." Lowering his voice, he continued. "I have a message for you from Governor Seay. I stopped by his office yesterday, and he asked me to deliver this to you." He withdrew an official-looking envelope from his pocket and passed it to the lawman, who nervously looked around and appeared on the verge of bolting from the room. It was with reluctance that he tore open the envelope to read its contents. Clayton waited a few minutes, but when the sheriff made no attempt to resume speaking with him, he returned to his previous post behind the solitary table opposite the Southbridge ladies.

Clayton endeavored to look unconcerned, but he couldn't help wondering what kind of hold Mason had on Lucy and her mother. He worried, too, concerning whether or not he could count on the sheriff for help. The lawman had been none too eager to speak with Clayton or accept the governor's letter. Clayton wasn't even certain the judge intended to return to the courtroom.

When the judge did walk through the door only a quarter of an hour late and the clerk asked everyone to rise, Clayton did so while struggling to hide a grimace. Whether he stood or sat for a prolonged period of time, his leg throbbed. The judge, making no attempt to hide his own scowl, which doubtless derived from a different source, lost no time in gaveling the court back into session.

As soon as everyone was seated, he spoke as though delivering a grand oration. "This court has no intention of disrupting the lives of Mr. Southbridge's widow or daughter on the basis of a counterfeit will, no doubt drawn up by that disloyal Southern dissident, Alfred Martindale, who masqueraded here as judge for forty years. Mr. Mason's claim to the Southbridge estate appears to be the stronger claim, and as Mr. Mason has informed me of his intention to wed Miss Southbridge and invite his bride's mother to make her home with them, I find in favor of—"

"One moment, Your Honor." Clayton, his features drawn into a cold, hard mask, paced toward the judge with one hand on his hip, drawing his coat back to reveal the revolver previously hidden by his coattails. The judge flinched and looked toward the sheriff for assistance. The sheriff gazed out a window, apparently paying little attention to the proceedings inside the courtroom.

"Sheriff, seize this man!" The sheriff continued to ignore the judge, who now wore a frantic expression on his face as he clutched at papers and attempted to rise.

Clayton continued to advance. "Before you make an official pronouncement, there is one more document you should read. It carries the seal of Governor Thomas Seay. He heard my case yesterday in Montgomery and ordered a warrant for Mr. Mason's arrest on a charge of attempted fraud. As for Mason's claim that he is about to marry Miss Southbridge, that too is a lie, as the young lady is already betrothed—to me."

CHAPTER TWENTY

CLAYTON HAD NO IDEA WHY he'd claimed Lucy was betrothed to him, but the more he thought about it, the more he wanted it to be true. As his wife and the mother of his children, there would be no more ludicrous claims against his right to the plantation. He'd admired the girl's spunk since that day when she'd held a gun on him, and her alerting him to the Yankee bounder's attempt to steal his property proved she was a woman of strong principles. But it was more than that.

All grown up, Lucy was a woman he wanted to claim as his own, but from the look of fury on her face, he'd made a mistake in publicly claiming her without discussing the matter with her privately first. Mary Beth didn't look too pleased with his assertion either. Arthur had told him a number of times that he was a clumsy fool when it came to women, and his experience with Lavinia certainly proved Arthur's assertion true.

"It appears," the sheriff turned his attention to the proceedings in the courtroom and rose to his feet in ponderous increments, "that this court has no jurisdiction in the matter at hand." He held up the letter Clayton had delivered to him and continued in an unhurried drawl. "Governor Seay informs me that you, Your Honor, have no valid appointment to the post you are occupying and that he is sending without delay a duly appointed judge to take over the judicial proceedings of this county. Until the new judge arrives, I am charged with maintaining order and adherence to the laws of Alabama."

"This is an outrage!" The judge pounded the desk with his gavel. "Turn in your badge. You're dismissed!"

"Meaning no disrespect," the sheriff ambled toward the judge's irate figure, "the voters of this county elected me, and until they elect someone else, I'm the law here. I suggest you find your way out of town without delay, or you may find yourself sharing a cell at my jail with your two friends here. I have warrants for both of their arrests." He turned to indicate Mr. Mason and his attorney, who were now both noticeably absent. Clayton hadn't noticed their hurried departure; he'd been too amazed by the sheriff's sudden entry into the fracas.

"Blast!" The sheriff waddled back to the chair where he'd left his hat, placed it on his head, and bustled toward the exit, muttering imprecations against inconsiderate crooks who expected him to chase after them in the blistering heat and without any regard for his bunions. When Clayton turned back from watching the sheriff's departure, he noticed the side door closing behind the judge. The clerk remained, his pen flying faster than before.

Gathering his courage, Clayton gathered up his walking stick. He approached the ladies, feeling unsure of his welcome.

"Mrs. Southbridge," Clayton attempted to speak to the woman sobbing on her daughter's shoulder. Mary Beth only sobbed louder, and Clayton felt helpless to know how to deal with the matter.

"Shouldn't you go after the buggy—if Mr. Mason hasn't absconded with it?" There was a chill in both Lucy's eyes and voice. Clayton decided he'd be wise to do as she suggested and fancied he appeared as ridiculous as the sheriff as he hobbled up the aisle after the lawman's departing figure.

Ignoring the ache in his leg, Clayton approached the stable in a wary fashion, his right hand hovering near the revolver hidden beneath his jacket. He wouldn't put it past the disappointed claim jumpers to lay a trap for him. He poked his head around the open doorway. Clayton found a man in overalls leaning against his pitchfork mumbling something unintelligible and assumed he was the stable master.

"Mrs. Southbridge and her daughter arrived earlier this morning. Would you have their horse and buggy made ready for them?" he interrupted the stable master's muttering.

The man scratched his beard and remained silent for several long minutes. "The ladies' rickety ol' buggy is ready anytime dey are, but dem fellas that rode in with dem this mawnin' took the horse and lit out o' here like dey's pants was afire, with both of 'em ridin' the old nag. Didn't pay dey bill neither."

Clayton drew a gold coin from his vest pocket and offered it to the man, who looked it over carefully before pocketing it. "See that mule under the big tree in front of the court house? Fetch him over here, and put him in the traces. I'll escort the ladies home."

"Yes, sir!" The man bolted from the stable, eager to fetch the mule.

On his way back to the courthouse, Clayton stopped to inform the sheriff of the missing horse. The man wiped his perspiring face with a large handkerchief and promised to add the theft of the horse to the wire he planned to send to the surrounding towns. Disgruntled, Clayton headed for the courthouse; he didn't expect there'd be any results to the sheriff's search for the thieves or the horse—even if he did get around to sending out a telegram. Clayton didn't suppose that all three men had been staying at the plantation, and he didn't expect that the sheriff would seek out their lodging. Clayton would do it himself, but he figured it wouldn't be wise to keep Lucy and Mary Beth waiting.

The two women were alone when he entered the courthouse. The clerk was gone, and Clayton suspected the judge had joined his cohorts and the three were already making plans to swindle someone else.

"Ahem!" He cleared his throat to draw the ladies' attention. "The carriage is ready."

The ride to the plantation passed in uncomfortable silence, and neither lady commented on the mule being in the traces instead of the old horse. As soon as they reached their destination, both women scurried to their bedrooms, leaving Clayton to wander about, reacquainting himself with the outbuildings and offering reassurance to Lucas and his sons' families, letting them know that they were wanted and needed to keep the plantation running. Hannah and Ruth were overjoyed to be asked to clear out the room Mr. Mason had been using.

The joy and approval voiced by Lucas's large family restored Clayton's good humor, but he found himself casting frequent glances toward the upstairs window he knew marked Lucy's bedroom.

Claiming a betrothal had been foolish, but he didn't understand why it upset Mary Beth. To his way of thinking, Elliot's widow should be relieved that she wouldn't have to seek lodging elsewhere and that her daughter could become mistress of the plantation. Sure, he had some rough edges, but he didn't think he was entirely objectionable as a prospective son-in-law.

A quick survey of his room brought some satisfaction. His locked trunk and the valise he'd carried on the train were both in their proper places. He'd have to remember to thank Lucas. Unlocking his trunk, he dug down through clothes and books until he reached the rifle that had lain there for four years. In recent weeks he'd had occasion to wish he'd had it in his possession, but now it wouldn't be far from his side until he was certain Mason and his friends had left the country.

Deciding it might be wise to examine the farm's books, he spent several hours in the library going over Elliot's careful entries. After Elliot's death, someone, he suspected Lucy because of the similarity in handwriting to the note she'd written him, had continued keeping meticulous records. A month earlier, the record keeping had ceased. He'd have to pay a visit to the local banker soon to determine if there were any funds left in the account he'd set up there for handling the plantation's expenses, and he'd have to contact Mr. Long to arrange the transfer of funds they'd discussed.

Feeling restless and hearing no movement from either of the Southbridge women, he made his way once more to the stable in search of Lucas. Clayton found the old man tending to a pair of mules in stalls near the mule he'd ridden earlier.

"You know, Lucas," Clayton said, "I didn't expect that scalawag to turn tail and run so easy. He might show up here after we're all in bed, bent on causing trouble. I'd appreciate it if your boys would arm themselves and spell me off keeping watch tonight."

"We ain't got no guns. It's agin the law for us folks to tote 'em."

"But I saw you with Grandpa's old shotgun when I was here before."

"Miz Mary Beth know nuthin' about de law. She happy thinkin' dat gun b'long to me an' I be shootin' dem squirrels and such 'stead of Miss Lucy."

"Just keep a big stick handy and wake me if you hear anything. I'll be sleeping on the verandah tonight."

Lucas's son James volunteered for the first watch, and though Clayton was tired, he had trouble drifting to sleep. He lay for what seemed liked hours listening to the hum of insects and the deep-throated croak of a bullfrog. He wished Mary Beth and Lucy would talk to him. Perhaps if he had a better picture of the events that had occurred over the past few months, he could put the whole thing behind him and move forward. Perhaps in time, Miss Lucy would even see him in a favorable light.

He must have drifted off because he jerked awake at the clamoring of a cowbell. He was on his feet before James reached him with a hissed warning that someone was coming through the woods. Clayton wondered why the man bothered to whisper when the cowbell had surely awakened everyone for miles around. Snatching up his rifle from where he'd left it under the edge of his bedroll, Clayton dashed toward the racket coming from the thick stand of trees that bordered the lawn and continued on for miles along the river. He was pleased to see that James followed, a thick tree limb brandished above his head.

Clayton turned to caution James to be silent, and they both slipped into the deep shadows of the woods. The clang of the cowbell ceased as abruptly as it started, and Clayton paused to get his bearings and to listen.

Someone *was* coming. He could pick out the faint sound of rapid footsteps coming toward them. Settling behind a large oak with his revolver, he motioned for James to hide and saw the man disappear behind a thick clump of honeysuckle on the other side of the overgrown path.

They didn't have to wait long. A slight figure burst past Clayton's hiding place, his steps almost soundless. Clayton was about to intercept the hurrying lad when he recognized the beat of heavier steps and the crashing and snapping of brush as someone heavier followed the first runner. Moments later a man paused inches away from Clayton to listen. It was too dark to identify the figure, but he had his suspicions.

As the man started forward again, Clayton saw he was armed. The distinctive shape of a pistol extended from one arm. Setting down his rifle, Clayton launched himself forward, tackling the intruder to the ground. They both landed hard, and the man beneath Clayton lay motionless. Clayton crawled off of the man he'd felled. He wasn't certain whether the motionless man was unconscious or just had the wind knocked out of him, but he began a search of his pockets for something with which to secure the man's hands. A voice interrupted his search.

"Get up real slow, and toss that gun you keep under your coat into the bushes. One sudden move and you're dead." Clayton ground his teeth as he did as he was told, but he attempted to toss the revolver in the direction James was hiding. He could only hope James would locate it and know what to do with it. Clayton berated himself for letting someone get the drop on him. He'd known there were three men involved in the scam meant to deprive him of the plantation. It wasn't like him to be so careless. He started turning to face the voice he recognized as Mason's attorney. He figured the man on the ground was Mason.

"Don't turn around. We're going for a little walk down by the river, and when I get back there won't be anyone who can dispute my friend's claim to this place. Start walking and remember I'm right behind you."

"You're forgetting I have a brother and that my will is on file in Montgomery." He wasn't certain whether he had a brother or not anymore. It had been four months since he'd last heard from Travis, but Clayton didn't want the hombre herding him along like a dumb steer to continue thinking the scammers' problems would be over if they killed him.

The only response from the so-called lawyer was a sharp jab in Clayton's back. Clayton walked as slowly as possible, racking his mind for a plan of escape.

A loud crack sounded behind him, and he dove for the shadows, expecting a bullet in his back. He rolled beneath a tangle of shrubs and then lay still. He hoped that if he didn't move, he wouldn't be found.

"I done kilt him!" James's voice was filled with panic. He stood in a small patch of moonlight holding the thick club he'd brought with him that night. The man who moments before had held a gun to Clayton's back lay sprawled at James's feet.

Clayton left his hiding place to examine the dark form to confirm that the man was indeed Mason's attorney. It was impossible to tell how severe his injury was, but the man wasn't moving. He was breathing, however, and Clayton's hands encountered a sticky wetness during his cursory examination.

"He's alive, and if anyone complains, I'll say I hit him," Clayton attempted to reassure the frightened black man. It didn't seem right to Clayton that James could hang for killing a white man in defense of another white man who happened to be his employer.

James continued to moan and wring his hands.

"Do you have anything we can use to tie his hands?" James produced a length of fish line but continued to whimper. Clayton secured the man's hands behind him. The phony lawyer groaned a few times, and James seemed to relax.

"I already tied up de other fella," James announced.

"We better keep our voices down," Clayton reminded him. "There's still another one out here someplace."

"You mean the one that ran past real fast? That be Miss Lucy. I 'spect she caught one of dem fellas in the snare she set on de path in de woods. He mos' likely be hangin' by his feet from a tree, waitin' for us to cut 'im down."

"Lucy?"

"Yes, sir. She real good at catchin' critters with snares, and she say she don't trust dat Mistah Mason. She make life real hard for him 'til her mama tell her to behave. That Miz Mary Beth allus tryin' to make a lady out o' Miss Lucy."

Clayton couldn't help the grin that spread across his face. Lucy was something, all right!

Taking the precaution of securing their prisoner's feet as well as his hands, they left him bound and hurried on toward the river. They hadn't gone far when a faint sound reached their ears. A few minutes later the path led them to a sight that made Clayton want to chuckle. The prisoner dangling from a stout tree branch by his feet was the pompous judge. He was nearly unconscious but revived enough to beg Clayton and James to release him.

James produced a small kitchen knife with which he hacked at the rope while Clayton searched for a means of lowering Lucy's catch to the ground. Clayton succeeded first.

Before the judge regained his ability to function, Clayton and James secured him with the rope and slowly dragged him back to the clearing, where the attorney was now awake and struggling to free himself. While James stood over the prisoners with the club he'd retrieved from the ground, Clayton hurried ahead to begin a search for his rifle and revolver. By the time he had them both in his possession again, Mr. Mason, their first prisoner, was groaning and struggling to free himself.

A commotion on the lawn drew Clayton's attention. Through the trees he could make out lanterns and a collection of excited people carrying weapons ranging from stout clubs to skillets. He recognized Lucas's voice. James shouted to them, and soon all three prisoners were being carried through the trees to be placed side by side on the lawn. Lucas looked them over, then summoned Hannah to bandage the crook James had hit over the head.

"Ain't much sense takin' those fellas to the sheriff tonight," Lucas decreed when the excited chatter ceased enough so he could be heard. "He be sleepin' 'bout now and he don' take kindly to folks who wake him when he be sleepin'. We kin shut dem in a shed for tonight." He motioned for one of the women who carried a lantern to bring it closer. He leaned over to inspect the bandage his daughter-in-law had fashioned for the luckless attorney. "Mighty fine job," he said, only he seemed to be speaking more to James than to Hannah.

Clayton looked around for Lucy but didn't see her. Disappointed, he turned back to securing the prisoners. "We better take turns guarding the shed," he said.

"I'll take the first watch," Israel, James's brother, offered.

After making certain the bound prisoners were firmly locked in the shed and Israel, armed with his brother's stout club, was posted outside the small building, Clayton wandered back to the verandah. He could seek out a bed in the room he'd come to think of as his but opted instead for his bedroll. Fatigue was beginning to set in, and he suspected he'd not have any trouble falling asleep. As he approached the steps leading up to the wide porch, he spied a forlorn figure sitting in a dejected heap atop the last step. His weariness fled.

"Evening, Miss Lucy," he said in a low voice.

"Evening, Mr. Telford," she responded in a subdued voice.

"Mind if I sit down?" He didn't wait for her to grant permission but settled a few feet away on the same step. Once his long legs were stretched out in front of him in a comfortable fashion, he continued. "I wish to thank you for sending me that letter—and for the trap you set in the woods tonight."

"Mother will be angry when she finds out, and we'll have to go away, but I couldn't let him steal your home without giving you a chance to put up a fight for it." A lock of hair had escaped her thick braid, and she pushed it behind her ear.

"Why should you have to go away? I told you to think of this as your home."

"That man, Mr. Mason, isn't really Papa's cousin, but Mama knows him from a long time ago."

"What do you mean, she knows him?" He couldn't believe Mary Beth had anything to do with the scam the three con men had concocted in order to steal his property.

"I don't know. It's just things he'd say, and Mama would look scared. It was better after he said he was going to marry me." Her voice ended with a little catch.

"Do you want to marry him?" He found himself almost holding his breath waiting for her answer.

He saw her shudder. "No, but Mama wanted me to say I would. I let her think I was going to say yes, but I couldn't ever marry a man I knew was a thief and a liar."

"Maybe your mama just wants to see you settled."

"I thought so at first, but there's more to it than that. She knows I don't like Maxwell Mason, and it's not like Mama to want me to marry someone I don't want to marry."

"Is it just the idea of getting married you don't like, or is it Mr. Mason? When I mentioned you might marry me, you didn't seem any happier at that prospect than you did about marrying Mr. Mason." He hadn't meant to mention his absurd assertion; it just seemed to come out. Still, he listened carefully for her response.

"I've been thinkin' on marrying you since I was fourteen." She rested her chin in her cupped hands and her shoulders slouched. She spoke so low he wasn't sure he'd heard right. He wasn't even sure whether he'd just proposed and if she'd accepted, but whatever the case might be, she didn't appear to be happy.

Clayton was silent for a long time. He found it difficult to comprehend that Lucy had set her sights on him the first day they'd met. It had never occurred to him until that moment in the courtroom that he might marry Lucy, but the longer he thought about it, the more the idea appealed to him. The problem was that he had no idea how to go about setting things right.

The moon was casting its light across the steps where they sat. Lucy was dressed much like she'd been the first time he'd seen her, though the masculine pants and shirt were a much snugger fit than they'd been back then. A long braid and several strands of hair had escaped one side of the crushed felt hat she wore. A warm feeling stole into his heart, and he knew Lucy meant far more to him than he'd realized. Wild tomboy or beautiful woman, he didn't care; he wanted her beside him during all the days before them.

"I'm surprised you set a snare instead of going after those scoundrels with Grandpa's squirrel gun." He smiled, trying to lighten Lucy's mood.

"Mama caught me with that rifle right after Maxwell showed up. I think she was afraid I'd shoot him, so she hid it. I suspect Lucas knows where it is, but he's too afraid of Maxwell to risk telling me where it is or getting caught with it himself."

CHAPTER TWENTY-ONE

It seemed Clayton had just closed his eyes when he was awakened by the sound of a buckboard rattling down the winding lane that passed the plantation and connected to the road leading into town. He was surprised to see the sun already up. He stood and made a few passes at his rumpled clothing in an effort to look presentable.

He was more surprised when he saw the wagon and recognized the horse tied to the back of the wagon as Dandy. In recent years the horse had been relegated to pulling the buggy when Mary Beth went to town. Holding the lines that snapped across the backs of a prime team of draft horses was the corpulent figure of the sheriff. He didn't look happy.

"Howdy!" Clayton stepped down from the verandah.

"Howdy," the sheriff returned his greeting. "Dang fool farmer woke me up before dawn to tell me somebody's horse was eating his wife's garden. He insisted I accompany him back to the few acres he's trying to scrape a living off of just down the river a piece. I recognized Miz Mary Beth's buggy horse right off."

"I appreciate your bringing him back."

"I would've waited 'til a more decent hour, but I expect that he's the horse that Mason fella and his friends rode off on, and it's my duty to warn you those crooks might be close by. They might even be looking for revenge."

"You're right about that. Last night they came sneaking through the woods, and one of them landed in a snare someone set in the woods. The other two dropped their guns when they saw we were on to them. You'll find them over yonder in the shed where James and Israel are keeping watch." He downplayed the night's adventure.

"That's right neighborly of you to keep 'em for me. Perhaps you and a couple of them boys could ride into town with me when I take 'em to jail. The governor sent a wire saying he'd send some federal troops to hustle 'em off to Montgomery for trial when I caught 'em." He puffed out his chest. "Don't suppose he expected I'd be taking him up on his offer this soon."

"I don't suppose you've had time for breakfast yet?" The sheriff had already accepted the invitation when Clayton remembered Mary Beth was put out with him and there might not be any breakfast waiting. He ushered the lawman inside and breathed a silent sigh of relief when the aroma of sausage and biscuits greeted them. He should have known Lucas would have sent one of his daughters-in-law to prepare breakfast the moment he recognized their early morning visitor.

Over breakfast Clayton suggested the prisoners be left where they were until the federal officers arrived. "There's no sense hauling them off to town then back out here to board the train, seeing as how you don't have any deputies. James and Israel can take turns watching, and I'll have some vittles sent out to them."

The sheriff took another forkful of biscuits and gravy, chewed for several moments, and then agreed to the plan. Clayton suspected the sheriff was pleased to escape the responsibility of caring for three prisoners but was uncertain how he'd be able to take the credit for their capture if they weren't housed in his jail.

"You might want to ride back out here when you find out which train the officers will be on, just so everything will be neat and official," Clayton suggested. The sheriff agreed it was his duty to turn over the prisoners personally and asked for another helping of biscuits and sausage gravy. Clayton tasted his own breakfast and thought he might offer Hannah a salary to cook his breakfast every morning.

* * *

Clayton decided he'd continue to sleep on the back porch until the state lawmen came for the prisoners, but he retired to his room to shave and don fresh clothes. Feeling somewhat refreshed, he made his way to the library, planning to go over the farm's accounts once more. He was anxious to take over day-to-day management and felt the best place to begin was with Elliot's careful records.

He wasn't surprised to find Lucy in her favorite chair with a ledger in her lap.

"That scoundrel never paid James and Israel. He lied to Mama, telling her to withdraw the money so he could pay them and purchase needed supplies. He didn't enter anything in the ledgers either! I don't know how much cotton was picked and sold or even if he collected payment and then pocketed the money!" It wasn't much of a greeting, but at least she was speaking to him.

Soon they were poring over the ledgers together, and Clayton was amazed at her knowledge of the workings of the estate. He felt a thrill of excitement when she expressed enthusiasm for his plans for expanding the number of acres under production and for acquiring a few horses. At one point they left the books behind to wander toward the stable, where Lucy pointed out the need for new shingles on the roof.

Clayton was careful to avoid bringing up his newfound feelings for Lucy, and she side-stepped mentioning any plans she and her mother might have regarding their future. She frowned on noticing Clayton's pronounced limp and demanded to know the details of the episode surrounding his injury. He was surprised by how easy it was to tell her of his adventure, though he took care to mention Mrs. Macintosh's assurance that the injury would heal with rest.

He enjoyed every minute he spent with Lucy, but Mary Beth still wasn't speaking to him. After two days of being in Lucy's presence and getting no closer to bringing their relationship to a more personal level, Clayton made up his mind to take drastic measures.

* * *

"This way, ma'am." Clayton conducted Mary Beth into the library. She'd been avoiding him since they'd returned from the sham court hearing, and she hadn't spoken a word to Lucy in that time either. He offered her a seat and then settled in the chair behind the desk. He looked at her for several minutes, hoping she'd begin the conversation. When she didn't, he cleared his throat.

"Mrs. Southbridge, have I done something to cost me your good graces? When I left here last, I thought we enjoyed an amiable relationship."

"Oh no, sir. You've been ever so kind to Elliot and me and our Lucinda."

"Then what is it? Do you disapprove of my clearly stated intentions toward your daughter?"

Mary Beth buried her face in her hands and dissolved in tears once more. Feeling uncertain of how to proceed, Clayton sat with shoulders slumped for several moments before digging out his handkerchief. He handed it to the sobbing woman. He'd never had any experience with a crying woman before and had no idea what to do.

"I thought you might be pleased to learn I've developed a fondness for Miss Lucinda, but if that is not the case, is there any hope that I might gain your approval to wed her?" Without sounding like a lovesick schoolboy, he wondered how he might convince Lucy's mother of his deep regard for her daughter and his conviction that he and Lucy were ideally suited to one another.

Mary Beth wiped at her face, and he watched her struggle to regain her composure. "You'd make a fine husband for my Lucinda, but . . . he threatened to tell . . . Oh, Mr. Telford, that wicked man will ruin Lucinda. She won't be accepted anywhere."

Clayton was growing impatient. Why couldn't the woman just come straight out and tell him what was troubling her?

"Was Mr. Mason blackmailing you?" He leaned forward to emphasize his expectation of a straightforward answer to his blunt question.

She shuddered, then began to speak in a slow but determined way. "Maxwell Mason is not Elliot's cousin." She paused to wipe her nose and dab at her eyes once more. Clayton hoped she was about to get to the point of her story.

"Elliot didn't have any kin," she managed to stammer.

"Who is he? And why didn't you denounce him as a fraud?" He was growing exasperated. He'd hoped a few minutes of quiet conversation and a restatement of his intentions would end the impasse.

Mary Beth sniffled once more, blew her nose again, and straightened her shoulders. "I apologize for my behavior," she said in a more formal tone. "You have been kind to us, and I've no right to withhold the truth of my birth from you." She took a deep breath to steady her nerves and began. "Maxwell Mason's father lived in the same small community as my mama and papa, and it seems the elder Mr. Mason passed on some ugly gossip concerning me to his son. As a child I was deeply hurt by the vicious tale. My mama died birthing me just hours after one of the household maids gave birth to a baby who never drew breath. The house slave became my wet nurse, but there were rumors that Papa was the father of the light-skinned girl's baby and that it was Mama's babe that died. Maxwell said that if I told anyone he wasn't Elliot's cousin or did anything to prevent him from becoming the master of the plantation, he would produce witnesses who would swear the slave girl was my real mama."

Her fingers turned white where she gripped the arms of the chair in which she sat. Clayton said nothing, waiting for her to resume her story.

"I was scorned by the best families and received no offers of marriage until Elliot came along. We had played together as children, and he knew about the gossip and didn't care whether it was true or not. He loved me and that was enough for him, even though it made our life more difficult and was the real reason he lost his farm. We had to leave the place where we grew up because racially mixed marriages are illegal in most of the South, even though slavery has been abolished. There were troublemakers who threatened us based on that old gossip, claiming we weren't really married and that our child was illegitimate and colored. Elliot couldn't manage the farm anymore by himself, and we knew the rumors would eventually destroy Lucinda's chances for finding a husband, so we gave in and left all we owned. We thought we were safe here because no one knew us. In five years no one had mentioned the old gossip.

"If I had only myself to think of, I wouldn't care what others think. It is Lucinda I worry about. If word gets out that there is even a possibility of her carrying "tainted" blood, she will be socially ostracized. When Maxwell offered to marry her, I believed he would keep her safe to protect his own reputation. Now he'll spread that story to get revenge." She burst into tears again.

"He'll not get a chance to speak with anyone. The sheriff is leaving him here until the federal officers arrive," Clayton attempted to reassure her. "He'll have no visitors."

"There'll be the trial, and even in prison he'll pass on the story to others. I know him. He'll stop at nothing to destroy me and Lucinda."

"We'll laugh it off. No one's going to believe a convicted liar. I doubt this is the first scam he's attempted, and if he tries to create trouble, I'll make it my business to find more charges to press against

him. Now how about it? Have I your permission to ask your daughter
to be my wife?"

To his astonishment, Mary Beth burst into tears again.

"So you still have objections to me?" He struggled to keep his
voice level, even though his pride felt bruised. *What further objections
could the woman have?*

"You're everything I could wish for my dear Lucinda." She wiped
at her eyes with her already soaked handkerchief. "It's just that I
always dreamed of her having a proper courtship."

"I'll do the best I can." He knew little of a proper Southern
courtship, but if that was what was required, he'd do his best. She
gave him an uncertain smile before she nodded her head.

* * *

Clayton remembered his mother had planted a rose garden behind
the house. He hadn't paid any attention to whether it was still there
on his previous visits, but now he determined to search it out. He
meant to get on with courting Lucy, and he'd read somewhere that
ladies liked their beaus to bring them flowers.

After a dedicated search, he found the bushes hidden in a jungle
of tall grass and overgrown shrubs. Cursing the thorns that stabbed
him as he cut the woody stems that sported yellow blossoms, he
collected as many roses as he could reach. If Mary Beth wanted Lucy
to be courted, he would court her. Once he deemed he had enough
blooms for a respectable bouquet, he retired to the stable to harness
the horse the sheriff had returned and hitch it to the buggy.

When all was ready, he hurried to the verandah. He paused to
brush away a few bits of foliage that clung to his clothes and ran
a hand through his hair. Instead of walking in, he gave the door
knocker a few good claps.

After a moment, Mary Beth opened the door and stared at him in
astonishment.

"I've come to call on Miss Lucinda Southbridge." He felt like a
fool standing at his own door, holding a bunch of prickly roses.

"I-I'll fetch her." Mary Beth snatched at her skirts and fled up
the stairs. "Lucinda, you have a gentleman caller," she called in a
breathless voice as she reached the landing.

Moments later Lucy peered over the railing. He saw trepidation turn to a fit of giggles before she rushed back to her room. He stood there glowering, suspecting he should have changed into his best suit and combed his hair with proper care before coming calling.

It was only a few moments before Lucy appeared again at the top of the stairs. This time she was attired in a gown with a bell-shaped skirt and she was holding a tiny scrap of lace in one hand. He gave her a stern glare. Taking her time, she sauntered down the curved staircase until she reached him.

"Here!" He thrust the flowers toward her. She accepted them, and Mary Beth, beaming with happiness, hurried forward.

"I'll put them in a vase for you." She hurried the flowers toward the kitchen.

Lucy looked up at him, waiting for him to speak.

"I've come to take you for a drive," he muttered.

"Just let me fetch my parasol." Her eyes fluttered, and she looked pleased or about to giggle before hurrying away to fetch a frilly bit of silk and lace that wouldn't be of much use if there should be a rainstorm.

On reaching the buggy, she paused for him to hand her in. Instead of offering his hand to assist her in climbing aboard, his hands went around her waist and he lifted her with ease to the seat. Something about his hands around her waist felt awfully good, and at this close range he discovered she smelled better than the roses he'd picked for her. He found that once she was seated, he was sorely tempted to keep his hands at her waist. It was with reluctance that he released her and hurried around to the other side of the buggy to take up the reins.

Sitting beside Lucy, he felt about ten feet tall. He slapped the reins across the horse's back, and the animal began a sedate walk down the lane. From the corner of his eye, he could see a pink flush on Lucy's cheeks and was pleased to note she'd remained where he'd set her and hadn't slid closer to the far edge of the narrow seat. Each time she moved, he felt a soft brush against his sleeve that made him want to drop the reins and clasp her to him.

They traveled for some distance before she ventured to ask him about his life out West. He found himself relating things he'd almost forgotten about the nomadic years he'd traveled about with Pa and

Travis. As their discussion of the West drifted to his recent years in Boston and finally to his plans for the plantation, their initial awkwardness fled. He realized with a jolt that those plans were no longer *his* plans, but *theirs*.

He brought the buggy to a halt beneath a canopy of thick tree limbs. He turned toward her and felt amazement that he'd never noticed what a brilliant blue her eyes were. Her bonnet had slid back, revealing a profusion of curls that gleamed like sunlight. He longed to place a kiss on each of the rosy spots that marked her high cheeks. One smile from her exquisite lips and he'd float right off the buggy seat.

"You really mean to stay?" she asked, bringing him back to earth.

"I do," he assured her. "This is my home and I want it to be yours too." He placed his hand over hers, and she made no move to free hers. He stared at her pink mouth and considered stealing a kiss but thought better of it. Lucy might not be comfortable with such a bold action.

"We'd best be getting back." If they stayed in the quiet bower, he feared his good intentions would be tossed to the wind. He lifted the reins, but before he could signal the horse to move on, a shadow leaped from the trees to drag Lucy over the side of the buggy. She went screaming and kicking. Clayton's hand dropped to the revolver at his side.

"Toss it on the ground or I'll slit her throat."

Seeing the large knife Maxwell Mason held to Lucy's throat, Clayton let the gun drop to the ground, though he took care to release it on the side farthest from the man holding Lucy captive. Rage consumed Clayton, and he had to force himself to remain outwardly calm. He'd do nothing that might endanger Lucy, but Mason would pay severely if he harmed her.

"Get down from the buggy," Mason ordered. Clayton moved toward the side of the buggy nearest the pair on the ground. He might get a chance to deliver a well-aimed kick. He wasn't going to allow any sidewinder to harm Lucy. For now, he'd appear to be following Mason's instructions.

"The other side! Get out of the buggy on the other side!" Mason increased the pressure against Lucy's throat, sending a thin red line trickling down her pale throat. The fear in Lucy's eyes nearly drove

Clayton mad, but he feared that showing any opposition would result in further harm to her. His knuckles turned white as he gripped the side of the buggy to begin his descent.

"Hurry up!" Mason hissed.

Clayton lowered himself from the far side of the buggy, his fists clenched in frustration. He had to find a way to turn the tables. Perhaps he could reach the pistol he'd dropped.

"Turn around and start walking! If you even look like you're bending to pick up that gun, I'll slit her throat before you can get off a shot." Clearly Mason didn't have a gun in his possession or he wouldn't be allowing Clayton to walk into the woods; Mason would simply shoot Clayton.

Holding his back ramrod stiff, Clayton moved toward the trees that lined the country road. Once in the trees he'd have a chance to do something. The area was heavily wooded, and he knew it well from the years he'd played there as a boy. As soon as he reached the trees, he'd circle back to the road, and this time he'd be the one springing a surprise attack.

Lucy screamed. Whirling around, Clayton saw that Lucy had crumpled to the ground and that the horse had trotted on a few steps. Mason was diving for the revolver now exposed because the buggy no longer stood between it and him. Clayton lunged toward the attacker. He couldn't possibly reach the gun before Mason did, but he had to try.

Mason grasped the revolver and thumbed back the hammer. His first shot went wild. Clayton continued his charge, narrowing the distance between himself and Mason. He expected a bullet to slam into his chest any moment. He didn't care. If Lucy was still alive, he had to give her every chance to escape.

CHAPTER TWENTY-TWO

THE SHOT CAME, BUT CLAYTON felt nothing. He continued to charge toward the man who had dared hurt Lucy. The gun fell from Mason's hand as Clayton slammed him backward several feet before he dropped like a lead weight onto the dusty road. Stunned, Clayton stared in confusion as blood poured from a gaping wound where the lower half of Mason's face had been.

Changing direction without taking time to assimilate what had happened, he rushed to Lucy. Kneeling in the dirt and weeds, he found his handkerchief, pressed it to the wound on her neck, and was relieved to see it was little more than a scratch.

"Lucy, dear Lucy," he whispered, stroking her face and pleading for her to still be alive.

She opened her eyes and blinked several times. Suddenly her eyes widened, and she threw her arms around his neck, burying her face in his shirtfront. Placing one hand beneath her chin, he lifted her face until their eyes met. At first it was enough to look at her beautiful face and assure himself she was alive, but then he growled, "Courting be hanged!" He lowered his head a few inches more until his lips touched hers. Her sweet lips returned the pressure with an intensity that took his breath away. It took several minutes for his senses to return and for him to recall their precarious position. He pulled back and Lucy clung for a moment longer, then she whispered, "I thought he'd killed you."

"I'm fine, but Maxwell Mason is dead."

"You killed him?"

Lucy thought he'd killed Mason; he hadn't, but someone had.

"No, I don't know who fired that shot." Chills swept down his back, and he considered carrying Lucy into the trees, where she'd be out of sight. The shot had been fired from some distance away, and perhaps Mason hadn't been the intended target. If Mason had escaped the shed, Clayton could only assume the others had too and could be as great a threat to Lucy's safety as Mason had been. No, it might be safer to put Lucy in the buggy and take her back to the house, then come back. Until he knew who shot Mason and the whereabouts of the other two prisoners, no one on the plantation would be safe.

Lucy started to rise, and Clayton turned her away from the body lying a short distance away.

"There are some sights a lady shouldn't have to witness." He was placing his arms beneath her to gather her up when the approaching sound of a wagon stopped him, and he estimated his chances of getting the both of them hidden before the wagon came into sight.

"Ho, there!" He was too late.

Recognizing the sheriff's voice, Clayton rose to his feet, with Lucy sheltered against his side. The lawman halted his wagon behind the buggy, where Dandy continued to graze on the grass that grew beside the road as though nothing had happened. A woman leaped from the high buckboard seat where she'd been hidden behind the lawman's wide frame and raced toward Lucy, crying her name.

"Lucinda, my baby. I thought that horrid man had killed you." She threw her arms around her daughter, sobbing and speaking incoherent words. Clayton chose not to examine her too closely, but he noticed that Mary Beth's gown was torn and there were black smudges on her hands and along one cheek.

While the two women cried and clung to each other, Clayton stepped toward the sheriff. Clayton was surprised to see old Lucas huddled in the back of the buckboard. Something about the way the old man watched Lucy and Mary Beth suggested to Clayton that he knew more about the events that had so recently occurred than he'd ever tell. At his feet lay the old, large bore squirrel gun. Sickness turned Clayton stomach. If Lucas was the shooter who'd saved him and Lucy, Lucas would likely hang. The Klan was active hereabouts, and it didn't matter why a black man killed a white man. If, in the unlikely event a jury cleared Lucas, he'd still be lynched.

"How'd Mason get loose?" Clayton asked.

"James took dem dey's dinner, and dey got the drop on 'im. Beat him bad—but he comin' round. That Mistah Mason take a knife from the young'ns playing mumblety-peg close by, but de other two run to the river. They stole my fishin' skiff and left Mistah Mason behind. Me and Israel follered Mason into the woods, but we lost 'im."

Clayton looked back at Mary Beth. Could Lucas be covering for her? Mary Beth would fare no better in court than the black man, and the rumors concerning her birth would be bound to come out if she should be charged with shooting Mason. He shook his head to clear it. What was he thinking? A genteel Southern lady like Mary Beth wouldn't know the first thing about handling a firearm. He looked up to see the sheriff watching him in a calculating manner.

"Sad business." The sheriff huffed and groaned as he made his way down from the wagon seat. He took dainty steps, doing his best to avoid the thick dust on the road that spilled onto his shoes, obscuring their fine shine. He stood for several minutes staring down at the body before reaching down to pick up Clayton's revolver that lay a few feet away.

"Suicide," the sheriff announced.

Clayton swallowed the protest that rose to his lips. Any fool could see the gaping wound in Mason's head wasn't put there by a bullet from a Colt. The shot had come from a good forty feet away, about the distance it would take for a shotgun to leave a good sized hole in whatever it hit.

"Lucas, come help load this body onto my wagon," the sheriff shouted. "Blamed fool killed himself."

Clayton shrugged his shoulders. He wasn't going to argue with a lawman.

* * *

Maxwell Mason was buried outside the fence of the town cemetery before the sun set, and the sheriff surprised Clayton by mustering a band of men to search the rivers and creeks for Lucas's dinghy. They had no success and called off the search when it grew too dark to see.

Clayton felt little interest in the search for the two missing men. If they were still in the area, he believed they would have aided

Mason in the attack on him and Lucy. He prowled the rooms of Southbridge, anxious to hear any word of Lucy and grew frustrated when Mary Beth insisted that her daughter could have no visitors and must rest. Mary Beth suggested he retire to his own room and give his injured leg a rest, but how could he sleep without first seeing Lucy and assuring himself she hadn't suffered serious harm?

Entering the library, he attempted to review the farm records. When that failed to distract his thoughts, he picked up a book Lucy had left lying on her favorite chair. It held no interest. Striding to the tall side window, he pulled back the heavy curtain and stared, unseeing, at the moonlit hill that sloped down toward the river.

Once he'd thought if he could study at the college in Boston and then return to claim Southbridge, he'd be the happiest man alive. Now he knew better, and perhaps he understood both his father and grandfather better. He'd come so close to losing Lucy, he realized that without her, no other dream mattered.

At last he lowered himself into the large chair behind the desk. His leg throbbed to match the pounding tempo in his head. Leaning forward, his head touched the oak surface. The house grew still, and he slept in spite of his certainty that he could not.

A sound awakened him, and he looked up to see what looked like an angel watching him from Lucy's chair. It took a moment to convince himself that he was really seeing Lucy. She wore something white and lacey over what he assumed was her nightgown. Her pale hair was loose and fell in rippling waves about her shoulders. A strip of white gauze circled her throat.

"Lucy!" His voice was hoarse. "Are you all right?"

"I shall be fine. The cut didn't go deep, and I only passed out because Maxwell crushed me so tightly I couldn't breathe."

Clayton rose to his feet and made his way around the desk until he stood beside her. "I thought I had lost you."

"I came to just enough to see you charge him and that he had a gun. I couldn't move. I couldn't do anything. Right then I wanted to die."

"I'm glad you didn't."

"Nor you." She smiled that mischievous smile that made his insides tingle.

Slowly, laboriously, he knelt.

"No! Please, your leg."

"It's all right. I'm only going to do this once in my life, and I want to do it right." He reached for her hand and she tightened her fingers around his.

"Miss Southbridge, my heart shall be yours from this day forward. I have come to esteem you above all others and will cherish you forever. Will you do me the great honor of becoming my wife?"

"Oh yes, a thousand times yes. There is nothing I long for more than to be your wife."

As Clayton leaned forward to seal their pledge with a kiss, his injured leg refused to bear his weight any longer, sending him sprawling on the carpet at Lucy's feet. With a quiet giggle, Lucy slipped from her chair to sit beside him. Gathering his head in her arms, she pressed her lips to his and he forgot all about his injured leg. It wasn't the way he'd planned it, but all in all, he believed the proposal had gone well.

CHAPTER TWENTY-THREE

A WEEK AFTER LUCY AND Clayton announced their engagement, a body was discovered downriver near Mobile. It was so bloated, identification was impossible, but the description sent to the sheriff sounded like the dead man might have been Mason's attorney. The judge was never found, but a rumor persisted that he'd caught a steamer headed for Jamaica.

With life settling down around him, Clayton was eager to begin implementing the plans for improving the plantation and putting his finances in order, but he hadn't considered that Lucy, Mary Beth, and all of Lucas's large family would insist on him resting his leg. For almost a week, he endured spending his days on the verandah with his injured leg propped on a pillow while he read or sketched the changes he envisioned.

He enjoyed the attention Lucy lavished on him when she and her mother weren't absorbed in planning her wedding dress, but he soon decided he wasn't a man meant to be idle. While eating breakfast one bright morning in early fall, he announced his intention of traveling that day to Montgomery to attend a horse auction.

"Perhaps another week—" Mary Beth began.

"I think that's a wonderful idea," Lucy interrupted. "While you look at horses, Mama and I shall search out a shop that carries lengths of yard goods."

Clayton turned over the suggestion in his mind while savoring the plate of eggs Hannah had set before him. The salary he paid the woman was worth every penny. He had to admit he liked sharing his breakfast table with the women and the feeling of having a family that went along with it. He was anxious to make Lucy and Mary Beth his family for real, and if inviting them to join him for the trip to Montgomery would hurry up the process, he was for it.

"Excellent!" he pronounced. "Since we shall arrive there late even if the train is on time, I think we should plan an overnight stay. We can stay at the hotel I've used before since it is centrally located."

Lucy's face lit with excitement, and Clayton suspected his fiancée had never stayed at a hotel. Chances were good she'd never ridden a train before either. He took a smug kind of pleasure in being first to introduce these experiences to his Lucy.

The three scattered to make their preparations for the trip. Both women were prepared for the journey in far shorter time than he expected, and he felt a swell of pride as he escorted them aboard the train and found them seats near a window. Mary Beth sat with her back erect and her hands clasped tight. A look of near panic crossed her face each time the train gave a spasmodic jerk. Lucy grinned and pressed her nose against the window. Once or twice, following a particularly hard jolt, she grasped for his hand and then giggled.

After arriving in Montgomery, Clayton engaged a conveyance to transport them to the hotel. He hid a smile as Lucy stared at the ornate lobby featuring smiling cherubs in the corners of the ceiling, a thick red and gold carpet, and French-designed sofas and chairs. He escorted them to their room to freshen up, then to a tearoom where black waiters brought their orders on silver trays held aloft by one hand.

Clayton finished his lunch before his companions and, excusing himself, stood. "I must hurry now and be off or the best horses will be already chosen." He bid the women farewell with a suggestion that they might wish to rest before beginning their shopping tour. He paused a moment to add, "Instruct the merchants to deliver your purchases to the hotel and have them applied to my account."

* * *

Lucy watched Clayton walk away and noted that his limp was almost unnoticeable now. He looked so handsome in his proper suit and gentleman's hat. She'd carried a picture in her heart for years of Clayton kneeling in the dirt, smiling over the rich texture of a handful of soil. And another of him standing in chest-deep water, his eyes dark with concern, as he reached for the nearly drowned child she held in her arms. Her picture didn't look at all like the man she'd pampered and conversed with on the wide verandah at Southbridge the past week. Nor did her picture look much like the man who fought Maxwell Mason in her defense. She wondered if she'd ever know all there was to know about the man who had captured her heart. She looked back at the elegant room and felt a moment's doubt. She should have stayed back at the farm. She wasn't an elegant Southern belle; all she knew how to be was a farm girl. How would she fit into the many parts of Clayton's world?

"Are you all right, dear?" Mary Beth reached across the table to touch her arm.

"I'm fine, Mama." She slid her chair back and rose to her feet with a forced smile. She was fine. What she didn't know, she'd learn. She loved Clayton, and wherever he went, she'd be at home there. "It's time to search out the most perfect fabric and lace for the most perfect dress."

* * *

Clayton had no trouble finding the barn where the sale was being held. He'd read about it in a circular Israel had brought back from town. The auction hadn't started yet, but he could see it wouldn't be long. Rough benches had been set up in the yard before a small platform where the auctioneer would stand. Clayton joined a parade of gentlemen and a few ladies who wandered up and down the aisle examining one horse after another. There was something about the sweaty odor of horses and straw, boarding stalls, and excited little boys darting between clusters of men discussing the merits of each animal that brought a wave of nostalgia Clayton's way.

It had been far too long since he'd heard from Travis. With all of the excitement of the past few months and especially since proposing to Lucy, he'd let his concern for his brother slide into the background. Tonight when he retired to his room, he'd compose letters to be sent to the address in Utah, to Mr. Sorensen, and to the Wichita bank, to be held by Mr. Long.

Leaning over the paneled gate of a stall, Clayton watched a golden yearling colt snort and dig at the floor with one hoof. His tail went up like a flag. The colt reminded Clayton of Zeus. The coloring was different, but there was something about the young animal's demeanor. Clayton made up his mind to bid on the yearling. He found an older mare he liked that appeared to have a few good years left. For the mare alone he wouldn't have planned to offer a bid, but beside her minced a delicate filly born to run—a perfect wedding gift for Lucy.

Minutes later, Clayton found himself seated toward the back of the crowd gathered for the auction. He watched and listened as the prices climbed for a number of excellent horses. When the yearling colt was led into the makeshift arena, it fought the lead rope and struggled to free itself. His reluctance to be shown resulted in a low starting bid, which Clayton upped. Another bid and then another quickly followed. Clearly Clayton wasn't the only buyer who saw the young horse's potential in spite of its feisty disposition.

The bids climbed higher, and Clayton felt a trickle of sweat beneath his coat. One by one the other bidders grew silent until only Clayton remained. The colt was his, and he struggled to hide his jubilant grin. Mentally he calculated his finances. He hadn't touched the money Travis had transferred to his account, and fortunately the cotton buyers hadn't sent their payments before Maxwell Mason had been ousted.

The mare, with the new filly at her side, was led into the circle. A few halfhearted bids were offered, and Clayton hesitated. He wanted that filly for Lucy, and a voice at the back of his head seemed to whisper that Travis would approve of his spending the money on a horse. Clayton lifted a finger and received a nod from the auctioneer. A few desultory bids later, Clayton placed the final bid.

He was already calculating the steps he needed to take to arrange for boarding the animals overnight and for transporting them by train the following day to Southbridge when he heard a familiar voice.

"Did you just buy that beautiful horse and her darling baby?"

Clayton turned to see Lucy seated beside him. He'd been so engrossed in the auction that he hadn't noticed her arrival.

"How did you get here?" He stared at her in amazement. She was wearing a blue gown he didn't recall seeing before. It was the color of her eyes.

"I hired a cab. The clerk at the hotel flagged one down for me."

He shook his head. Though there were a few women present, he wasn't sure a public auction was a proper place for an unattached female, considering all the sorts of men she might encounter, and he didn't care to dwell on the possible dangers that might befall a young woman traveling unescorted across town. He considered scolding her but instead slid closer and placed his hand over her gloved fingers. Lucy was Lucy, and he loved her. He'd just have to grow accustomed to the unexpected.

"Well, did you?"

"Did I what?" He'd lost track of the thread of their conversation.

"Did you buy that horse and her baby?"

"Yes, ma'am. If it suits a certain young lady whom I adore just the way she is, the little filly shall be her wedding gift." She clapped her hands and snuggled closer. He grinned at her, enjoying her pleasure in the gift.

* * *

Clayton stood in the front parlor watching the grand staircase, waiting for Lucy to appear. He resisted the urge to loosen the stiff collar that rose above the lapels of his jacket. The day that had been slow in coming now seemed to be rushing toward him. He patted his pocket where he'd placed the telegram that had arrived that morning. He'd memorized the words.

> *Got letters Utah STOP delayed early snow STOP horse buyer contract STOP congratulations STOP kiss bride for me STOP Travis*

The telegram brought more questions than answers, but the important part came through. Travis was alive and cared enough to wish him well.

A flutter of sound from the top of the stairs alerted him that Lucinda was coming. His eyes searched the dim hall above and found her stepping into the light given off by dozens of candles. He'd discovered months ago that she was beautiful, but beautiful didn't begin to describe her appearance as she stepped onto the first stair, trailing a cloud of white behind her. Her skin appeared pink and gold in the candlelight and her eyes as blue as the Texas sky. Long gold ringlets cascaded from high on her head and fell over her shoulder, just the way her braid often did. He couldn't describe her gown if he tried. To him it was swirls of silk and lace that highlighted her tiny waist and made her look like an angel floating down the stairs.

When she reached his side, he took her hand in his and felt his breath catch as their eyes met. The minister from town had to clear his throat twice to get Clayton's attention. Clayton spoke his responses in a firm voice that belied his shaking knees and felt something tremble deep inside his chest as he listened to Lucy repeat her vows.

"I now pronounce you man and wife. You may kiss the bride," the minister intoned.

Clayton knew it was customary to deliver a soft, chaste kiss at the conclusion of the wedding ceremony, but when his lips touched Lucy's and he felt a soft movement beneath his own, he couldn't resist taking the kiss deeper. Her response followed with a matching urgency. Lucy was now his wife!

A soft snicker reminded him that they had an audience, and he reluctantly brought the kiss to an end. Lucy ducked her head, and streaks of red lit her cheeks. He kept a consoling arm around her, but he couldn't help grinning.

Lifting his head for just a fraction of a second, he thought he saw Mama and Pa standing a bit apart from the wedding guests, smiling their approval. He blinked, and it was old Lucas's beaming face that came into focus. Slowly the old man closed one eye in a broad wink as if to remind Clayton, "It be fambly what matter de most."

The candles had burned to their nubs and their guests had departed when Clayton swept Lucy up in his arms to carry her up the staircase. He had the strangest feeling that, at last, he'd come home.

ABOUT THE AUTHOR

JENNIE HANSEN LIVED A NOMADIC life during her early years and can remember living in twenty-two different houses and attending eight schools. The two colleges where she earned degrees, Ricks and Westminster, made ten. She worked as a model, secretary, newspaper reporter and editor, legislative page, teacher, and librarian. Through it all, she kept writing. To date she has twenty-three published novels, numerous short stories, and many magazine and newspaper articles to her credit. She has written reviews of LDS fiction for *Meridian Magazine* since 2001.

She and her husband have five children, all of whom are married to wonderful people, and eleven grandchildren. Two days each week Jennie and her husband can be found serving at the Oquirrh Mountain Temple, a fifteen-minute drive from their Utah home.

You can learn more about Jennie Hansen by visiting her blog at http://notesfromjenniesdesk.blogspot.com or by contacting her publisher at Covenant Communications, P.O. Box 416, American Fork, Utah 84003-0416.